BOLDLY

BREAKERS HOCKEY #2

ELISE FABER

BOLDLY
BY ELISE FABER

This is a work of fiction. Names, places, characters, and events are fictitious in every regard. Any similarities to actual events and persons, living or dead, are purely coincidental. Any trademarks, service marks, product names, or named features are assumed to be the property of their respective owners and are used only for reference. There is no implied endorsement if any of these terms are used. Except for review purposes, the reproduction of this book in whole or part, electronically or mechanically, constitutes a copyright violation.

BREAKERS HOCKEY SERIES

PROLOGUE

Oliver, Nine Months Before

THE SCORE WAS TIED.

I was exhausted.

It was double-overtime, game seven of the Stanley Cup Finals, and my legs were dead—and not just *my* legs, everyone on both teams' legs were dead—and that meant plays were getting sloppy, turnovers were happening left and right, and collisions were getting gnarly. It also probably meant that the game-winning goal would be some garbage shot that ricocheted off a trio of players—*and* someone's ass—before creeping home.

But for whose side, I didn't know.

I hoped it would be for us, of course, but truly, it could go either way.

Marcel banked the puck off the boards, and I could see it wasn't going to clear the blue line, so I hauled ass to pick it up, to clear it out.

I managed to get it over that line, to give my team a little breathing room, to get it deep enough to get fresh players on the ice.

But I paid the price, taking a hard slash on the wrists, pain lancing up my arms.

I nearly dropped my stick, my hands going numb for a brief moment, but I powered through it, held tight, and continued driving forward.

Even though I took another hit, this one to the back.

Not that the refs were going to call anything.

Double-overtime in the final game of the playoffs? Yeah, no. Nothing outside of the most egregious of hits was going to be called.

But, fuck, I'd appreciate it if Mark Goddamned Shelby would stop trying to pound my spine into my body. Former teammate and all-around asshole, Shelby had been unceremoniously traded to the Kings, and he had made it his personal mission to make every Breaker pay for the insult.

So much so that I knew I'd be black and blue tomorrow.

Totally worth it, though, if I was able to hoist the Cup. Especially if me doing so meant that Shelby wasn't.

Still, risk of bruises or not, I battled along the boards, gaining a few inches.

But when I glanced over my shoulder, saw Mark was winding up again, I let my instincts take over.

I kicked the puck forward, dodged to the right.

Shelby missed the crosscheck and stumbled.

I saw the empty lane ahead, the chance to advance. A sudden surge of adrenaline had me bursting forward on tired legs to retrieve the puck, to pick it up on my stick and streak toward the Kings' net.

I had space. I had opportunity.

I was going to end this.

Fifty feet from the net. Thirty. Ten.

Just me and the goalie...and a glimpse of an opening on the short side.

I held my breath. Fuck, maybe I even closed my eyes when I shot that puck. Maybe that was why I didn't see it.

But whether it was a mere blink or an unconscious close of my eyelids, they snapped open at the sound.

Thunk.

Not the *ping* of a crossbar or post being hit, the puck deflecting out without crossing the goal line, but the solid *thunk* of the biscuit colliding with the wrapped metal support...at the back of the net.

The buzzer went.

The red goal light flicked on.

The crowd erupted.

And in all that joy and cacophony and chaos, I didn't see Shelby coming.

Just felt the heavy impact.

Saw the ice coming up fast.

Then pain, so much pain...and the world went black.

Oliver

I WALKED into the practice facility for the first time since the previous season.

Walked might be a loose term.

Or, at least, it was a very different type of walk than I'd done nine months before.

This walk that took me in from the parking lot, in through the rink doors, into the cold air of the practice ice the team used still required some concentration.

Because I was down a leg.

A bad break, the bones in my lower leg essentially crushed between the goalpost and the boards. I'd scored the game-winning goal, won the Cup for my team, and I hadn't even gotten to enjoy it. Instead, I'd been in an ambulance, heading to the hospital.

Then in surgery to keep my badly broken leg. I hadn't gotten to heft the Cup, though the guys had brought it to the hospital, so I'd seen it when I'd woken up from anesthesia, held it, thinking at that point I was going to rehab my way back onto the ice. Because the doctors had done their job. I'd been healing. Then...

Infection.

A persistent, antibiotic-resistant infection that had ultimately—four surgeries later—left me without my right leg.

Bye, NHL career.

Bye, captaincy.

Bye, life as I knew it.

Now, I was up and walking. Getting around on the prosthesis. My pain was under control. I was moving on, and I was doing that by coming back to the rink.

My eyes drifted to the ice, watching the guys skating around aimlessly, shooting pucks without really aiming, just warming up before practice began. Something I'd taken for granted.

Something I missed.

I couldn't lie.

The cool air on my face, the feel of my stick in my hands, the crunch of the ice beneath my skates.

I missed a lot of things.

But...there was no going back. I couldn't be what I was, not the least of which was because I was missing a fucking leg.

"Hey," Luc said.

I stiffened, and it was harder than I wanted it to be to tear my gaze from the ice, from where *my* teammates were practicing, getting ready to defend the Cup, their record at nearly three-quarters of the way through the season making the prospects of going for two in a row possible.

There was no doubt that was the plan.

They certainly had the talent and experience to do it.

I started to face Luc, who had asked me to come to the rink. The man had pretty much become a fixture at my house after my injury, and strangely (because I would have never thought it possible), the GM of the Breakers had become less boss and more good friend. Strange, considering I had always kept myself removed from those in positions of authority, but ultimately a good thing. I couldn't have made it through the last nine months without Luc and his wife, Lexi.

"Hey," I said, but before I managed to say anything else, the guys noticed I was there and came over to the boards, acknowledging me through the glass with nods and the occasional wave. Smitty actually opened the door, started to stride down the steps when Coach—Tommy Franklin—came onto the ice and blew his whistle.

Smitty paused, made a face, then mouthed, "Fuck. Talk later?"

I nodded. Smitty had become another regular fixture at my place. Mostly because my friend was stubborn and wouldn't leave me alone.

Smitty jerked his chin up before heading back onto the ice, closing the door behind him.

Tommy said a few words, and the guys started moving.

I let out a breath, stifled my longing.

I'd seen my teammates a lot since my injury, but paired with being in the rink, seeing a practice I would have been participating in if not for the dirty hit from Mark Shelby, and I felt raw inside. I wanted to be out there.

I knew there was no point in dwelling on it.

I wouldn't be back on the ice in any capacity that I wanted, not ever again.

"Come on," Luc said, clapping me lightly on the shoulder. I nodded to the hall that led to the offices in the back of the practice facility. As we walked, I got the glances. First, just out of the corner of Luc's eye, directed low, probably assessing my stride (smooth, because I'd PTd the fuck out of getting my movements to look as normal as possible). Next, it was pointed at my face, probably attempting to judge how raw I was feeling (which, of course, the answer was really fucking raw, but eyes forward, thoughts forward). Last, it was another long stare that was punctuated by, "How're you feeling?"

And fuck, *that* was a question I was tired of hearing.

Also, so tired of hearing it in *that* tone.

The worried, pitying tone.

Yes, I'd lost my career, my leg. Yes, my entire life had changed.

But...that was the past, and I didn't live in the past.

Never had.

I hadn't been able to afford to. Not ever.

"Fine," I said, following Luc.

The GM glanced at me, and I deliberately kept my gaze pointed forward, not staring at the ice, not like I wanted to, studying the drills the guys were doing, being part of the plan to win that second Cup.

Missed that so fucking much.

Wanted that so *fucking* much.

But wasn't going to get it, so...moving on.

"Right," Luc said after a moment, and we strode into his office. Luc nodded to the chair in front of his desk, and I sat down, thinking that the last time I'd been in this position, shit had been so fucking different.

I'd been worried about the team back then, worried I wasn't the right captain for the team, worried I couldn't do the job.

Now, everything had changed.

There was still a job to be done.

Just not by me.

Luc sank down into his chair on the opposite side of the desk and picked up a folder sitting on top, flipping through some papers and then passing them over to me. "Here," he said, rather unceremoniously.

I scrambled to take the sheaf, and it was lucky that it was stapled together because I caught it by the top paper—nearly ripping it off—before I pulled it into my lap. Then I noticed what was at the top. What the—? I started reading, my eyes flying across the words on the first page and then the next.

And then the next.

My gaze flew up.

"I don't understand."

"I want you to head the Player Development department."

"But"—I continued reading, somehow unable to stop now that I'd started—"why?"

"Marco's leaving, and you already know that Allie and Chad have moved on to new posts. The department needs someone capable to take it on, to rework it into something that'll bring us to the next level."

They'd won the Cup.

What was the next level beyond that?

A dynasty? Just a repeat? A solid team for years to come?

All of that, I suppose.

"Why?" I still found myself asking, and though I left off the *me*, I knew that Luc heard it anyway.

Namely because Luc was silent long enough that I looked up from where I'd been conducting a study of my hands (big, scarred, maybe a bit too hairy on the knuckles) and realized that was what Luc had been waiting for: Me to look at him. "Because you're one of the best fundamental players I've ever seen. Because you're good at teaching the guys—I saw you plenty of times pointing out some small way they could change their play, and it made a big difference. Tommy"—Coach—

"agrees. We both saw the way the guys respected you, and that's saying something, considering the egos that come along with professional athletes."

"I—we all brainstormed. It's not like..."

"You said anything special?"

I shrugged.

"Well," Luc said. "*I* saw something special. Tommy saw something special. We both agree we want that special helping our guys win the Cup again. Especially since we won't have you on the ice leading us."

I winced.

I knew I did, couldn't help it, couldn't hold it back.

And, of course, Luc noticed.

"Fuck," my friend said, features drawn tight, "I didn't mean it like that."

I sucked in a breath, released it slowly. "I know."

And I did. Luc was a good guy.

"Look, I know you lost everything, and I know—" He cut himself off. "I can't say I know how you feel. When I hurt my knee, I lost my career, but I didn't lose my..." Luc trailed off, scrubbed a hand over my face. "It's just...I know that shit gets real when the rug gets yanked out from beneath you, but this isn't about that. This isn't about me just trying to throw you a bone. I know you're the right man for this job. You'd be an asset to the team whether you're on or off the ice." He straightened in his chair. "And because I can't have you on it, I want you off it. If you're ready for that. If *you* want that, too."

I sucked in a breath, released it slowly. "Luc, man, I don't have any real experience coaching. Not even kids. I—I wouldn't know what I was doing."

"You have good instincts."

I sighed.

I couldn't lie and say this job wouldn't be a fucking

godsend. I missed the team, missed the ice, missed doing something normal, even if that was just coming to the rink every day.

This was the type of opportunity former players would kill for, leg or no leg.

But... "Do you really think I'd be a good fit for this?"

Luc stood and rounded the desk, sitting on the edge and crossing his arms over his chest. "Look, you know me. You know I don't blow sunshine up people's asses. If I think you'll be an asset, I *know* you'll be an asset. I'm not about to give a cut of my budget to someone I think can't hack it. You were the captain of this team. You led us to a Cup win, despite the disastrous start to the season. We were the *last* place seed. We fought for every game. And the guys did that because *you* were the leader, *you* bolstered them when they didn't think they could do it, *you* were the one who put that game-winning goal in the net."

My breath slid out of me, shaky as fuck.

"I want you in the position. *You*. Because you're the best person for the job. Now," he said, when I just continued to breathe, "tell me first, is this something you might even want?"

"What?" My eyes shot up. "Of course, I want it. I miss being part of the team, of something that's bigger than me. I just—"

Doubts.

I'd had doubts my entire life, and this wasn't any different.

"Okay," Luc said, no nonsense as ever, "so now *that* part is out of the way, I have two conditions for this offer."

Bracing now, I held Luc's gaze.

"First, you'll take a coaching course I recommend."

Well, that wouldn't be so bad.

"Okay," I said

"Second, you have mandatory sessions with Hazel."

Um.

"Hazel?"

The team psychologist.

She was beautiful, kind, and had a body that screamed sex.

And last time I'd seen my had been in the hospital, horror written into the lines of my face.

TWO

Hazel

I DIDN'T HAVE a traditional job.

I wasn't the type of psychologist who had a fancy couch and a large office, expensive artwork on the walls.

I was the type of psychologist who had a slightly beat-up couch shoved into one corner, a very beat-up desk in another, a half-wilted potted plant shoved in one of the others, and a stand-up punching bag in the final one, thus clearing as much of the floor space as possible.

Because my guys didn't like to sit still while they dealt with the shit that was troubling them.

They did it moving. Pacing.

Sometimes punching that upright bag I had in the corner.

My most expensive purchase, aside from the fancy rug that covered the industrial carpeting.

The guys deserved something nice to pace over.

Even if it got trampled.

They also deserved...or maybe *needed* that punching bag.

So, it wasn't like I'd developed some magical treatment plan to help professional athletes—unless punching and pacing could be considered magic. I just...tried to give them what they needed.

But now...

I didn't know if I could do it.

Mostly because I'd fucked up so much the first time I'd tried to help.

Which was why *I* was the one pacing.

Why I was seriously considering wailing on that bag in the corner. Because. I. Had. Fucked. Up. So. Fucking. Bad.

The knock at the door stopped me from doing just that— from wailing, both aloud and on the bag.

He was here.

A deep breath in. A deep breath out.

I needed to own my shit, apologize, and hope we could move past it. Otherwise, I would have to refer him to someone else and—

Another knock.

"Fuck," I breathed, hurrying to the door and swinging it open.

And there he was.

So fucking gorgeous. A sharp jawline, stubble on his cheeks, pale blue eyes, brown hair. He wore slacks and a button-down, and he wasn't as bulky as he'd been the season before, having lost some of his muscle mass.

He was still in shape.

Just less muscular.

And...I liked him less bulky.

His brows rose, and I realized I was just staring at him. Quickly, I hopped back. "Please, come in."

He gave me a sharp look, probably because my voice

sounded like I'd become intimately familiar with deep-throating the twelve-inch dildo my friends had gotten me for my bachelorette party.

A bachelorette party that had coincided with my fiancé's *bachelor* party.

A bachelor party that had then coincided with the end of my engagement.

Because how could *a man* be expected to not partake in variety when it was right there in front of him?

Turned out, Trevor wasn't a one-woman man.

And I considered myself to have dodged a bullet—no, a grenade—to have found that out before I'd walked down the aisle.

Of course, I would have rather known that before I'd put down the deposit for the venue and bought my dress and signed contracts with the caterer and florist and photographer. But I *definitely* would have rather known before he'd given me the ring, or even before we'd moved in together.

Sighing, I rubbed my fingers over my forehead.

"I don't have to do this, you know?" Oliver said, his voice as calm and gentle as always, though I detected a thread of hurt.

And why wouldn't he be hurt?

Based on the staring and our disastrous last meeting and—

He shifted.

I blinked, realized I'd gone way down the rabbit hole and was into serious Fuck Land.

It was an amusement park for screwed-up people—therapists being right there at the top of the list because what was that about contractors' houses never getting fixed? Oh yeah, when someone spent the majority of their time analyzing everyone else's lives, it was easy to pretend their own life was fine, if only to spare them the brainpower.

And I'd been sparing myself a lot of brainpower lately.

So anyway, Fuck Land had Ferris wheels that spun people out of control, cotton candy that gifted consumers food poisoning, a carousel that had anal beads instead of saddles (because at Fuck Land one got *fucked*), and one of those mirrored houses that made everyone look the worst versions of themselves (my: pimples, braces, ratty hair, and unibrow for days...yay!)

But I was a goddamned professional—screwed-up thoughts of Fuck Land aside—so, I had to lock it down.

"I think you have to do this," I said mildly, "if only to fulfill the terms of your contract."

His gaze came to mine, and God, his eyes were beautiful. "I can do it with someone else." A beat. "If..." There he trailed off, and I was reminded again of the apology I needed to give him.

And not just because of my trip to Fuck Land.

"Please, sit down," I said in my patented mix of gentle and firm. Gentle because I found that most of the guys responded to me going soft and sweet (hello, patriarchy), and firm because the other half of them liked to go toe-to-toe with someone who could hold their own.

When he didn't move, probably because before his injury, he would have been one of those guys pacing back and forth on my rug, I dragged my chair out from behind my desk. It was wood, scarred, but with a kick-ass cushion that supported my back and butt like I was floating on a heavenly cloud. I placed it dead center of the couch and sank down onto it. I normally wouldn't have pushed this, but I wasn't certain if standing on his prosthesis for too long would hurt him.

I'd need to broach the subject.

Just not the first day.

Oliver was quiet for a moment before he moved.

I shouldn't be cataloging the movement, the way he walked —so smooth it was almost unnoticeable that he'd been so severely injured. But I had cataloged a lot of things about

Oliver, okay, *everything* about him from the first moment I'd met him.

He was gorgeous but quiet.

A puzzle I wanted to untangle.

But this wasn't about that.

"First," I said, after he'd eased himself onto the worn leather of the couch, "I owe you an apology. I definitely am happy to work with you, and I'm sorry if I gave you the impression otherwise." I rubbed my temple again, the constant throb that had invaded my temple from the moment Trevor had shown up on my porch that morning intensifying.

"Are you not feeling well?" Oliver asked, voice soft, and I thought he might know something of mixing gentle and firm.

"Just a headache."

I stood and went to my desk, pulling out a bottle of acetaminophen and taking two tablets dry.

Because I was that good.

Because I couldn't risk taking my migraine meds and being drowsy for the rest of my workday.

Or maybe just because headaches were kind of my thing.

Along with a season pass to Fuck Land and having formerly been engaged to a man who'd decided to take up polygamy.

Noticing Oliver staring at me, I dropped the bottle back into my drawer, returned to my chair, and sank down into that cloud-like cushion. "That'll help," I said. "Next—"

"Do you get headaches a lot?"

My fingers had made their way back to my temples, and I consciously forced them down. "Yes, unfortunately. But it'll go away. They always do." Except for the ones that chased me all day and forced me into an early bedtime, and then were there greeting me so sweetly in the morning. "Okay, so the next—"

"What causes them?"

I stopped, studied him.

Avoidance or interest?

I didn't know him well enough to say which one it was for sure. But I didn't really want to get into a battle of wills during our first session.

So, I gave him the honest answer. "Stress. Too much caffeine. Not *enough* caffeine. Occasionally, too much alcohol. The wind deciding to blow. The flowers blooming. The sun being really sunny." My lips curved. "My computer making a whirring sound that makes my ears unhappy—"

He pushed to his feet. "Your computer's making a sound?" He moved to my desk, picked up my laptop and listened.

Sure enough, it was making the noise that made me want to punch myself in my throat.

"Hmm," he said, bringing it back onto the couch and flipping it open on his lap. Then, surprising the shit out of me, he turned it over, pulled out a tiny toolkit from his pants pocket, and started unscrewing things. "What else?" he asked as he worked.

Thank God I'd backed up all my files that morning.

I wasn't sure I trusted a hockey player to provide tech support on my computer.

"What else?" he repeated, when I debated between asking him to stop and hoping that he might be able to fix it. And, oh, also I lost myself for a minute watching those long fingers work so efficiently as they removed the plastic cover on my laptop.

Where else might they work so efficiently?

"Hmm?" I asked, gaze on his hands.

There were some scars on the backs of them, white lines marring the olive skin, probably from fights on the ice. I wanted to study them, to tally all those tiny hurts, to ask him about each one and then kiss away the pain.

And then I wanted his hands on my body.

Yeah, that would be...well, better than nice.

"What else causes your headaches?" he asked.

"Besides the sun being sunny?"

A smile flickered at the corners of his mouth. "Yes, aside from the sun being sunny."

"I—" I sighed. "It's nothing concrete. I wear a super, sexy mouthguard at night because I used to grind my teeth"—*too much information, Reid,* I thought to myself, even as my heart started fluttering because the corners of that lush mouth had curved further, twisted up into a smile—"and my ex-fiancé is really good at pushing my buttons and bringing them on." His lips flattened, so I hurried to add, "but anyway, no one has been able to figure out a single trigger. It's just..." I shook my head, shrugged. "Something that happens."

"Hmm." A beat, then, "What's your guess for the one today?" Pale eyes on mine, holding me in place.

I stilled in my chair, the answer on the tip of my tongue.

He was good.

Getting me to relax, to internalize, to easily give answers, and then...boom! Time to pounce.

Well, I should pounce myself.

"I owe you an apology," I said.

Eyes flicking to mine. Then back down to the laptop. "You already did that."

"Not for today." I started to lift my hand, caught myself, and clutched them both in my lap. "For the hospital. I...reacted poorly, and made you feel self-conscious, and I'm so sorry for that."

His gaze was on mine, holding me in place, eyes unreadable, and yet there was something beneath the surface that called out to me, something that needed to be teased free and dealt with. Then he shrugged, and the roiling below disappeared. "It was an intense situation. Not everyone is good with seeing someone like that."

That being with a newly amputated leg, covered in wires and tubes, a man I'd formerly seen as huge and untouchable reduced to something breakable.

The latter was my problem since no one was unbreakable.

It was...it just hurt me to see him suffering.

But I could deal with all of that, could logic and think and control my reaction to all of that, if not for...

"The blood," I blurted. "I...um...have an aversion to blood, and that's the only reason I reacted the way I did. It's illogical and unfair and had absolutely nothing to do with you. But when I see it, especially in person, I...have a reaction that isn't... good," I finished lamely.

"Okay." This time, his voice was all gentle.

"It wasn't you, it was..." I trailed off before I could say "me," and tore my gaze from his, studying the painting that hung over the couch. Swathes of blue—turquoise to royal with a dash of white in between—covered the canvas. It was chaotic and rife with color...and it was also peace.

"Hazel."

I glanced back to him, knowing when I saw him staring at the painting, that this session had gotten out of my control, and yet not knowing how to get it back.

"Yeah?"

"Our time's up."

He stood, set my laptop—now all back together—onto my desk. My gaze flew to my watch, saw that the hour had indeed passed. Somehow, I'd stared in silence at a painting during the majority of his session and talked about myself for the rest of it.

Fuck.

I sucked ass.

"I'm sorry," I whispered.

"I'm not," he said, and then he stroked his knuckles down my cheek.

My lips parted on a gasp.

Then he was gone.

THREE

Oliver

I SAT in the office that had been assigned to me, wearing a suit that was a little too big for me, staring at a computer, and hoping like hell I could meet this challenge.

The class—a series of online seminars, homework, and then a video conference at the beginning of next week—was going well.

So far, I hadn't learned a ton.

Not to say it wasn't helpful.

Just that most of the material was something I'd learned from my coaches over the years, and the rest was intuitive.

Now that I'd begun making good progress on the coaching course, I was going through the motions of trying to understand the system already in place in the development department.

I needed to hire a couple of new people.

The two assistant directors had gone off to run departments at other teams, and the current head, Marco, would only be around for another couple of weeks. He was retiring to his beach house in Florida.

Which meant that I had a stack of files on my desk to go through.

And the one I'd happened to open to start with?

My own.

"Fuck," I muttered, resisting the urge to toss it aside and forcing myself to start at the beginning, to take note of the way the file was formatted, the things that had been jotted down.

The information was good, all things that had been appropriate about my game play (before I'd stopped playing) and the skills earmarked for improvement were on point as well. It was just...this was a paper fucking file. Why was this information not computerized when everything else in the Breakers organization was of the highest tech?

I knew the answer to that.

Marco.

Old school.

The man had an allergy to computers but was good at his job. Which was why I put my file to the side—gently—then moved onto the next, reading through information about Smitty and Marcel and Raph.

All of it precise.

All of it exactly what the guys needed.

And that was the moment I started to get excited. I knew drills that could help with the weaknesses called out in those files. Knew that there was equipment the team could bring out to build up what was lacking, bolster what needed support.

For the first time since Luc had offered me the job the week before, I thought that, yeah, I could be of use.

Which felt really fucking good.

Smiling, I moved on to the next file just as there was a knock at the door.

Glancing up, since the panel was open, I saw Connor Smith—Smitty—leaning against the jamb, arms and ankles crossed. "Lunch?" he asked.

I wanted to turn him down.

Not because I didn't want to see or hang out with my friend, but because I wanted to dive into the files, get caught up, and then start developing a computerized system where I could dump all this information.

Just the thought of spreadsheets and coding them got me excited.

What could I say? I might be an athlete, but I loved anything tech-related, and though I was better at the hardware stuff than the software, I could make my way through a bit of base code.

Plus, I knew a couple of people who were way better at it, and I'd bet at least one of them would take on the project.

Then I could hire some assistants to replace those who'd gone their own way.

"Ollie?"

I blinked. "Sorry." I closed the folder, stood. "I was thinking about all the things I needed to do."

"Is it a lot?"

Snagging my cell as I moved around my desk, I nodded. "A lot, but I think it'll be good."

"And *you're* good with it? With working in the back office instead of playing?"

That was Smitty.

Let it hang right out there.

Luckily, I was used to dealing with him, and I wasn't easily offended. "I'm as good with it as I can be, Smitty. Would I rather be playing? Yes. Would I rather have my leg? Fuck, yes. But do I? No. So, I'm dealing with it."

"Dealing with it how?"

"I'm getting on with my life."

Connor's lips pressed flat. "Right."

"Smitty, look. I appreciate you being concerned, but I'm *fine*."

"Fine," Smitty repeated.

And his face told me he didn't get it.

It was infuriating. It was...what it was.

"Come on," I said, grabbing my suit jacket and shrugging into it. "Food, and then you get to do all the fun conditioning on the ice while I get to mess around on my computer."

Smitty moved out of the door when I walked toward it, but I didn't miss that my friend's eyes still held concern, still held worry.

Stifling a sigh, I slipped out into the hall and tried for a joke.

"Since you still have that big contract, you're buying."

But Smitty didn't laugh.

And lunch was...too damned quiet, filled with too many awkward pauses.

"What do you think?" I asked Luc that Friday.

A week since I'd agreed to the job.

Three days since my time with Hazel, since I'd found out her ex was an ex, since I'd understood the horror on her face wasn't because of me, or at least not really about me.

Blood.

It had been so much clearer when she'd said that.

Pale skin. Wide eyes. Wavering on her feet.

Not because she was disgusted with me, but because she had some phobia that had nothing to do with me.

And somehow that made it better.

"I think I'd better show you the budget for your department."

My heart sank.

Luc clicked a few times with his mouse then turned his computer screen so that I could see.

It took a few minutes to process the line and the amount.

"That's yours to use as you see fit," Luc said. "For new hires. For whatever incidentals or needs your department has. This"—he nodded toward the proposal I had brought in for the electronic system I wanted my friend Kailey to build—"falls under the category of incidentals. You need it, there's a budget for it. I trust you, which means you want to do something like this, you want to hire someone, you do it. But you want my opinion on something, you want to check in with me, want me to be a sounding board? I'm there. I just want to be certain you understand that you don't need to ask permission to do your job."

I sucked in a breath.

"I trusted you to do right by the team on the ice. I trust you'll use those same skills—and learn any additional ones you might need—to do right by the team now that you're off it."

I released the breath, released the tension that had been knotting my insides and...relaxed. I could do this.

"Okay?" Luc asked and yawned.

I nodded. "Okay." Luc yawned again. "What about you?" I asked, noting the dark circles beneath Luc's eyes. "Are *you* okay?"

A nod. "Noah's decided he doesn't like to sleep."

"Has he *ever* liked to sleep?"

"I"—another yawn—"no. The kid seems to make it his mission to *not* sleep."

I winced. "Shit, man, that's rough."

"There's a reason they use sleep deprivation for torture."

Luc chuckled, shoved a hand through his hair. "But I love the little bastard."

"I think that's a requirement."

Luc nodded, lips curving. "For me it is, anyway." Another yawn.

"On that note," I said as I stood. "I'm going to let you get out of here. I'll let Kailey know she can get started on the program."

"Oh, before you go. Any luck on your search for assistant directors?"

"Prudence Hansley is coming on for a trial period. She doesn't want to leave her NWHL team unless she's certain she has a future here."

"She'd stop playing?"

"Apparently, she's not certain how many seasons she has left, or if she'll make it through this one. Her back is giving her trouble, so she wants to plan for what she'll do once she can't play anymore but doesn't want to give it up any sooner than she has to if working here isn't a good fit."

"Makes sense." Luc stacked some papers. "You can also work a deal where she does both. Their season is shorter and with limited travel." That was true. Since the professional women's league was relatively new and still building its infrastructure and fan base, it obviously wasn't at the same level as the NHL. "If you find someone who can be here full-time, she may be able to do something part-time remote and part-time here."

"That might tempt her if the trial goes well."

"Good." Luc nodded. "Let me know if you need any help getting that sorted with HR. I'd hate for her to give up playing if she's not ready." The GM froze, and I watched my boss's jaw clench. Probably at the reminder that we'd both been forced to stop playing before we'd wanted.

I cleared my throat, adopted a tone that was much more business-like. "We need to support the women's league where we can, and Pru is one of their bigger stars."

"Agreed."

"Good," Luc said again. "You still coming to dinner tonight?"

"Depends. What are we having?"

Luc grinned. "Udon."

"I'm in. I'll meet you at your house. Want to finish up a few things here." With that, I stood, headed for the door.

"Ollie?"

The nickname—the one the guys used when I was still playing—hurt, but only just a little bit.

Better.

It was all getting better.

"Yeah?" I asked, turning back to face Luc.

"You've got this."

FOUR

Hazel

A WEEK after our first session, and I was ready for the knock.

Meaning, I didn't make him wait for me to answer the door, nor did I stare at him, though he was absolutely beautiful with the light from the hallway shining down on him, caressing the strong lines of his cheekbones, his jaw, his nose, made sexier for the bump that was in the middle of it.

But I was prepared for this session.

I didn't have a headache.

And I hadn't had a run-in with Trevor that morning.

Plus, I had a game plan.

Ignoring the sexual attraction I felt for him.

See? It was a good plan. A great one, even. Because I wouldn't be taking a turn on one of those fucked-up rides in Fucked Land.

I stepped back, smiling at him. "Come in," I murmured. "It's good to see you. Are you well?"

There. That was perfect.

Warm with the perfect amount of patient-doctor politeness.

Though I should probably refrain from questions of wellness, based on the way his eyes tightened at my inquiry.

"Fine," he said, and moved by me, striding to my desk, and dragging my chair over to the couch, so it was centered exactly like last time. Then he sat on the sofa and opened his mouth.

I was prepared for his distracting questions this time.

"Have you started your new position?" I asked before he could jump in.

His gaze went to mine, held for a moment, probably judging to see if I could be distracted again, could be pushed off my plan to talk about him. I wouldn't be, so I lifted my chin, stared back at him. And waited.

Something flickered in his eyes. He shifted slightly on the couch, and then he spoke in that quiet, easy voice of his. "I just finished the training course Luc wanted me to take."

Success!

Careful now.

I asked casually, "And was the course helpful to get you over your anxiety of taking the job?"

Brows raising, he leaned back into the cushions.

I elaborated. "Luc shared that you felt like you were under-qualified for the role."

"I am."

Said baldly.

"Why do you think that?"

Did this have to do with his injury?

A shrug. "I don't have any coaching experience. I would think to coach players, I would need to have a baseline amount of it, especially since we're talking about coaching in the NHL."

He had a point there, and there didn't seem to be any self-pity. Just resolution and reality, and I got the notion that this man was markedly well adjusted after what had happened to him.

Though I supposed he'd had time to come to terms with that.

But...did anyone ever really come to terms with such a thing?

I wasn't sure.

Oliver had experienced a violent attack, premeditated and completely outside the bounds of play. Mark Shelby had gotten himself banned from the league for it, was currently fighting criminal assault charges.

Because the hit that had so severely broken Oliver's leg had been egregious.

After the buzzer.

After the game-winning goal had been scored.

Mark Shelby had ended Oliver's career and didn't even seem to be sorry for it. Oh, he'd done the media apology—"I'm sorry he got hurt," and "I'm sorry it turned out that way for him"—but never once did he take accountability for his actions.

He didn't reach out, at least not according to Luc.

He didn't apologize to Oliver directly, again coming from Luc.

And all the while, Oliver had been focused on his recovery, on healing, and he'd been a rock, apparently. Hell, I'd seen that firsthand when *I'd* nearly passed out in his hospital room and had run away. He hadn't held it against me the next time I'd seen him (i.e., last week). In fact, he'd been polite, kind, then had fixed my computer from making that god-awful whirring noise.

Even.

Accepting.

No rage. No anger. No self-pity.

Again, those revelations had come from Luc, and I trusted the GM. Luc had spent a lot of time with Oliver.

So, if he said that I needed to talk to him, felt it was important enough to require it as part of his contract, then I was going to do my part to help him slay any demons that might be floating around his mind.

Even if that meant starting with his lack of coaching experience.

Especially, if it meant starting with his lack of coaching experience.

Because it was something personal, somewhere he didn't feel like he was measuring up, *and* it might be a start to get to the other things, the turmoil I'd just barely gotten a glimpse at the week before.

"While you don't have any coaching experience, you have a lot of player experience, and I would think that those in the development program would benefit from a player's perspective, especially if you bolster your experience by learning different methods of coaching." I paused, lifted a brow. "I'm assuming that was the purpose of the course you mentioned earlier."

A nod.

"So, the barrier, or at least part of it, has been removed. Do you feel better about taking the job?"

He was quiet for a long time. "I think I can be helpful to the team."

That was it.

"Are you excited about finding a new role?"

Those blue eyes held mine, and I couldn't get a read on a single emotion. Just...placid.

It was unnerving. Unnatural.

Then he softened. "I'm happy to be of use. I don't know what my life would be like if I didn't have hockey."

Hmm.

But also, he'd worked his whole life to make it to the NHL. He was twenty-nine. He should have had years ahead of him in the league. So, it wasn't exactly a surprise that he'd feel lost without it.

"What about your family?"

Luc hadn't mentioned them.

"Dead."

I blinked.

The word wasn't clipped out. But it did have a tinge of cold on the edges. "How did they die?"

He shrugged. "Overdose. I went into the system. Eventually got a foster family that adopted me. They're gone, too."

Staccato.

Short.

Bare facts recited.

I weighed for a moment how to proceed. "How old were you?"

"A baby when my bio parents died. Ten when I got to that foster family. Twelve adopted. Nineteen when they passed in a car accident."

Sympathy welled in me, but I didn't let it show.

That wasn't what Oliver needed in this moment.

"Did they support you playing?"

He nodded, seeming to relax when I brought up hockey. "My dad was the one who dragged me onto the ice that first time. I was lucky. I started late but had natural ability and people who supported me. There was no way that I should have made it as far as I did, but...things aligned. I loved it. Lived, breathed it."

And now, it was gone.

I also didn't miss that he'd referred to his adopted father as his dad. That certainly was understandable, but it was also another trauma.

"Did you play in the minors?"

A nod. "Just over a season. I was one of the lucky ones. Made my way to the league quickly and luckier still to stay here." He shifted his gaze away from me. "So, why that painting?"

Deflection.

But he'd given me something, so deflection was something I was going to give him. At least for a few minutes.

"My parents bought it for me. They have a winter house in Florida now. On the beach, and I love to go down there when it's ridiculously cold here and watch the waves." I smiled when he looked back at me. "I literally just sit on the sand and stare at the waves." A shrug. "There's something about them rolling in, slow and steady and unchanging, that I love. It's my happy place and part of why I like living near the ocean. Though I wouldn't say I'm tempted to put my feet in the water, at least not here."

"Too cold?"

"*Florida's* water is too cold for me." His lips tipped up and mine followed suit. "I'm more of a bathtub and hot tub kind of girl."

"Or just a *tub* kind of girl," he joked.

I drew my brows together, honestly thinking. "Are there other types of tubs?"

He paused, seemed to be considering that. "I can't think of any...oh, organizing tubs! That's a thing, right?"

Laughter danced on my tongue, but I swallowed it down. "It's a thing," I agreed then swept a hand around my office. The furniture shoved against the walls, my messy desk, the papers and books stacked on every flat surface. "Though, I can't say that I've had cause to use them."

Humor.

In the lines of his face. In his eyes.

I liked that a hell of a lot better than the deflection, the staccato from before.

"So, waves," he prompted.

I nodded. "Ocean waves—though I'll take them on the lake, too, or even a river sliding over rocks." I paused, turned the conversation back to him. "What's something you enjoy?"

That seemed to halt him in his tracks.

He went stiff. His jaw clenched.

I waited for implosion—well, if I were being honest, I braced for an explosion. Because that glimpse of emotion roiling beneath the surface was no longer hidden below it.

That turmoil was there. In the open.

And—

He shot to his feet.

I stayed still.

He paced to the punching bag, lifted a fist, and...rested it against the black leather. Then his forehead.

"I used to love the feel of the air in the rink."

"And now?" I breathed, not daring to give any strength to the question.

"Now it's torture." A long pause, his shoulders rising and falling. Slowly. Measured. "*Now* it's still the best fucking feeling in the world, even though I can't get back out on the ice —or at least not in the same way as before." Still inhaling and exhaling slowly, purposefully.

Then he turned to face me. "Why is your fiancé an ex-fiancé? I remember seeing him with you last year at one of the games. He was majorly in love with you."

I didn't think he meant that as a blow.

But it felt like one.

So, I didn't answer.

Oliver walked back to me, settling himself on the couch, and I tried to turn the subject back to him. "How else are you going to prepare yourself so that you're ready to get on the ice as a coach?"

Silence.

"Do you mean logistically or emotionally?"

"Which have you considered?"

A twist of his lips. "Both."

"Do you want to tell me about them?"

"Do you want to tell me about your ex-fiancé?"

I clicked the pen I held, not that I'd brought it to the notepad. I'd been too riveted by Oliver to jot anything down, too swept up in the web of him—male, confident, sexy, conflicted, just shy of tortured. Kryptonite. "I don't want to tell you about him, namely because this is about you, but also because he's an ex for a reason."

"Ah. He broke up with you."

Irritation welled in my veins. "No, actually. I dumped him."

"Hmm."

A sigh filled my lungs, but I forced myself to release it slowly, incrementally, letting it wash away my anger. Did I want to battle him on this? No. Did withholding this piece of information make any bit of difference considering I'd already told Lexi about the piece of shit my ex had been (though not nearly as shitty as Lexi's ex had been) and it was probably common knowledge amongst the Breakers' front office and support staff, which meant that it wouldn't take any bit of effort for Oliver to find out, if he really wanted to? Also, no.

Did some part of me *want* to tell him because, despite the deflection and semi-placidness, he seemed nice?

Okay, maybe yes.

And that maybe yes was why I found myself telling Oliver

everything, when normally I would *never* talk about my personal life with a client.

But Oliver wasn't a normal client.

Of course, he wasn't.

I wanted him.

He was there as a requirement of his contract.

I'd already blurred the lines between us more than a half dozen times, and we'd had one session together.

So, this wasn't going to be traditional. This wasn't going to be my helping a player get some mental clarity because he wasn't producing as he thought he should. This was building some connection that would help him release that tension he continued to try to bury.

This was me helping him.

And if I had to bare my soul to do it, expose my weaknesses to the light...then I would.

Because Oliver was worth it.

FIVE

Oliver

HER EXPRESSION WAS FILLED with irritation.

And then it wasn't.

As though one of the waves she loved had come to shore and washed a sandcastle away and left nothing but smooth, blank sand in its wake.

She was beautiful.

But I rather liked putting the befuddled look on her face, same as the irritated one. I didn't like this blank bullshit, the careful professional distance she kept trying to erect between us—and yeah, maybe that professional distance was the right thing, considering I was supposed to be her patient for the time being, and then we'd be working together, at least in some sort of professional capacity in the near future, but I didn't want any distance between us.

The *only* reason I hadn't asked her out within about ten seconds of meeting her that first time was the giant diamond ring on her finger.

A ring that was no longer there.

I felt like I'd been existing in a vacuum since the injury—and maybe that was something I should be telling her, something I should disclose. But that vacuum, that sense of suspension, had disappeared the moment I'd walked into her office. It had cleared in the hospital room, too. Just for a moment before she ran. And even before that, upon our first meeting.

Because while I would like to say that my vacuum existence had begun after I'd been hurt, that would be a lie.

Separate.

Always separate. Always with careful walls. Always carefully curated.

I would bleed for the team—and had. I would give them everything—and nearly had.

But I didn't take.

Because accepting meant gratitude, meant owing something back, meant...being vulnerable in a way I despised.

It was so much easier to be the one giving. I got to be the hero without any of the strings.

But you took the job, didn't you?

I had.

Because...I needed it.

And taking the job, even the required sessions with Hazel. I'd needed them both, needed to feel alive and out of that fucking vacuum and—

"My ex is an ex because he fucked around during his bachelor party"—she met my gaze, her eyes steely—"and by *fucked around* I mean, literally, fucked around. He banged three girls in the club they went to and then got a blowy from another. Four times in one night"—a shake of her head, her lips turning up, trying to force a smile, trying to make it all a joke—"*I never got that kind of stamina.*"

But the hurt was there, and I found myself sitting up straighter, wanting to reach for her, but not wanting to break the spell.

Because I wanted to know everything about Hazel Reid.

Even the bad.

A deep inhale. A shaky exhale. But her eyes remained dry. Over it enough for it to still hurt but not enough to make her break down.

"He told me himself."

I felt my eyes go wide.

"Walked straight into our condo the following morning, sat on the edge of the bed and told me what he'd done. And then —" Another shaking exhale. "He told me he'd decided he wasn't a one-woman man and that he didn't actually believe in marriage."

Silence.

On my front because I was trying to hold back my temper. I didn't think it would be particularly helpful to tell Hazel that her ex was a fucking douche canoe. On her front, she seemed to be lost in thoughts that I wouldn't be able to delve into.

A shrug, her voice markedly lighter.

"He still wanted to be together, wanted an open relationship. Yeah, like that was going to happen." She laughed quietly, though it wasn't in true humor. "It was good he told me before we got married, though. An easier...end." She cleared her throat. "I gave him his ring back, left while he packed his bags, and then...that was it. Three years, and one night, and we were done."

My heart pulsed. "It hurt."

She blinked, as though coming out of a trance, and nodded. "Yeah. It hurt. I felt betrayed in any number of ways, not the least of which was the cheating. But there was no going back, and luckily I didn't have to deal with trying to get a divorce if he hadn't learned of his preferences that night."

If he hadn't learned of his preferences?

The man was an asshole.

He *knew*. He just didn't care.

But bringing that truth up wouldn't help anyone. "You dodged a bullet."

She grinned. "I like to think of it as having dodged a grenade."

The joke surprised me, and I was caught off-guard by my laugh, not because anything about Hazel's situation was particularly joke-worthy, but because she was laying it out there so straight.

Calm. Her pain banked, her eyes looking forward.

Since that was my motto, I respected it a whole lot. Respected *her* a whole lot.

"There," she said, "now you know about my ex. Which is something I'd appreciate not circling the locker room if it hasn't. It's not like I'm trying to hide anything. I just..."

"Don't want everyone up in your business?"

She nodded.

I chuckled. "That might be hard for this crew."

Her eyes warmed. "Isn't that great?"

It was. It was fucking incredible, especially considering the dysfunction we'd begun with the previous season—mostly due to He Who Should Not Be Named—okay, due to Mark Shelby.

Shelby had been a talented player, but he was a cancer in the locker room, eating away at the good things, returning it as bad shit. He'd fucked Marcel's girlfriend, intentionally tried to injure people on the ice (even before his intentional hit on me that had gotten everyone to this point), and he constantly undermined anything positive.

Someone commented on a good play. Shelby commented with something snide.

Someone had a date. Shelby tried to get in there first.

Someone needed time with the trainers. All of a sudden, Shelby's "injuries" took top priority.

And that didn't even include the fucked up shit he'd said about Conner ("Smitty" for his last name of, unoriginally, Smith), Luca ("Cas" for Castillo, also another unoriginal nickname from his last name), and Raph (short for Raphael, perhaps the most uninteresting nickname of all).

Those guys were professionals, able to let it roll off their backs, a la water off a duck's feathery spine, but taken all at once?

The spirit in the locker room had been grim.

Luckily, Luc had stepped in, and though I knew I'd made a mistake not going to the GM with the issues and instead trying to handle them myself, Luc had guided me forward. Luc *should* have taken the captaincy from me because I hadn't handled the situation correctly. At the first sign of big trouble, I should have gone to the coaching staff, to Luc, should have worked out something with the assistant captains, Smitty and Cas. But I hadn't. I thought I had to handle it all myself, and the team had suffered. Despite all that, Luc had stuck with me.

Because Luc didn't punish people for making mistakes.

Because he was a good GM and Luc understood that I had been trying my best (even though it was a fucked-up best). We'd sat down together and figured out a way forward.

First step of that? Trading Shelby.

Next? Team building activities, including a plant growing contest that Lexi had begun us on. One I'd won, by the way, considering my plant, KiKi was still alive. Though I couldn't reasonably take credit for the last *after* my injury, since Lexi had used her green thumb (hell, the woman had two green hands) to keep it alive while I was recovering.

Not that it mattered.

My plant had survived the rest of the season.

No one else's had.

Come to think of that, I'd never gotten my spoils for winning the contest. I'd have to find Lexi and get her to give up the goods.

"It *is* great," I said. "In fact, the entire team is great."

They were.

They'd been there for me over the last months, the front office and support staff, too.

Food stocked in my fridge. My laundry done. My house cleaned. Company on my couch. A ride to doctors' appointments. A plethora of dumbasses taking up every bit of floor space in my living room so we could all play *Call of Duty*.

I hadn't been alone.

And that was why I was fine and moving on and focused on the future. No sense in looking back; that shit did no one any good, least of all me.

It didn't help to wish my parents hadn't OD'd.

To wish I hadn't ended up in foster care because my biological family wasn't willing to take me in.

To mourn my adoptive parents and wish I'd had them longer.

I was alone, but not by myself, if that made one fucking bit of sense.

To my brain, it did.

But maybe not to anyone else.

Because I was used to being on the periphery. Even as a player, as a captain, I'd been part of the team, but also had held a slice of myself back. That innermost piece I had to protect because if I gave that away and people left, if the rug was pulled out from beneath me again, as it had many times before, I wouldn't have anything left.

Being captain made that slightly easier.

The leadership meant that I had to be aware of the example I was setting.

And it was easier to protect that little piece.

"You got quiet," she murmured.

Not a question.

But still one anyway.

I met her gaze. "I think everyone keeps expecting me to lose it."

She set her pen down. I'd been watching her twirling it, spinning it between her fingers, not clicking it, but pulling up on the little tab at the top then letting it go. Then repeating the process again. The only time she wasn't playing with her pen was when she was spinning the glittering flower in her earlobe —around and around and *around*.

Not once had she actually written on the pad.

Which, perhaps, was why I said that.

Why I *admitted* it.

Hazel sat up a little straighter, held my eyes. "Why do you think that?"

I fell silent.

She waited.

So eventually, I continued admitting. "Everyone walks around me on eggshells. Everyone keeps asking me how I am, and when I tell the truth, when I say I'm fine, they look at me in disbelief."

More quiet.

Then, "You had something very traumatic happen to you. It would be completely understandable if you were not fine."

Nine months of this shit.

Nine fucking months of people expecting me to react a certain way.

Nine *fucking* months of people tiptoeing around.

Even Luc, the person who'd been most straight with me, hadn't pressed when he wanted to call me out on something. He just let it go. *Everyone* let it go. And maybe that should make me and my sliver of armored, protected self feel safe. Secure. But instead, it just kept pissing me off. Because fuck, why couldn't they see that I was doing *fine?*

The circumstances were shit.

But I was moving forward.

"I *am* fine."

Brown eyes on mine. Pretty with a breadth of colors I'd never seen before. Gorgeous, like some beautiful work of blown glass.

Except they held pity.

And sadness.

And were looking at me with the distinct impression that she thought I *wasn't* fine.

It was as though someone had flipped a switch.

One second, I *was* fine. The next I was *furious.*

I burst to my feet, and the words just flew from me, bullets flying out of a gun, clipped before I could smother them.

"I am more than a fucking leg!" I roared.

Probably loud enough for the entire building to hear, but fury had my hands clenched into fists, my teeth grinding together, red hazing my vision and making it so that I could hardly see those beautiful eyes, that gorgeous face.

Red. *Red.*

I leaned down, not so far gone as to not notice the way fear crept into her face, how her eyes went wide, hating myself for being the cause of it and yet, unable to stop.

I wanted to shake her, to make her understand.

But I'd never laid hands on a woman like that.

And I wouldn't start today.

Sucking in a breath, I turned, strode to the door, yanked it open, and got the fuck out of there.

Before I did something I might regret.

Like instead of shaking some sense into her...

Deciding I needed to kiss that sense into her.

SIX

Hazel

I WAS STILL SHAKING.

It had been ten freaking hours.

And I still felt like a shit bag.

I needed to refer him to a therapist who wasn't me. I wasn't qualified for this. I helped athletes visualize getting on the scoreboard or perfecting the ideal slap shot.

Dealing with the trauma of losing a limb wasn't in my wheelhouse.

I am more than a fucking leg!

He was.

And I and everyone else had reduced him to that.

"Fuck," I breathed.

Well, the first step to making it right was being here tonight. Luc had invited me to dinner at his home, and the first step was telling him that I was going to give Oliver a referral to another therapist, but that it should be up to him if he wanted to use it.

Ultimately, it needed to be up to Oliver if he wanted to unpack this all with someone.

But—more—ultimately, that person shouldn't be me.

Not when I was practically salivating over the man and off my game...and then making him feel like crap because I'd been so fucking reductive.

I am more than a fucking leg!

Guilt washed over me again—my best friend for the last ten hours—as I knocked on the door.

Footsteps on the other side.

The wooden panel opening...

To reveal Oliver.

Um...

His eyes widened, and he started to speak, but then Lexi was there, holding her baby, a gorgeous green-eyed little boy with wavy brown hair. Oliver stepped back to let me into the hall.

"Ah!" I squealed, moving forward to squish the little baby's cheeks. The infant pushing me beyond my guilt and firmly into cuddle mode. "How's my little Noah?"

Lexi smiled, despite the black circles beneath her eyes. "Not sleeping like he's going for a gold medal in the event."

"Oh, no." I plucked him from Lexi's arms, cuddling him close. "Why aren't you sleeping, baby boy?" A kiss to his forehead, those wide green eyes on my. "Are you trying to torture your mommy and daddy?"

Lexi yawned.

Noah smiled and giggled.

The scamp.

"All right," I ordered, tucking him onto my hip. "You go run yourself a bath. I've got Noah for an hour."

Lexi's brows furrowed. "But I've got to order dinner."

"Funny, I didn't realize I had a phone that could order Udon off DoorDash."

"I know I should have cooked—"

"No, you shouldn't have," Oliver murmured, closing the door behind us and ushering us down the hall. "We'll order the food. You take your bath."

Lexi's expression went chagrined. "You don't know what I want."

I recited her order.

Lexi bit her bottom lip, glanced between me, Oliver, and Noah. "What if he cries?"

"Honey, your house is nice," I said gently, "but it's not a mansion. If he cries, I'll take care of it. If I can't soothe him, I'll just walk up the stairs and knock on your bathroom door. Okay?"

"I—" More lip biting. "A bath does sound nice."

"Go," I ordered.

Lexi smiled, hugged me around Noah. "You're the best, Hazel." A beat. "And Oliver, I didn't mean to imply that you're not—"

"Go," he ordered.

Another moment of hesitation. Then I was gone, and I was standing in the hall next to Oliver and cradling an adorable baby.

"Where's Luc?" I asked as the silence stretched.

Oliver chuckled. "Passed out in his office. His dark circles had circles, so I suggested he close his eyes for a few minutes. It took approximately two seconds for him to pass out."

I grinned.

Then remembered why I'd needed to speak to my boss and sobered. "Oliver," I began, "I need to apologize to you." *Again.* It seemed I was always apologizing to him, always messing up.

His brows drew together. "Why?"

"I...um..." I bit the inside of my cheek, sucked in a breath through my nose and released it, finding my voice, finding the words I owed him. "I upset you this morning. You *are* more than your leg, and what I said is unforgivable, and—"

"Haze."

I blinked.

"It's fine."

"It's not fine," I told him. "I shouldn't have agreed to see you." His face clouded, and I hurried to add, "Not because of you. It's just...I'm a sports psychologist, and I'm not qualified to conduct therapy like I was trying to give you. I thought because we'd worked together before, it would be okay, but it's not. I'm not a good fit for what you need." My words came fast and furious. "So, I'm going to get you a referral for someone who is qualified for that kind of therapy, and I'm going to talk to Luc and tell him that he needs to take the sessions off as a condition of your contract because that should be your choice and not something you're forced into, and then—"

"Hazel."

"—I'm going to give you my referral's contact information, and then you'll only reach out to them if you believe that you want to talk to them and—"

He stepped forward, closed the distance between us as much as he was able, considering I was still holding Noah.

"Um..." I whispered before soldiering on. "And then I'm going to stick with counseling players about staying calm during a game or getting on the scoreboard and leave any coaxing out of trauma to the professionals."

That was the point I ran out of steam.

"You done?" he asked.

I nodded.

"Good." He shifted, put his hand on my back, and coaxed me forward, leading me into the kitchen almost as if it were his house instead of Lexi and Luc's. "First, thank you for apologizing. That was unnecessary but appreciated. Second, I'm the one who should be asking for your forgiveness. I shouldn't have yelled, and I certainly shouldn't have walked out like that. I—"

He hesitated long enough that I found myself filling in that blank.

"It's a big change, what happened to you," I whispered. "But it's not *my* change. It happened to you, and you're allowed to feel the way you feel. But more than that, what happened to you doesn't define your life. You're not Oliver James because you overcame something. You're not Oliver James *despite* something. You're just Oliver James, and that's enough, and it should be enough for everyone around you."

I'd been talking for long enough to have reached the kitchen, to have sunk into a chair at the table, cuddling Noah close.

I did that talking, not realizing that Oliver had dropped his hand from my back and was standing there, staring at me.

Intently staring at me.

Then he blinked and started moving again, his face going placid as he moved toward me.

Then *kept* moving toward me.

Not stopping until he was just inches away.

His fingers brushed my cheek, so lightly, so quickly—the slightest flash of a movement—and then he sank into the chair opposite my and pulled out his phone.

For a moment, I thought he was just going to sit there and chill on his phone while I held a dozing Noah, and for few minutes, that was what he did, tapping away at the screen, eyes on the device.

I stood. "I should go check on Lexi, make sure she didn't pass out in the tub."

Fingers on my hip, stalling me. "I've got Luc and Lexi's

order. What do you want? I'll put it in before you go check on her."

"For what?"

A flicker of humor. "Udon. You came over for dinner, right?"

Oh, right.

"Um..." My eyes drifted away. "You don't have to do that. I'll watch Noah for a bit and then go home and eat."

"Hazel."

My gaze slid back to his, unable to stay away.

"What do you want to eat?"

"I—" A breath. "You don't need to pay for me."

"You can get the next one."

Next...*one?*

"I—"

Noah squawked.

"Food, babe."

"I—"

"And not just for him," he said, standing up and scooping Noah out of my arms, moving toward the fridge and pulling out a bottle with a practiced ease that told me this wasn't the first time he'd taken care of the baby for Luc and Lexi. He used one hand to screw a nipple on the bottle, plunked it in the electric warmer, and then paced back and forth, bouncing Noah in his arms.

The man looked good with a baby.

Damned good.

Strong arms dwarfing the little guy, big hands cupping Noah's back, the baby's head covered in downy hair, Oliver's kissable mouth moving as he murmured to the baby, warm but indistinguishable words rumbling across the room, transfixing me as I stood there watching the pair.

The bottle warmer turned off.

Oliver checked the milk, plunked the nipple into Noah's mouth, and then turned to face me.

"Babe."

I blinked.

"Food."

"Um...what?" I breathed.

He smiled at me, and it was so fucking gorgeous that I just blinked again.

Then he was in my space again, and he smelled good and was gorgeous and...was *right there.* "Go check on Lexi, babe. I'll order you something."

"What?"

His fingers on my cheek again. His scent still in my nose, but his words processed, albeit slowly. "You. Lexi. Bath. Me. Food."

That trickled into my brain.

And then all I could think was that *God,* I needed to get it together if he was speaking to me in Caveman.

A breath.

Another.

Then I whispered, my cheeks no doubt bright red, "I'll go check on Lexi in the bath."

Spinning, I all but sprinted from the kitchen and hit the stairs.

God, I hoped that Lexi hadn't drowned in the tub while I had been making an idiot of myself in the kitchen.

Moving quietly, I knocked on the master bedroom door, and when Lexi didn't answer, moved inside, intending to avert my eyes if Lexi was getting out or if the tub came in sight and my friend was naked inside it.

But I didn't get that far.

Lexi was still completely dressed...and passed out on the foot of her bed. As though she'd sat there just a second, her hands having gone to the button of her pants, but she hadn't made it further than that before slipping into sleep.

Poor exhausted woman.

It was enough to make me want to get my tubes tied.

If I hadn't just cuddled the adorable Noah, I might be tempted, just purely from viewing the pure exhaustion on my friends' faces.

Now, however, I pushed down my pity (and my thoughts of permanent birth control) and tugged the covers down, folding them over my friend.

Then I tiptoed out of the bedroom, closing the door behind me.

SEVEN

Oliver

I'D GOTTEN over my fear of holding Noah several months ago.

Then my fear of holding Noah while standing on my prosthesis.

Now I could just hold and stare at the miracle—still tiny, though not as tiny as during those first few months after he'd been born, when Lexi had descended on my house, saying she needed to water my plants because horticulturicide wasn't going to be committed on her watch. The baby had grown, but I remembered the first time I'd held Noah.

Tiny fingers.

Chubby cheeks.

Eyes that seemed to bore into me even though the kid couldn't have seen more than a foot in front of his face.

That was the turning point for me.

Because I couldn't imagine how my own parents could have left me, drugs or not.

How they could have left an innocent child.

How my grandparents or aunts or uncles hadn't taken me in.

They'd left me to a system that was known to fail. They'd left me to a life without a lot of good in it. Until Teresa and Alex.

Ten years of dreary gray, and suddenly my life was in color.

Until I'd lost them.

But I'd struggled to hold on to the technicolor, knowing that was what they would have wanted for me. Even after my injury, after I'd lost everything, Teresa wouldn't have wanted me to end up back in all that gray.

Noah had reminded me of that.

When I'd been slipping back down that slope, the innocent newborn had pulled me out, and despite what the rest of the world thought, I really was *fine*.

Not normal. Not yet. But I'd get there.

Because, as I'd not so nicely yelled at Hazel, I wasn't defined by my leg. By the loss of it. By the loss of a career.

And if I continued saying that and moving forward and having my eyes up and aware and on the fucking puck, I would be okay. The parts of me that hated where I was, hated Mark Shelby, hated that I wasn't in that locker room or on the ice or handing a game-used stick over the boards to some kid who would be so excited to receive it she'd be sleeping with it under the covers next to her would eventually fade into the background.

I knew it.

I'd experienced it.

Just...eye on the puck.

A flicker of movement in the hall caught my focus, and I saw Hazel standing there, her face soft and her eyes warm.

When she noticed me looking at her, she smiled and moved into the kitchen. "You're good with him."

I shifted and leaned against the counter. "He's a good baby."

"Except about the whole not sleeping thing."

"Except, about the whole not sleeping at the *right time* thing," I countered, and watched amusement glimmer through those pretty brown eyes.

"That's true." She tucked a strand of her hair—short, curly, and just reaching her jaw—behind her ear. "It's enough to make a woman never want to have kids."

That made something in me stand up and take notice.

Something I'd been ignoring since I'd found out about her ex now being an ex. Something I knew I probably shouldn't act on.

But something I was realizing I was going to act on anyway.

"Kids aren't something you want?"

She moved toward me, pausing just a foot away, her eyes no longer on me but on Noah, and while I didn't like that, the look on her face as she glanced down at the sleeping baby was so fucking gorgeous it took my breath away.

Wonderment. Gentleness. Love, even though it wasn't her kid.

I'd had that.

It was the best drug on the planet—a woman's love, a mother's love.

"I want kids," she murmured. A corner of her mouth hitched up, and I was close enough to see that one day lines would form there, lines born of humor and happiness and inside jokes.

I *wanted* that with a sudden urgency that nearly sent me to my knees.

"I just"—a finger brushing along Noah's downy cheek—

"wish they'd come with the ability to sleep." Her eyes hit my, and I could almost see the laugh lines forming around those pretty brown depths, too, the lines she'd earn with age and would only make her more beautiful. "Because I really like to sleep."

She laughed, and I joined in, quieting the sound when Noah jumped, though the baby slept on, thus proving that he *could* sleep, but that he just preferred to do it in someone's arms and during the day, rather than in his crib and at night.

"Can I hold him?" she asked when we quieted again.

"Of course."

We made the switch, and I watched her shift into Mom Mode, or rather move with that instinctual motion that soothed and allowed Noah to sleep on, the movement that came from somewhere deep inside, maybe programmed into a woman's DNA all the way back to the caveman days.

And if I'd ever voiced that thought aloud, my adopted mom, Teresa, would have smacked me upside the head and then threatened to never make me brownies again—because not all women wanted to be mothers, and me assuming that it was written into Hazel's DNA, but not my own was patriarchy defined. Hence, head-smacking and brownie-hostaging.

But Teresa wasn't around any longer, and thinking about the loss of her rather than the look my dad would have given me had I voiced my instinctual, caveman thoughts (namely that Alex would have cracked up, huge smile turning up the edges of his mustache, and then he would have ruffled my hair the same way he had when I was ten, the same way he *always* would have, no matter my age if the car accident hadn't taken them both from my life), was too painful.

So, I focused on caveman DNA.

On brownie hostages and head smacks that didn't hurt.

And Hazel.

"You're good with him," I murmured. *God*. And seriously, I had a beautiful woman in front of me and I could only repeat the same inane statements over and over again?

I used to be charming.

Now I was...out of practice.

Luckily, Hazel didn't seem to notice. Her smile grew as she smoothed Noah's hair back. She slowed her swaying and gazed up at me, eyes twinkling. "He's a good baby." Okay, maybe she did notice my lack of conversation skills, but at least she was still smiling, her voice soft when she said, "But you know that."

There was a question there.

Laid down quietly, but also like an olive branch.

How had I become so familiar with Noah and his routine? With this house.

"Lexi and Luc spent a lot of time at my place after I was discharged from the hospital, and I spent a lot of time here after Noah was born."

She nodded, taking in the answer to her question that hadn't been asked.

"You know about him, too," I said.

Another nod. "Lexi heard about my breakup and descended on my place with ice cream, wine, and Noah." Sad flickering across her face.

I ground my teeth together, forced my voice to be gentle. "I'm sorry your ex was a dick."

"He *was* that." She sighed. "But I think..." She trailed off and shook her head, eyes drifting to the window, the one that looked out onto the back yard and the lush oasis Lexi had created there.

My feet—one made of metal and composite, the other flesh and blood, but both belonging to me—took me to her, close enough to smell her shampoo, something sweet and floral, to smell *her*. Clean. Woman. *Hazel*. "You think what?" I asked softly.

Her body jerked slightly, as though she hadn't heard me moving, as though she'd been too lost in thought to hear me. "I think..." She turned and her lips parted, eyes flaring, words halting.

Our gazes connected.

I watched the shiver skate down her spine.

Then her lips pressed together, heat dipping into her irises, a blush sliding onto her cheeks.

"Hazel?"

"Hmm?" she murmured.

"What do you think?" I asked. "About your ex?"

The heat banked and while I didn't like that, I also really wanted this piece to the puzzle of her.

"I think," she said, turning back to the window, "that I'm more sad because I think that I should be *more sad*." A shake of her head. "That doesn't even make sense. I *am* sad my engagement ended, especially the way it did. I'm sad that I misread someone so completely to get to the point where I had a dress and a date and had gone cake tasting without understanding who he was. I'm sad that I failed myself in knowing who he was when he should have been the most important decision in my life."

"And you failed."

Her gaze remained out the glass. "Now you sound like my mother."

I winced.

She must have caught it in the reflection of the window. "She's great," she said quickly, turning to face me. "Sorry, I just meant that tone is very much my mother, and usually paired with something along the lines of *You hold yourself to too high a standard, Hazel Montgomery Reid,* or *People fail,*

Pumpkin, or *You can't always do everything exactly right, sugar pie.*"

I grinned. "Sugar pie?"

She did, too. "That along with honey cakes, banana blossom, apple sweetkins, and"—her brows drew together—"an iteration on pretty much any other baked good she's ever consumed. It was torture in high school." Pink on her cheeks, eyes back on the window. "And now I'm blabbering to you about my ex *and* my high school experience. Cool."

Fuck, she was sweet.

A sigh. "My point was, my mom has always been intrinsically herself and never fails to call it like she sees it, including if calling it means showing her daughter that she loves her by calling her Banana Bread Sweetums in front of her entire school while emceeing the talent show"—more pink on her cheeks—"a show I refused to participate in but was forced to volunteer at and work the concession stand because my mom... is my mom."

I chuckled.

"See?" she said. "It's terrible." A begrudging smile. "But it's also pretty awesome because my mom is always the same, always just *her,* and she makes it easy to be her daughter."

"Even though she calls you Banana Bread Sweetums?" I teased.

Her smile grew. "Even though."

We stood there grinning at each other, and I found myself drifting closer, even though I was already close. But there was something about Hazel that drew me in, a tractor beam to the Millennium Falcon, a lure drawing a fish into a hook.

I thought that her mom must have rubbed off on her.

She was herself.

Open and sweet and self-deprecating.

I liked it. I liked *her.*

"Your mom is right," I murmured.

"Hmm?"

"You *are* too hard on yourself."

A flash of consternation drifted across her face. "Oliver."

I touched her cheekbone—high and tinged with pink. "You've apologized to me like a hundred times since we started meeting, all for things that weren't a big deal."

"Me nearly passing out in your hospital room because I'm a weakling about blood and you thinking it was related to you wasn't a big deal?"

I shrugged. "You explained. It's done."

"Me making you furious enough to leave a session—rightly so, of course—because I made it about your injury instead of you?"

"Again. I explained. You explained. You apologized. I apologized." Another shrug. "Not a big deal."

"Oliver, I—"

"Hazel."

Her eyes narrowed. "It wasn't a big deal for me to agree to Luc's scheme to fix you when you didn't need fixing?" She scowled. "I should have told him that in the first place instead of thinking I was going to swoop in on my white horse, a knight in shining armor, waving my sword around."

I grinned, imagining her on horseback, waving that sword through the air.

But then she looked so torn up about it that my grin faded, and I found myself running my knuckles over her cheek, something that, every time I did it, I told himself I shouldn't. Still, it was something I couldn't stop myself from doing because her skin was like silk, and touching her was...

Everything.

"Ask me why I agreed to those sessions," I murmured.

"Even when I was still thinking it was my injury that had terri-fied you."

"I..." Her brows dragged together. "What?"

I tried another way. "Ask me why I didn't tell Luc to fuck off when he told me about the sessions with you."

A beat, then, "Why?"

"Because they were with *you*."

Her lips parted.

I shifted closer. "Because the first moment I saw you, I wanted to ask you out."

We parted farther.

"Because I would have told Luc to fuck off if those sessions were with anyone but you."

Farther still.

And I knew the world could be ending, but I still would have to taste those lips.

So, I did.

EIGHT

Hazel

HE WAS LEANING IN.

His mouth brushed mine.

He tasted...*wonderful.* I leaned in, shifting to not squish Noah, but then that was the last conscious thought I had because his hands slid into my hair, he murmured, "These fucking curls," against my lips, and then he kissed me.

The world stopped spinning.

Gravity ceased being a thing.

I was floating and drifting through a cloud of desire.

The doorbell rang

And I plummeted toward the ground.

Oh shit. Oh. *Shit.*

I was kissing Oliver James. My client. I was kissing my client. Oh, fucking hell. I was a psychologist and kissing a client and—

"I lost her," Oliver murmured, pulling back slightly, enough that I could see the humor in his eyes. "I guess I'll just have to try harder." He leaned back in.

"O—"

The doorbell rang again.

A sigh. From him? Me? I didn't know. But he didn't seem particularly upset, so I figured it was from me and the weird push-pull in my gut rather than Oliver, especially when he smiled gently and kissed the tip of my nose. "I'll get the door. You try not to freak out."

Yeah.

Like that was going to happen.

But before the sound of disbelief made it up my throat and out through my lips, he was striding into the hallway and I heard him open the door, the crinkle of him accepting a bag—our dinner, I supposed—and his footsteps returning.

Then he was back, smiling, calm, and assured, as though he hadn't kissed me in a way that changed everything...*and* I'd only gotten a marginal amount of tongue.

As in, it had been in my mouth, stroking along mine, coaxing mine out to play, and giving me the best kiss of my life —and that included those given to me by *Trevor*, the freaking man I was supposed to have married, kisses that I'd thought were fucking fantastic considering Trevor could use his lips and tongue in a way that was hot, not sloppy, and didn't leave me wiping my mouth on the back of my hand after we'd finished.

So yeah, I still had more trauma from my high school days, and that didn't end with my mom calling me Banana Bread Sweetums in front of the entire teenage populace.

First boyfriend.

First kiss.

First time I'd been slobbered on.

That made me shudder.

And fingers found my cheek again, that light brush of Oliver's knuckles over my skin, causing me to shudder again, though this time for a completely different reason than the previous one. Namely, that every time he'd done that—*did* that —it made my imagine him doing that on different parts of my body.

Naked.

And by different parts, I meant *everywhere.*

"Cold?" he murmured, setting the bag on the table.

"No."

It was a whisper. One that drew his focus.

"Freaking out?"

"No."

Still a whisper.

"Then why are you trembling like you're in the rink in a bikini?"

That had my mouth twitching and my tongue—unfortunately in my own mouth and not being coaxed out to play by *his* supremely more talented one—loosening. "First, it was a shudder because I was thinking about our kiss and how it was good, better than even Trevor's, and that got me thinking about the bad, and how my first kiss had warranted a rub-off afterward."

His brows rose, something like displeasure flitted across his face.

Defensiveness crept into my tone. "What?"

"Rub-off?"

I paused, brows drawn together for a long moment, then gasp. "Not *that* kind of rub-off. I meant having to rub the spit off my lips because he tried to Hoover my mouth."

"Ah."

A glare. "*That's* all you have to say?" I demanded.

"Well, in fairness, I didn't know what kind of *rub-off* you were referring to."

The fucker's eyes were twinkling, as though he had tiny stars glittering in his irises.

"I wouldn't jerk off a boy in high school after *one* kiss. Hell, I wouldn't do that *now*. That's third date stuff or fifth or—"

"Babe."

"*Sixtieth* date stuff and—"

"*Babe.*"

"What?" I snapped.

"I wasn't talking about you jerking him off. I was talking about *you* rubbing one out."

"And it's up to me if I grab a cock or not and *when* I want —" I continued to snap at him, for no reason except because he was being presumptuous, and I wasn't going to allow him to be presumptuous, not on my time—"so long as the man whose cock I'm grabbing wants that, too, because consent is a thing and—" Then his words processed. "Rub. One. *Out?*" My mouth gaped open, and I stared up at him.

The sparkling stars were still in his pale blue eyes.

But now they'd been joined by heat and—holy *hell*—was that some *heat*. Christ. The man was threatening to set me on fire.

"Yeah, babe," he said, like he was completely unaffected. "I'm assuming you touch yourself?"

I nodded.

"But I'm also guessing, based on your reaction and the aforementioned Hoovering, that it wasn't in relation to *that* kiss."

I nodded again.

Knuckles on my cheek. "When do you do it?"

A silken question, one that almost had me telling him.

But then I remembered myself, remembered where I was and who I was with, and was I seriously discussing my masturbating habits with Oliver James, who was still a client, in my *boss's* house, while holding my boss's baby.

Seriously.

What. The. Fuck. Was. Wrong. With. Me?

I was holding a *baby*.

I resisted the urge to earmuff his tiny little head so he wouldn't hear, even though the damage would have already been done to his developing brain at this point if he'd been able to understand a word of what we were talking about with our discussion of rubbing.

Fuck.

Okay, I was starting to save up for his therapy fund now, *and* I'd start gathering referrals immediately.

"I've lost her again," Oliver murmured.

I narrowed my eyes.

"Second?"

I blinked.

"You said first." He was close again, those knuckles on my skin, sliding down over my jaw and along my throat. "So, what's second? Why else were you trembling earlier?"

The man had magical powers.

That was it.

He'd wielded his imaginary wand and put some charm on me that made everything running through my mind slid right off my tongue.

Okay.

It wasn't him.

At work I often had to bite my tongue, though not as much as if I'd been a therapist who counseled people on their lives instead of hockey players who needed to get their head in the game and who most of the time preferred that I give it to them straight instead of going easy (though some of them definitely *did* need easy, especially if they'd been on the snide—not scoring—for a while). But outside of my work, I tended to fly free and loose. My mom was...herself and never met a tongue she liked to bite. My dad was chill and laidback but didn't have any qualms about being honest either—whether that was when my mom made something new for dinner (or he did because they took turns cooking, though his experiments often ended in the trash and then my parents ended up with takeout) or if he thought I was dating someone he didn't like.

For the record, Trevor had been almost at the top of that list while we were dating and engaged and had moved to that absolute top spot after our engagement had broken off in the way it had.

Which was the only reason I could think of later for why I told Oliver what I did.

"Second," I blurted, "I was trembling because the kiss was good. *Really* good, and it was *so* good that I wish we hadn't done it because I can't pursue this because you're a client—"

"I thought you were cutting me loose as a client."

"—and now," I said, ignoring him and giving him the rest of it because that was my, and fuck if I was going to be anything but myself, even with gorgeous Oliver James and his pale blue eyes and hair I wanted to grab tight while he rubbed one out on *my* was standing six inches from me, "I'm going to be thinking of that kiss every time I have to work with you—"

"Which you just said was never, babe," he pointed out.

Annoyingly.

"And," I went on with more ignoring because I was on a roll, "I liked kissing you because your tongue has some serious fucking skill, and I can't help but imagine what that might feel like stroking over my clit."

He stiffened. "*Babe.*"

I inhaled, let it out slowly. "Right. It might have been a mistake to tell you that."

"Not a mistake." His voice was a rasp, and then I dropped my gaze...to his pelvis. Okay, not his pelvis. That was me pretending I didn't see what I saw. Which was lower.

And harder.

Oliver's cock was hard and pressing against the zipper of his jeans.

Lovingly cupped by his already tight jeans because even though he was less bulky than before his injury, his ass was still a hockey player's ass, and that meant there wasn't a whole lot of space in that denim. As thus, his erection was emphasized by that material, and...

I wanted to touch.

Clearing my throat, I shifted away from him. "I'll put Noah down, check on Luc and Lexi." I didn't want to give up my shield—which probably said horrible things about my being willing to use a baby as a human shield so I didn't touch Oliver's lovingly cupped cock—but I'd corrupted Noah enough already.

And it was really hard to earmuff with only one free hand.

Plus, sometime during this dangerous conversation, Noah had gone out. Not just dozing. But out. *Way* out. So I'd put him into his crib and hoped that he slept long enough that his parents emerged from the other side of their naps semi-human again.

"Babe?"

It probably also said something bad about me that I shivered when Oliver called me babe in that slightly raspy voice. And that I stopped and turned back to face him without hesitation, without commenting on the endearment.

Letting it go when I should be telling him to stop.

Instead, all I said was, "Yeah?"

"It wasn't a mistake to tell me that."

Shivers and shudders and trembling.

I had them the entire way to Noah's room, while trying to put him down (super not conducive to keeping the infant asleep while I did so, though I managed), and while peeking into the master bedroom and then the den, finding Lexi and Luc, respectively, both still asleep, both snoring quietly, their faces slack, their bodies relaxed.

I still had those shivers when I forced myself to walk back into the kitchen—both because I wasn't a coward and because Oliver was in there and I couldn't make myself walk out the front door.

Expecting a confrontation or at least some conversation that would have necessitated earmuffs for Noah, had he been in my arms still, I was surprised to find two containers of udon set out on the table, utensils at their sides, Lexi's candle lit and set in the middle of the table, soft music playing from...somewhere (his phone I realized on closer examination). The bag was gone, Lexi and Luc's food hopefully stowed in the fridge, and Oliver was standing there studying me—

While I studied the space.

His face was unfathomable.

Then he smiled, and it made my heart skip a beat.

"Hungry?"

I was.

But it wasn't for udon.

NINE

Oliver

I SIPPED THE BROTH, not hot like I would get at a restaurant since it had been sitting for a bit now, but still delicious, especially with the noodles and veggies.

Seriously, one of my favorites ever since Lexi had turned me on to it.

Hazel was similarly engaged in her food, after she'd stared at the kitchen with the candle, dimmed lights, and music playing like it was a rattlesnake and she was just about to step on it, fangs exposed, rattle shaking.

Which had made me wonder if it was because she read into the effort for what it was.

Because I *had* tried to bring a little romance, considering we weren't in either one of our houses and we were alone, but my and Hazel's boss and coworker were currently sleeping off their fatigue only rooms away.

But it had also made me wonder if the lights and candle and music had surprised her in a way that wasn't because I was trying for romance, but because no one had done it for her before.

That was what I had read from her reaction, from the wide eyes and stuttered steps, from the way her face went soft, her eyes warmed.

Had her asshole of an ex not given her any romance?

They'd been engaged, for God's sake.

And this was one three-wick candle, a Spotify playlist, and a dimmer switch slid halfway down.

"Babe?"

"Hmm?" Her eyes stayed on her spoon, on the noodle she was carefully piling onto it using her chopsticks.

"Was your ex a bigger asshole than I already suspect he was?"

The noodles plopped into her bowl. "Um, what?"

"I lit a candle and put a playlist on, Haze. I flicked a light switch. And you came in looking around like you'd never had that before."

She set down the spoon. "I—"

"Don't bullshit me."

A frown gathered on her features. "I don't owe you an explanation of my life."

"No, you don't," I agreed. "But I want to hear all about it anyway."

Her shoulders rose and fell on a breath. "Pushy."

I shrugged.

A sigh. Then, "You're right," she said very, very softly. "I haven't had...*that*. Stupid, really. It's small, but it was sweet, and it...surprised me, I guess, especially when you just invited me to eat and know that you can't get anything out of it."

There was a lot to unpack there.

Starting with me only doing something so I could get something in return.

And ending with her not having had candles and music. What the fuck kind of man had her ex been?

Considering that he'd left her after fucking around on her at his bachelor party, I supposed I already knew, and it made me want to get the fucker's name and address and then show him a little of what I used to give guys on the ice.

But instead, I asked the question I thought was more important.

Which was, "How do you know I can't get anything out of it?"

Her brows lifted. "Because we're in Luc and Lexi's house."

"If you think for a second any man wouldn't take the opportunity to fuck you senseless—just because his boss was sleeping in the next room—" I shift closer. "You have no clue what your appeal is."

She gaped.

I reached over and brushed my knuckles on her cheek. "But, you're right, it's not a first date thing." Certainly, not with a woman like Hazel. "Though, I can't commit to not stealing another kiss tonight because that *is* a first date thing," I added, just because I wanted to see if she would get befuddled and what she would say.

Or more befuddled, anyway, because she'd gotten that adorable frown between her eyes, rosy pink cheeks, and parted lips when I had talked about fucking her senseless.

"*Another* kiss?"

"You said you liked it, baby."

She shook herself, and fuck, if I didn't like her, didn't like the way she made me feel. Like a man. Whole and untarnished with none of the past drawing me down. Like I could look forward and build a future and...

Just be.

A beat of hesitation. Then she lifted her chin and said, "I did."

"Well then." I reached across the table and handed her the spoon. "Eat up, and we'll see how the future goes."

***

AFTER WE'D FINISHED our udon, Noah had woken up, not because he was hungry but because he needed to be in someone's arms to sleep.

So, we were standing on the back patio taking turns holding the munchkin and talking about nothing.

Different from the conversations we'd had in her office.

She was relaxed and open and a lot of fun.

We discussed the usual pop culture stuff, movies and TV shows, and what streaming service we couldn't live without, but then she surprised me and asked, "When did you get into computers?"

She hadn't mentioned me fixing her laptop the previous week, and I'd thought that since she'd been trying to kick that headache and hadn't been feeling a hundred percent herself, that she might have forgotten all about it.

But now she was walking Noah back and forth, bouncing him and trying to settle his little colicky soul and waiting for me to answer.

"I like taking things apart and putting them back together." My lips twitched.

"What's that for?" Hazel drifted closer, touched the corner of my mouth. "You're smiling."

"I was thinking about Teresa. She and Alex bought me a computer one Christmas because I had begged and begged for it. We thought I was too young—God, I had to have been thirteen, fourteen? And we had a family desktop. But I wanted my own, and I was going to get it. So, I started saving money and doing extra chores, determined to buy it myself." My heart squeezed. "And then I opened my present on Christmas morning, and they'd gotten me my own computer."

"That's sweet."

It had been.

"They told me to use my money to buy all the cool things a teenager was desperate for—the light-up cooling fan, the keyboard that had built-in LEDs, the mouse that was red and black and had fancy buttons." Fuck, I'd been so proud of my keyboard. "So, I did, but I also had enough money left over to buy some books on computers. Which also meant that I was curious about the inner components and took apart the computer."

Hazel gasped.

"Teresa nearly lost her shit."

"Did you put it back together?"

"What do you think?"

A pause then her pretty brown eyes drifted to my, studying me closely. "I think yes."

I grinned, pushed off the rail, snagged Noah (because it seemed like Hazel couldn't help herself from coming close when I did that), and returned to the railing because my thigh was aching. My evil genius plan worked because Hazel trailed me, leaning next to me, her hand smoothing up and down Noah's tummy.

Which meant that she was pressed into my side.

But I wasn't going to say anything.

Not when I got that sweet and floral scent of her. Not when I got her breast grazing my arm and sending tendrils of desire snaking through my body.

"Well?" she prompted, studying Noah.

"I put it back together."

She smirked, fist-pumped with her free hand. "I knew it." A beat. "Teresa was your adopted mom?"

I nodded, heart pulsing again. "Yeah."

"What was she like?"

"A lot like your mom, I think. Or at least, how you've described her. She was warm and funny and didn't care that I was a ten-year-old boy who'd never been shown love or affection. She gave it to me without reservation. She gave it even when I'd convinced myself I didn't want it."

"That sounds wonderful."

"It was an adjustment," I said. "After being on my own for so long, I wasn't used to relying on other people."

"Still aren't, I'd wager." It was a murmur, but not one I could ignore.

"No," I agreed. "I'm definitely not used to people taking care of me or looking out for me. I'm still...I don't know, not open in that way. When you grew up the way I did, you learn to protect yourself. You bury the things that hurt and move on because there isn't any time for you to process it. Survival is most important."

"I can understand why you needed that." A squeeze of my arm. "Even if it makes me sad that you had to go through that."

No judgment.

No pity.

Just empathy and understanding.

I fell right there for her. Just a little bit. Okay, maybe more than that considering I'd pulled out romance in the form of a candle, music, and dimmed lights in my boss's house.

But how couldn't I?

She was incredible.

And because of that, I found myself still talking. "Teresa basically bullied her way into loving me, dragging Alex behind her—he wasn't the bullying type. He was quiet and patient and could out-wait the *fuck* out of me."

Hazel giggled, and it wasn't lost on me that she still had her hand on my arm.

"My dad is like that, too," she said. "He's so chill that it seems like he's just letting everything go and then *bam,* you find yourself on the other side of his piercing stare, and you just blabber like you're a seven-year-old trying to pretend you didn't eat the last cookie."

Amusement hit me hard, building in my gut, filling my chest, bubbling in my veins. Funny and smart and sweet.

Perfect.

"And Luc and Lexi?" she asked. "They seem to get through the protective barriers." A comment, albeit a gentle probing one. But since it wasn't filled with pity or—too much—pressure, I found it easy to answer.

"Have you met those two? They're as stubborn as they are pig-headed. I couldn't *not* let them in. Even if I tried, they would have barreled their way right through any protective barriers after my injury."

"Says the man who keeps stealing the baby from me because he's worried my arms are going to get tired."

I pretended to flex, as much as I could do so with a baby in my arms. "Look at these muscles compared to your puny biceps."

"Hey!" She tugged up the short sleeve of her blouse and flexed, showing off a surprisingly toned upper arm. "I do pilates four days a week! I'm strong enough to cart around that little one." Her body drifted to me, her head dropping to my shoulder for a moment, and my breath caught at the sheer inti-macy of having her that close while cuddling a baby. She seemed to realize the same because she stepped back and before I could process the loss of her against me, she asked,

"Did you expect anything different of Luc and Lexi? Or the team?"

"No." I shook my head. "I'd be there, doing the same if it was any of the other guys. But because it was me..."

Gentle brown eyes on me. "Weird?"

A snort. "Weirder than anything I've experienced. Made harder by everyone expecting me to freak out."

"I think it would be normal to freak out."

My pulse sped. "And what would that get me?"

Her voice was even. "Closure? An emotional release? Acceptance?"

Anger coiled in my stomach, pushing out the humor and sensation of falling hard and happily. "And how will that change anything?"

"I'm not saying this as a therapist," she said softly. *Carefully*. And I was brought back into her office earlier that day, to me losing my shit, to the guilt that I'd carried until I'd seen her that evening. Because she wasn't a punching bag, and this wasn't her fault.

Neither was the conversation.

She'd been open.

I was doing the same.

"I'm saying it as your friend," she went on, just as soft, just as careful, and I tempered my reaction, "as the woman who really, *really* enjoyed that kiss in the kitchen. Not that you're going to get another one," she added quickly, and a curl of amusement wrapped around me—bare feet walking along the shore, a wave dancing up the sand and just barely washing over my toes. But it was there, and the urge to lash out and push her away, to keep myself safe, dissipated. "I think there could be something helpful in a freak-out. I...had my fair share of them after Trevor decided to end things, and it released some of the fury that was tearing me up inside."

I reached out, rubbed one of her curls between my fingers. "I wish you didn't have to go through that."

She rested her hand on my chest, leaned a little heavier into my side, still careful of the baby. "Right back at ya, big guy. And I think that's why Luc, Lexi, and company are so worried. Luc especially, since he had that injury that ended his career. It threw him for a loop in a way that couldn't have been easy to come back from, and for all intents and purposes, your injury was worse, you know?"

I processed that, still rubbing that curl, back and forth, back and forth.

I knew.

I understood that.

So, I nodded.

"But what he needs to understand, and the part I missed enumerating to him, is that your feelings are *your* feelings. You don't grieve via a playbook. You do it under your own terms and timeline, and that's why you and I never would have worked."

"Babe," I warned.

She softened. "I'm referring to required therapy sessions, honey."

I pulled lightly on the curl. "And not to the fact that both of us are considering how you and I might work in other ways?"

"Oliver," she warned. But she didn't back away, didn't tug her head—her curl—out of my grip. She kept her body to mine, her curl between my fingers, her scent to my nose.

"Don't give me that bullshit about me being a client and you a therapist," I said.

"It's not bullshit, I—"

I fixed her with a glare. "We had two sessions together, and during the first one, I fixed your computer and asked you questions about yourself—which you answered, by the way, and based on the therapists that came to my room while I was in the hospital was very *not* therapist-esque."

She winced, hurt streaking across her beautiful face.

Fuck. Shifting, I released her hair and caught her jaw instead. "Not a comment on you or your abilities, babe. You're talented and smart, and I know that not just because I've spent time with you, but because Luc wouldn't have hired you otherwise."

Her throat worked.

I kept going. "So, the way I see it is that our first date was in your office, me fixing your laptop, you telling me about yourself. Our second date was this morning, and I almost blew it, but I redeemed myself with udon, dimmed lights, a candle, and music for our third date." My thumb brushed her bottom lip. "And I waited until the third date for a kiss, even though I was desperate to do it from the moment I first saw you walking into the practice facility last year."

Wide eyes on mine. "You were?"

A nod. "Until I saw that diamond ring on your left hand and realized someone had got there first." Another brush of her bottom lip before I leaned close and whispered in her ear, "And I was still desperate to do it even *after* I saw the ring."

She shuddered. "So, the music wasn't just about doing something nice?"

"Hell no." I nipped her earlobe. "It was about you and me and making it clear to you that I am as far away from a client as I can be." I straightened, her curls clinging to the stubble on my cheek, wafting that floral and sweet scent into the air. "It wasn't about me getting something. It was me making a point that you're a woman I want to know better. Though what I already know about you means that you deserve the romance, the candles and music and dimmed lights and a hell of a lot more than that." A brush of my knuckles over her skin. "It was me telling you that in no way do I consider our relationship anything resembling doctor-patient, and I hope to fuck that you don't because I want to take you out on date four."

The only noise was the breeze through the trees, rattling the leaves, mingling in with the sound of our breaths, the soft hoot of an owl, the occasional rumble of a car driving in the distance. For far too long that was it.

I'd laid it out there.

And she'd gone silent.

And stiff.

I couldn't miss that either. She was still next to me, her front pressed to my side, her hand on my chest, but she might as well have become a statue instead of a living, breathing woman.

But I'd just given her a lot to process, so I waited.

Quietly.

Absorbing the noise of the busier street in the distance, the critters making themselves at home during the night, the leaves rustling, the way her breathing had been short and staccato and a bit loud, but how it was now slowing and evening out and growing quiet.

I knew she was going to speak before her soft words filled the air. I'd sensed something in her body, the way the space around her shifted, the slightest bit of easing in the tension filling her frame.

"I liked the music," she whispered.

My breath slid from my lips on a long, slow exhale, heart pounding because some part of me had been worried she would deny it—the draw, the connection, the tractor beam pulling us together.

"I did, too."

She relaxed. Her head came against my shoulder, and we stood there, the night sounds surrounding us all over again.

At least until I said, "So, am I going to get a date four?"

Tilting her head up brought her body away from my—which I didn't like—but it brought her mouth in line with my—which I liked for obvious reasons. Then she smiled, and I knew I had to taste her, date four on the line or not.

I bent, felt her warm breath on my lips.

And then the sliding glass door opened behind us.

Luc stumbled out onto the patio, his hair askew, his shirt wrinkled, and if I was seeing correctly, the imprint of his watch on his cheek.

"Argh," Luc grunted, not quite human yet as he rubbed his eyes.

Hazel stepped away.

"Why don't you go back to sleep?" she said. "We have Noah."

Green eyes were slowly clearing. "I—"

Footsteps on the wood floor behind Luc, Lexi slipping through and shutting the door that Luc had left open. She'd been asleep for a shorter amount of time, but it appeared to have refreshed her. Either that or she just was better upon waking, because those dark circles were still there, fatigue was still written into the lines of her face. I made a mental note to talk to Luc about a night nurse.

Hazel took another step back.

Lexi scooped up Noah. "My baby," she crooned to the sleeping infant—sleeping because he appeared to have absolutely no problem with going to bed...so long as that bed was someone's arms. Luc stumbled over, rubbed a hand over his face, and stared down at his son with such adoration that it made my heart skip a beat.

The moment thoroughly broken, Hazel bustled toward the house. "If you two won't go back to sleep," she said all business-like, "let's at least get you something to eat." She headed for the kitchen, tossing over her shoulder for them to follow, telling them about the dinner they'd missed that could be easily heated up.

Lexi stroked a finger down Noah's nose then followed.

Luc trailed her—a ship to a tractor beam.

Just like I followed Hazel, slipping into the kitchen and helping with the heating up. Because Luc and Lexi needed to eat, but also, because...Hazel.

We fed the tired parents.

We chatted for a few minutes.

Then we let the tired parents get on with their evening, Luc and Lexi walking us to the door, waving goodbye from the porch as Hazel and I got into our respective cars.

Which meant that, in the end, I didn't get another opportunity for a second kiss.

Nor for confirmation of that "fourth" date.

TEN

Hazel

I SLEPT SOUNDLY through the night, very glad I didn't have a newborn.

The next morning, I woke with sunlight glimmering through a piece of stained glass hanging on my window that made little rainbows appear on my bedspread. Blues and greens and purples. My favorite. Mixed with a bit of orange—my mom's favorite—and gray—my dad's.

Yup.

My dad's favorite color was gray.

Well, graphite, if I were being precise.

Which I wasn't.

It was Wednesday morning and that was my late day and *that* meant I got to sleep in and not worry about being precise or getting to the rink early.

I could lounge in bed, read for an hour, stumble downstairs for coffee, and then slowly greet the day.

So that's what I did.

Lounging. Trying not to drop my paperback on my face when I rolled over from one side to the other while continuing to read. Then, eventually, tugging on a pair of old jeans, a Breakers hoodie, and doing that stumbling so I could ingest some caffeine.

Hair into a ponytail.

Feet in sneakers.

The team was away and so I would play.

It was after ten by the time I rolled into the practice facility, sipping on a traveler mug of coffee, still smiling from the happily ever after I'd read, and anxious to get started on my work. I'd come up with a new plan for Marcel, who had been struggling the last couple of games. Truthfully, he hadn't been right since Mark Shelby had fucked his girlfriend—and seriously, Shelby had a special place in Hell reserved just for him. Marcel had pulled it together for the most part, but he was streaky, and that made it difficult for the coaching staff to rely on him.

Which Marcel knew.

Which then made Marcel even more insecure and even more streaky, even though he worked really, really hard at being consistent.

He was at the rink before everyone else, stayed longer, worked hard. Always did extra reps, extra conditioning, extra skating. All in all, he was a totally awesome guy, was beyond sweet, and was just too much in his head. So...I would find a way to get him out of his head.

That was where my plan came in.

For now, though, I had some paperwork to complete, some emails to send, and then some pieces to put into place for my plan with Marcel.

I was grinning about that, about my book, about the really nice night I'd had with Oliver last night, so that might be why I didn't immediately notice that my couch wasn't empty.

Dropping my purse into the bottom drawer of my desk, opening my laptop, settling into my chair, fingers on my mouse to click—

"Holy fucking mother of fuck!" I gasped, my hand coming to my chest.

Because Oliver was on my couch.

Sprawled out, hands folded behind his head, and smiling at me like it was the most natural thing in the world for him to be on my couch.

"That's a twist on the f-word I haven't heard before," he said, sitting up and crossing to me.

"Wha-what are you doing in here?"

He perched on the edge of my desk. "I brought you coffee." He nodded next to my laptop—where I was now noticing there was a cup of coffee with Oliver's name written on the outside of the paper cup. "I just expected you in..." He glanced at his smartwatch. "Two hours ago..."

"You've been on my couch for *two* hours?"

What the actual—

"No."

I relaxed.

"I've been on your couch"—another glance at his watch—"two hours and twenty-three minutes." He bent, ran his knuckles over my cheek. "Worth every minute of it to see you walking in here with that gorgeous smile on your face."

My lips parted, whatever I might have said just flitting out of my mind.

"I—what?"

"Why were you smiling, gorgeous?"

He was the one who was gorgeous. *He* was the one who was smiling.

But again, my being comfortable with saying whatever was flitting through my mind last night was rearing its not-so-ugly head that morning because...I just told him what had made me smile. "My book, my plan for Marcel, and...you."

That sent him rocking back slightly, his fingers gripping the edge of my desk. "Me?"

"Last night."

Smug approval sliding across his face. "Date four?"

I didn't touch that. Just lifted my brows.

Amusement joined the approval, and he bent at the waist, his fingers coming to my jaw, stroking lightly along it. "I see I may have to go for that second kiss before I get you to agree to that."

My heart thudded. Hard. "What?"

"What book were you reading?"

My brows drew together. "What?" I asked again.

"What were you reading that put a smile on your face, babe?"

I told him. Again.

"Romance?" he asked when he heard the title, his lips curving.

I didn't like that smile, didn't like where that was likely going, the derision that would follow. I brushed his hand aside, poked him in the chest. "Yes. *Romance.* And don't give me any crap about reading smut or books with happy endings. I love it and the world needs more books written by women and for women from a woman's point of view. Plus, normalizing sex is a good thing, especially healthy and kinky and fun sex. And—"

"Babe."

"I don't care what you say about it," I went on. "I—"

My words cut off because...they were spoken against his tongue.

Because he was taking that second kiss. Though maybe I

was the one giving it because the moment his lips hit mine, I took over. I opened my mouth, thrust my tongue into his, launched myself out of my chair and wrapped my arms around him, knocking us both into the desk. Things rattled, something hit the ground, and I had half a heartbeat to worry about it being my coffee before Oliver yanked me closer, *his* arms banded around me, and then I wasn't thinking about books or sex scenes or female authors.

I was kissing the sexy, gorgeous man who had me plastered against his chest.

And *fuck*, but I was kissing him.

How was it possible for a kiss to be this good? There was no fumbling or hesitation. It was as though I'd fallen into the hottest kiss of my life and there was no build-up needed. Straight into the flames, and I was thrilled for it.

A moan flowed up my throat and into his mouth, and he swallowed it whole, drawing me closer, a groan rumbling from him to me, vibrating over my tongue.

And swear to *fuck* if that didn't arrow straight toward my vagina.

I slid a hand down his chest, reached for the button of his jeans and flicked it open.

His fingers slid from my ass to between us and snagged my hand, tugging it away as he tore his mouth from mine.

A kiss to my palm. His breathing accelerated when he asked, "Did I say anything?"

I was in kiss mode, so I had no idea what the fuck he was talking about.

Something he seemed to realize when he smiled at me, resting my hand against his chest and nuzzling my neck. "I think it's cool you read romance, babe. Gives us plenty of ideas of things to do when we're in bed."

I sucked in a breath, heat pooling between my thighs.

Because the idea of acting out anything with Oliver was... yeah. It was the hottest fucking fantasy of my life.

"So, you read something," he said, "and when we're ready for it and you want to do it, I'm all over it. I'll be your tortured hero, or your dom between the sheets, or your cowboy who keeps forgetting to wear a shirt, or—"

I lifted my hand and covered my mouth. "Desk sex," I blurted.

His brows lifted, tongue flicking out to taste my palm.

"I want desk sex," I said. "The book was an office romance, and the hero cleared everything off the surface and fucked her on it until she couldn't stand and—"

Now *his* hand covered my mouth.

"I am all over desk sex, babe," he said. "But not before we've had date four, which I know I teased you about being number four, but it's really number one, and you're the kind of woman who deserves to be wined and dined and romanced. And you say you're not a date one to four kind of girl, but a date six kind of girl, and that means..." He pressed his lips to my forehead. "That means"—a breath—"we have time, love. Though," he murmured, kissing his way down to my ear, "I will be keeping a mental list, so keep telling me, okay?"

"I—" A breath before I settled on the only thing I could. Which was, "Okay."

He gently unwound my arms from around him, nudging me back into my chair, before bending to snag, not the coffee thankfully (that was safely sitting on my desk), but a stack of papers.

He wobbled, almost went down before he steadied himself on the edge of my desk, and took a moment.

"I can—"

His eyes looked over my shoulder, frost tempering the

desire that had been in those pale blue depths a moment before. "I got it."

Firm.

Not necessarily mean.

But *definitely* firm.

And he *did* have it.

He bent and got the folders, and I didn't do him the disservice of watching him. Instead, I drew in my chair, straightened the items on my desk, and then continued logging on to my laptop.

By the time I got into my Breakers email account, he had straightened and set the folders on the wooden surface. Only when he returned to leaning on the edge of my desk did I glance up at him, seeing the strain in his eyes, the slight sheen of sweat on his forehead.

And the bit of defensiveness in his expression.

Expecting me to comment.

Well, I wasn't about that.

I'd told him that this wasn't my area of expertise, that he wasn't my client. Hell, I'd been tongue fucking him on my desk all of three minutes before. That put us firmly out of the realm of therapist and client.

"Thanks," I murmured, nodding at the folders.

The tension bled out of his frame, but he didn't say anything.

"Will you just promise me one thing?"

Silence.

I pressed on. "Will you just promise to be honest with me if something is too much? Not because any part of you is weak, because you're one of the strongest people I know. But because I'll promise to do the same."

More silence, and I found myself holding still.

He picked up my hand, started stroking his fingers along

my palm, a gentle abrasion that made my shiver. Then said simply, "You got it, babe."

And this time, the tension bled out of me.

Relief had me nodding and going quiet, but as I stared at my laptop screen without really seeing the emails piled up in the inbox, I was thinking that he'd given—or at least, he'd pursued—and shared his interest. I was thinking that I liked his pursuit, liked how he was with me (minus the outburst he'd apologized for the other day).

I liked *him*.

So maybe it was time for me to take a step in his direction.

"Oliver?"

"Yeah?" A cautious answer.

"I was thinking."

Now there was a thread of amusement in his voice when he said, "About what?"

"I have an idea."

"About what?" More amusement.

"Trust me?"

His eyes came to mine, and he said, without hesitation. "Yeah."

That was big. As in, it made *me* feel big, feel like he'd just given me the best Christmas present ever—better than puppies popping out of wrapped packages, Tiffany boxes under the tree, a lifetime supply of chocolate filling my pantry. That trust without hesitation was a fucking gift.

And I wasn't going to squander it.

"This is..." Oliver trailed off as he stared at the space around us.

I sucked in a breath, held it.

"*...amazing.*"

He spun back to face me, grinning wide.

Every cell in my body settled, and I released that breath before I passed out. "My plan is to take Marcel here."

His head jerked, gaze going from mine back to the room. "Damn, babe. You're good."

That made me feel...well, it made me *feel*.

This man, who barely knew me, who was attracted to and interested in me and hadn't even tried to hide it, he made me feel *awesome*.

Pride in his voice, in his body language, in his face.

Something Trevor had never given me.

And Oliver had just tossed it out into the air without strings.

Something else Trevor had never given me, I realized.

God, I really *had* dodged a bullet with him, hadn't I?

"Babe?"

God, but seriously, Trevor was the biggest dick around and for too long I'd thought that was on me. That I'd made a bad choice or had caused him to treat me poorly. That I should have done something, *anything* to make it better.

But when I compared Trevor to Oliver, I knew.

I. *Knew*.

Whatever we'd had was broken from the start.

Cracks in the foundation, mortar crumbling out of the brick walls. Destined to fall apart.

Because he wasn't like Oliver.

It was even more than him not being a "one-woman man." Trevor wasn't a man for *me*. He never could be. Not when he didn't love or care about me the right way.

That right way being...unconditionally and generously and without keeping a tally of who did what. And seriously, I was done thinking about Trevor, thinking about what happened. If

Oliver could put his head down and move forward with all that had happened to him, then I could put a broken engagement behind me.

Hell, I hadn't even kept the ring.

Hadn't wanted the memory.

And that made something else click in my mind. *That* was what Oliver was doing.

Processing.

Letting go.

It was time I let the dredges of Trevor go. Time to give Oliver the space and support to allow him to let go on his terms.

Fingers on my cheek—no *knuckles* on my cheek. That gentle touch that I already loved because it was Oliver touching me, because the look that came into his eyes when he stroked my skin like that—gentle, sweet, a dash of affection—made me feel amazing, different, special.

"Babe?" he asked again.

"I'm good."

His brows lifted.

I picked up a bat, twirled it in an arc. "Am I going to be the only one doing this?"

Those brows rose further.

"Chicken?" I asked archly.

A grin, then he matched my movements—reaching for a bat and swinging it through the air. "Not a chicken, babe. Just don't like whatever thought went through your head to make you look like that."

"Like what?"

"Like someone had punched you in the stomach."

My lungs froze, and then I forced myself to breathe. "Reality strikes sometimes without warning. But," I added when concern rippled across his face. "Sometimes, that reality strikes in a way that makes a person, makes *me*, realize that

things weren't the way they were supposed to be. Especially"—
I moved toward him, cupped the side of his neck—"when
someone"—a squeeze so he knew that someone was him—"gives
pride and encouragement so easily, it makes a woman think
about why she was with a man who didn't give that to her
before, because I deserve that."

I finished on a whisper.

His face was a study in wonder. In *fury*. "I hate that
happened to you."

"I hate that I accepted it as my due." A beat. "I deserve
more."

Now it was back to wonder. "You do."

There. That was out of the way. I stepped back and waved
the bat again. "Okay, so I know that we're not going to have
countertop sex in here—"

"Another for my list?"

I nodded, fighting a grin. "—with the windows and cameras
and people in the front lobby," I went on without otherwise
acknowledging him. "So, what do you say that we start
swinging?"

"Big bat energy?"

I snorted.

Actually snorted.

Then said, "Exactly."

Then I swung the bat and got to work.

ELEVEN

Oliver

THIS WAS WILD.

This was out there.

This was *amazing*.

I didn't know where Hazel had found this place, but it was a fucking blast. And by blast, I meant that I got to *blast* shit apart. With a baseball bat. Or a golf club. Or—something I hadn't touched because it felt too raw—a hockey stick.

"It's a rage room," she said, taking a breather, her chest heaving, her eyes glimmering with happiness. There was a flush on her cheeks, and her skin shone with sweat.

Because breaking shit was hard work.

I paused next to her, absently rubbing my thigh, and didn't miss her eyes going there.

She didn't comment, though, in that she trusted me to tell her if it was too much—a promise I'd given with the intention of keeping because she'd done the same—meant a lot.

"But I think," she went on, still panting, the bat hanging at her side, tendrils of her hair sticking to her temples, her neck. I tuned out for a moment, thinking about how else I might be able to get her sweaty, how else I might be able to see that flush on her cheeks. Albeit with her naked and beneath me and studying every inch of her body for more blushes. Would it spread across her chest? Tease the tops of her breasts?

I hoped so because I wanted to kiss and touch every inch of rosy skin.

"Oliver?"

"Hmm?"

"It's not helpful when you keep looking at me like you want to jump me."

I started, focused. "Sorry."

"Why do I feel like I hear an unspoken *not sorry* there?"

A grin curved the edges of my mouth. "Because you do?"

Snorting, she moved to the far wall, to the rack of "weapons" that were available to us to destroy the contents of this room. Furniture. Plates. Appliances. Glasses. Even a lamp in the far corner.

"As I was *saying*," she went on as she perused, "I think this will be good for Marcel because he banks all of his fury and frustration until it explodes."

It did explode—oftentimes on the ice when he picked a fight and ended up bloody. The kid wasn't an enforcer, though he was built and could handle himself. But the team needed his hands steady and bruise-free. They needed his stability, especially without me captaining.

Not to brag, but once I'd figured out my path, I thought I'd been a good captain.

I cared about the guys, tried to lead by example.

Tried to do right by them and leave it all on the ice.

I supposed I had.

Literally.

"If I can find a way for me to release the steam before I gets to that point, I think it'll help." She picked up the hockey stick, tested it in her hands. "What do you think?"

I swallowed, eyes on that stick, longing in me. "I think it'll help me."

My voice was wrong.

I knew it. She knew it.

Without a word, she turned back to the rack and set the stick down, picking up the golf club instead. "Good," she murmured. "Because I think it's going to help me too. Especially when I imagine this as my shit-bag ex's face." Then she started wailing on an old school computer, one that looked like it was heavy as shit and took up half the table on the far side of the room. "Fuck you, Trevor!"

I grinned as I adjusted my safety goggles, glad she could start working through some of the emotions that made her so sad, glad that aching pain was burning hot, transforming into anger, scorching through her so she could put it out, eventually put it behind her.

I swung around, took a breath, and hit my way through a toaster, a blender, and a fridge that was apparently supposed to plug into the cigarette charger in a car.

Ridiculous contraption.

But it felt fucking great to see it explode into pieces.

I glanced around the room, started to head toward a stack of porcelain teacups, concentrating as I moved, because although I'd gotten good on the prosthesis, it didn't quite feel like an extension of me under these circumstances. That being, the floor littered with debris, meaning the chances of slipping and eating it were substantial, even for those humans with two normal legs. I had worked hard to get comfortable with my prosthesis and had gone through a couple of different iterations and fittings before everything felt right. I also had a couple of different attachments for running and exercising versus day to day. Kneeling was still shit and didn't feel super stable, nor did stairs, but I was getting better at both.

Mostly because I was a stubborn bastard.

But that wasn't what had me stopping before hitting those teacups, nor was it the floor covered with debris.

It was the hockey stick sitting in the rack.

Slightly askew, since Hazel had set it down without really paying attention to lining it up with the other stick. And that was the reason I was telling myself that I crossed over to it, why my fingers hit the wood—not the normal composite material that I'd used in the league, and that was probably a good call since that could get expensive. But I wasn't even sure they made wooden sticks any longer, let alone where they'd gotten one.

Probably where they'd gotten the Stone Age computer.

Smiling, I straightened the stick, lining it up like was proper —shaft to shaft (which sounded like a bad title for a porn film), blade to blade. But they just looked better that way. Neatly placed in a row.

But when I started to turn away, something stopped me, and I turned back, my fingers going to the wood again, circling the shaft (more bad porn film titles), and I found myself lifting it from the rack.

My hands instinctively went to where they should—right hand halfway down palm out, left hand at the top—and it felt...

Like coming home.

And also a little wrong because I couldn't go home, not in the same way anymore.

I started to put the stick back, but then I glanced over my shoulder, saw that Hazel was going to town on a bookcase, and hesitated.

And...I picked up the stick again.

For a while I just held it, soaked in what I was feeling, right and wrong all tangled together, foreign and familiar, but ultimately just...natural.

Instinct to hold it correctly, to place the blade on the floor and press down, checking the flex.

"Would you..." I glanced up, not having processed Hazel stopping her work on the bookcase. "It doesn't have to be today, but maybe would you teach me how to use it?"

No.

That was my first instinct.

Well, *that* and tossing it back on the rack and running from the room.

Except...I *wanted* to teach her, I wanted her to know the pleasure that came from shooting a puck, from the first time lifting it off the ice and the crack of the blade as it made contact. I wanted her to feel the surge of pleasure when she scored a goal, the breeze on her cheeks, the fist bumps from teammates, the roar of the crowd, the—

"Another time," she whispered, stepping back and leaving me to it.

But I didn't want her to leave.

I didn't want her to step back.

I wanted *her,* and I wanted to give her the experiences I'd had, wanted to take back some for myself.

But mostly, I didn't want her to leave.

"Wait." Lungs tight, I caught her arm.

She stopped instantly, turning to face me. But she didn't give me pressure or sass that I'd changed my mind. She just gave me time and patience and...I found that I could take a breath, could focus on her and not what I'd lost.

I inhaled and got flowers on my nose.

An exhale. Another breath.

And then...it just got easier.

I brought my arms around her, holding the stick in front of her body and placing her hands on it. "Like this," I said, positioning her bottom hand so it was facing the right direction, the top so that its grip was better. The stick was too tall for her, but that didn't matter, not right then with my arms around her and her body pressed to my. "Bend your knees a little," I murmured, and yeah, my voice went a little gruff.

Mostly because her body against me made me hard.

But also, because when she moved to bend those knees, her ass brushed against my cock and then she glanced up over her shoulder and I was rethinking countertop sex, even with that huge ass window revealing us to anyone who might walk into the lobby.

"Like this?"

Her voice wasn't gruff. It was liquid heat that told me she was feeling everything I was, that she was feeling every *inch* of me.

I nodded, coaxed her forward slightly, just enough so that her weight was on the balls of her feet.

And fuck, if that wasn't better.

Her ass to my crotch. Her body close. My arms wrapped tight.

"Yeah, baby," I rasped.

A moment passed, and for my part, I was soaking in the way she felt against me, trying to concentrate when every bit of blood in my body seemed to be in my dick. For hers, well, I couldn't read her mind, but I knew she was enjoying it as much as I was.

This was because her hips were working, just slightly, as though the motion was out of her control, but they were *moving,* and by moving, I meant rocking back against me, making my cock go from half-mast to full, taking the rest of my body and diverting it solely to my pelvis, and basically driving me insane in the best possible way.

And when she spoke again, I knew she was there, too. "What's"—another shift of that sexy ass against me—"next?"

"Bend over."

That wasn't *exactly* next, bending over was a rookie mistake borne of weak legs and poor discipline, but I couldn't resist.

Totally worth it too when she did it, when she again glanced at me over her shoulder, and my mind filled with possibilities.

But she must have gotten a glimpse of my semi-nefarious intentions because she glared, straightened, and I thought she would step out of the circle of my arms and move away from me. Instead, she shifted closer and her hips—her *ass*—moved with intention this time, rubbing in a slow rhythm I was desperate to find again when we were both naked.

"Thinking about me doing that while we're both naked and partaking in countertop sex is your punishment."

Then she stepped away from me, moving to the rack, and snagging the other stick.

She tossed it.

I caught it without thinking.

"Next you'll teach me to shoot," she said. "But we only have ten minutes left. Let's get down to fucking up the rest of this room."

She moved to a china cabinet.

Grinning, I returned to the teacups.

A swipe had them flying off the shelves, shattering into a million pieces. Another had the row above cleared. But when one remained unscathed, piled on the broken remains of its brethren, I did something else instinctual—scooping and lifting the cup onto the blade of my stick, balancing it as I gently tossed it up and down, and then just because I could still do it, I launched it into the corner of the room.

It exploded into tiny pieces.

"Whoa."

I turned, saw that Hazel was gaping at me.

"Do that again," she demanded.

Not about to deny her anything, I shot the stick out toward another shelf, scooping up another cup, bouncing it a couple of times before I repeated the shot against the wall.

"Oh my God," she gasped, dropping her stick onto the rack. "I knew you guys were good with your sticks, but...how...I—" She shook her head while I was grinning about her saying I was good with my stick (also a bad name for a porno) and picked up a vase. "Can you do it with this?"

"Probably."

She held it out.

I scooped it up.

"Aim for the red splotch on the wall," she demanded.

Now I was grinning because I was showing off, because it felt good that she was impressed by me.

This one was a bit harder to balance, both because it was bigger and because its shape made it wobble against the curve of the stick's blade. But after a few movements, I got the feel for it, and then I launched it at the wall.

It hit the red spot she'd pointed out with a *thunk* and shattered.

She squealed. "That is *so* cool." Her gaze moved around the mostly decimated space. "What else, what else?" She kicked debris out of her way and snagged a ceramic bowl filled with plastic and Styrofoam fruit. Then began tossing one at a time, calling out targets.

Fake apple. Exploded in the corner.

Foam pear. Colliding with the shelving.

Bunch of plastic bananas. Right for that old-ass computer.

The ceramic bowl. That went right at a truly disgusting painting of a swamp. Pink porcelain mixed with puke green in a way that brought absolutely nothing good aesthetically but felt incredible when the shards embedded themselves into the canvas.

Hazel whooped and clapped her hands.

And then our time was up.

I was sweating and breathing hard. She had a piece of plastic tangled in her curls. We both had impressions on our foreheads and cheeks from the safety goggles.

But I was flying anyway.

"That was *fun!*" she exclaimed after we pushed out onto the sidewalk and started heading for her car.

It had been fun. Really fucking fun.

But it had also been *big*.

Because Hazel might not have realized it, but for all my talk of giving her the experiences I'd had—showing her the feel of the puck, a goal, the cool air—she'd been the one to give *me* something.

She'd given me hockey back.

The joy of the sport, not the pain of missing it.

And I made a promise right then and there, the cold air swirling around us, the sun barely poking out from beneath the clouds but still making her curls shine as they bounced around her head, her excitement given form in words that kept pouring out of her mouth.

I would give this woman everything.

Even if *everything* ended up being every single piece of myself.

TWELVE

Hazel

"NO, MOM," I said, "it's fine. I totally have time to talk, as long as you don't mind listening to me pack up as I do so."

"Hazel Abigail Reid, do *not* tell me that you're still at work."

Uh-oh.

Mom Voice had come out.

It was always best to head this off in the beginning.

"It's Wednesday, Mom. It's my late-start day."

"It's nearly nine o'clock at night."

I winced. Because it *was* that. But I'd started late and then Oliver had been in my office and we'd discussed all that desktop fucking (and other things I supposed). Then we'd gone to Rage—the wreck room I'd discovered by chance—and I'd thought that Oliver might have some anger to let go of, too, and I had some myself, and, truthfully, I just wanted to spend more time with him.

Say what you want, I liked the man.

A lot.

Which was why the hour spent tearing through that room and culminating in Oliver showing off his stick skills had been a blast.

Laughter and activity.

Breaking shit, and I hoped, putting just a few of the pieces back together.

Not that I saw him as a project—or a client any longer because clearly that ship had sailed about two minutes after he'd walked into my office for our first session—but I liked helping people, and I liked Oliver.

But I especially liked the smile that had come onto his face when I'd launched plastic and foam fruit at him and demanded he hit the targets I pointed out.

He had, without fail.

And that smile had stayed.

So, I had asked if he had time for lunch—he had—and we'd gone down to a little place near the waterfront, and we'd had soup and sandwiches, huddled together on a bench. Because the sun might have been out, but it was still winter in Baltimore (though almost spring). So while there wasn't snow on the ground, when the breeze picked up, especially off the water, I'd felt like I was turning into a popsicle.

Even with my heavy coat and scarf.

But oddly enough (Ha! There was nothing odd about it), I'd felt much warmer when Oliver had slid an arm around me and tugged me so my body was pressed to his.

Which meant we'd stayed there for a while.

Long enough that I was working until nine at night.

"I repeat, I had a late start," I said when my mom continued to rant and rave about my working myself to the bone (I was too thin apparently), and being too tired to function properly (apparently my mom could see my dark circles through the airwaves), and needing proper rest or else my face would be full of wrinkles (oh, and by the way, had I been using my eye cream?).

"Weren't you the one who told me that wrinkles are just God's way of telling me you lived properly?" I asked.

A scoff. "Well, I'm *old*, Peanut Brittle Princess—"

I smiled. That was a new one.

"—which means I have to make excuses for my wrinkles. You, on the other hand, are young and beautiful and not married—"

"Oh Lord, here we go," I muttered. "You realize that I only broke up with Trevor six months ago."

"Seven, my Strawberry Daiquiri Darling. That means it's time to move on and get me those grandbabies."

"You do realize you already *have* grandbabies, don't you?"

"From my son."

I hit the button for speakerphone because I was getting a crick in my neck trying to hold it as I gathered my things. And while I loved my job and had loved my day with Oliver, I was tired and ready to go home. "And your oldest daughter," I pointed out, feeling like it was my duty as the youngest child to remind my mother that grandbaby duty didn't fall solely to me.

There was a soft knock at the door, and I glanced up in time to see Oliver poke his head in.

And...fuck, he was pretty.

Just the sight of him made my heart beat a little faster, my fingers clench with the need to touch, my feet ache, wanting to carry my body over to his and pick up where we'd left off cuddling on that bench.

I waved him in, right as my mom said, "But I don't have grandbabies from *you*, Pecan Pie Pumpkin. I want a little girl with curls and your brown eyes."

Oliver jerked his head to the door, silently asking if I wanted him to go.

But since his eyes were dancing and his lips were twitching (rather than him running off screaming for the hills because my mom mentioned grandbabies), I shook my head and pointed to the couch. "I'm not sure Pecan Pie Pumpkin makes sense, Mom," I said.

A sniff.

"And I want kids, but I don't know when that's going to happen, okay? I thought things were going a different way"—I saw Oliver stiffen and forced myself to bring my gaze to his—"but I'm glad things ended before I had kids with Trevor. It's just...kids aren't exactly priority number one right now for me."

His face gentled.

My mom's voice didn't. "Well, it's priority one for me, Darling Donut, and you know what that means."

I groaned. "You're not fixing me up, Mom. I'm—"

"He's a perfectly nice man, Hazelnut. He's got a good job and is nice. Plus, I saw him with his shirt off at Suzy Duncan's hot tub and let me tell you, that man works out. Hell, I haven't seen abs like that on a man since—"

"You streamed *Thor: Ragnarok* last week?"

A pause, probably because I had guessed right.

My mom had—rightfully so—an obsession with all things Hemsworth.

"You make a good point," my mom said, "but he also doesn't have a movie studio's budget or a personal trainer, professional chef, and whatever other services those fancy actors have to help him get that body. So, trust me, Muffin Mop, you would be doing the world a service to get up close and personal with those abs, let alone if you managed to get Eddie into a pair of gray sweats—"

There was a lot there, and a lot of it that sent my brows

high up on my forehead, but first and foremost was wondering how my mom knew about gray sweats.

Then again, I got most of my book recs from my mom.

Actually thinking about it, I had probably learned about the gloriousness of tight sweatpants from my mom and not on my own.

But I didn't have a chance to fully process all things sweats or to say anything to cut off the hard sell of Eddie and his glorious abs. Which, face it, wouldn't be a hard sell if the man who I'd lusted after for ages wasn't currently in my office looking like he was either going to burst into laughter or track down Eddie and make sure he never got within five hundred feet of me. The first I liked a whole lot and was why I wasn't turning my phone off speaker.

Because my mom was my mom, and if he couldn't hack my mom on the phone, then there was no way he'd be able to hack her in person.

The second—the glimpse of jealous and protective—I supposed I should hate, but truthfully, it made my belly feel a little squishy.

Hand in my feminist card immediately.

But, ah well, a girl had to live in fantasy everyone once in a while.

While I was thinking that—and it must be said, while my mother was waxing poetic about abs and sweatpants and hot tubs—Oliver was moving.

Toward me.

Oh. I liked *that*.

His knuckles trailed down my cheek. I sighed and shifted closer, winding my arms around his neck, suddenly needing to taste him.

What Mom on the phone?

But as I'd reached for him, my hand hit the cell and knocked it from the desk.

It clattered on the floor.

"What was that?" my mom demanded. "Hazelnut Puff, are you there?"

Oliver grinned, unwound my arms and bent. This time I did watch him, mostly because his ass in those pants was *chef's kiss*. A moment later, he'd snagged the cell (much faster than that morning with the folders, so maybe he'd figured out how to make that movement easier on himself) and set it on the desk. "We're here, Hazel's mom."

He snaked an arm around my waist and tugged me close, lips brushing my cheek.

"*We're?*" my mom asked.

I rushed in. "Mom, meet Oliver." It was weird doing an introduction this way. "Oliver, my mom, Toni. Mom, sorry you're on speakerphone, obviously and Oliver is a coworker."

"Hi, Mrs. Reid," he said. "It's lovely to meet you."

Charming.

Genuine.

My mom felt it, I could tell, even as she asked, "Coworker?"

"Yes," he said simply, not biting—good strategy. "But also, the man hoping to score a fourth date with your daughter," he said, so silkily that I didn't immediately process what he'd said.

Then I did.

Then...I swatted him.

Right about the time my mom screeched, "*Fourth?*"

Because seriously?

"He's teasing, Mom," I said, reaching for the phone, intending to take it off speaker. "I haven't agreed to go out with him yet."

He moved the cell out of my reach. "What was today if not a date?"

"Today?" my mom squawked.

"I miscounted," Oliver said, still silkily, still charming. "I'm trying to get your daughter to agree to a fifth date."

"Hmm." A pause, and I braced myself for what would next come out of my mom's mouth. "How're his abs, Honey Cakes?"

Without missing a beat, Oliver tugged up the edge of his shirt, revealing...

"Holy hell," I breathed.

"Oh, I wish I was FaceTiming right now, Strawberry Shortcake. Please, tell me he's showing them to you right now and they're *glorious*."

"*Hngah*." I didn't know exactly what kind of sound I made, only that it was instinctual and paired with an intense urge to go all grabby hands—grabby *tongue*—all over his torso.

"Queen Croissantia? Are you alive?"

I blinked, managed to squeeze out, "Barely."

"I'll keep Eddie's number just in case," my mom murmured.

"I—"

"Oliver?"

The man was grinning, but he slowly lowered his shirt. "Yes, Mrs. Reid?"

A pause, and fuck the man was charming the *shit* out of my mom. Seriously, how was he this good? Then my mom got it together (easier because she didn't have the mental imprint of Oliver's abs on her eyelids). "Hazel's coming to our house next Sunday. I'll expect you to join her for dinner."

"Mom—" I began.

"You'd better have secured dates six through eight in the meantime."

Oliver smiled. "On it."

"*Mom!*"

"Good," my mom said, completely ignoring my protest.

"Love you, Banana Bread Baby. Talk soon." A beat. "Oh, I sent you a couple of books to your Kindle!"

Then I hung up.

In like a hurricane.

Leaving...someone that was silent and begrudgingly charmed (me) while the person on the other end of the line was running to gleefully dish all the details of her daughter's five non-dates and Oliver's abs (my mom, obviously)—which she hadn't seen but based on my reaction were fantastic (a rightful assessment).

Knuckles on my cheek. An amused voice saying, "I guess I'd better keep working on my abs."

"Umm..."

Not the most intelligent statement.

But there was a lot to process.

The best, perhaps, was the sight of those glorious abs.

THIRTEEN

Oliver

I DROPPED my bag just inside the door and walked through my empty house.

Wide open spaces.

Large windows.

Furniture that wasn't a bachelor pad, but instead was decent quality, not super expensive but still was something that wasn't going to fall apart in a couple of years.

I liked my place.

But it reflected that I'd never really been good at letting people in. My home wasn't lived in, not like Lexi and Luc's with their plants and baby stuff and pictures cramming the walls. My space looked like a hotel.

Impersonal.

I'd thought I liked it that way.

But today, looking around at it, I realized that it had been a crutch, a way of bracing that barrier so that it wouldn't fall.

I'd left Hazel at her car, and I'd wanted to follow her home, barrel into her house, to take her to bed and fuck her senseless then maybe make love to her if we had the energy after spending that hour breaking shit and then working the rest of the day. But she was more important, and she still hadn't agreed to go out with me.

Even though she'd stroked a hand over my jaw, pressed a light kiss to my lips before telling me goodnight.

Now I was home, thinking about Hazel and how special she was and knowing that I wanted my place to be a *home*, to be someplace she would find warm and inviting, and I was wondering why I'd spent my whole life thinking I couldn't have that.

My parents OD'ing. Foster care. Those were the obvious reasons.

Teresa and Alex's house. My adoption. The car accident. Perhaps still obvious but also dug a little deeper. Because I hadn't known my bio parents, but I'd known my adopted ones. And losing them had hurt.

But it had been easier to focus on hockey.

Because it had happened in the middle of the season, and the playoff push was real, so I'd organized their funeral, made sure the other kids they'd fostered were as okay as they could be under the circumstances, and then I'd gone back to work.

Skating was easier than dealing with the loss.

But now skating was gone, my leg was gone, and my job—which was going well—wasn't taking up the same type of all-consuming attention that hockey had before.

I'd had hockey to get over Teresa and Alex.

My recovery and PT to push down what happened with my leg.

And now Hazel to forget that I'd lost hockey.

I wanted to make her my new obsession, to use her to chase all those demons away, and maybe I would have done it without quite understanding what I was doing and what it might mean to use her in that way.

But then I'd overheard her mom call her Darling Donut and ask about grandbabies and...

It was like Teresa had dropped down out of the clouds and shook me, had yelled in my ear to pay attention. I knew that I'd liked Hazel, liked her a whole hell of a lot. But she wasn't a woman to just like. She was a woman to *love*.

A woman I could easily love if things kept going that way.

Which meant she deserved a home and a man without barriers propping up the concrete and barbed wire surrounding me.

I moved to my couch, wincing when I sat down, muscles I hadn't used for months burning from my little show with the fake fruit and bowl—my obliques, the sides of my pecs, the tops of my thighs. And she'd given that to me without pressure, facing hockey in a way that I hadn't been able to deal with yet (because it wouldn't be the same, wouldn't feel the same, *I* wouldn't be the same).

It had been fun.

I'd found the joy.

And I meant to keep my promise I'd made on the sidewalk earlier that day, when I'd seen her hair shining and her eyes filled with happiness.

I was going to make her happy.

I just needed to get her to agree to a date first.

THE FOLLOWING AFTERNOON, I strode down the hall to the locker room and poked my head in.

Hazel had been in meetings all morning, and that meant I had time to enact my plan. The first part, I'd been able to take care of. The second part was...going to require a bit of assistance. Luckily, I knew exactly where to find a bunch of nosy fuckers who'd be happy to be part of something that they might be able to give me shit for later.

The guys had just finished with a short practice, just something quick and easy to keep the legs moving and keep the cobwebs off.

Smitty was sitting next to Marcel, a towel around his waist, his chest bare.

Honestly, I was surprised the man bothered with the towel at all. Smitty loved being naked. Hell, I had seen a lot of dick in my life in various locker rooms, but I'd seen Smitty's an uncommon amount of times.

Marcel was mostly dressed—meaning he had boxer briefs and a T-shirt on—and the two of them were quietly talking. Well, Marcel quietly, Smitty was booming.

As usual.

At least until Smitty saw me.

Which was pretty much the same time that the rest of the guys saw me.

The room went silent.

So silent that I could hear the water dripping into the drains in the attached showers.

I opened my mouth to say...*something*.

But Smitty beat me to it. "Get your ass in here, Ollie! We were talking about getting beers tonight. Fucking loss last night sucked. Can't believe we gave up that lead. You're coming with us."

Not a request.

I might have still treated it as one, if not for last night.

Home. It wasn't just a place.

And yes, fuck, that sounded sappy as hell. But also, it was true. I was realizing that home was also *this* place, these guys, the joking and shit-giving, and God forbid, Smitty and his dick that never stayed behind a towel. It was being on the ice and grabbing beers when hockey was done. It was video games at Marcel's sitting on lawn chairs because my girlfriend had taken the furniture in a final fuck-you and he hadn't gotten around to buying new stuff. It was...this team.

But not because they were a distraction.

Because they were important.

They'd shown up for me. In the hospital. Afterward. My fridge had been stocked. I'd been chauffeured around when I wasn't ready to drive yet. And when the season started, they'd still checked in.

Less because they were working and the job of playing hockey professionally took a lot of time.

Less because I'd purposefully pulled back, knowing they needed that space to do their job.

But still there.

Smitty moved over and patted the bench next to him. "What's with that face?" he asked. Another pat. "Come and tell Daddy all about it."

"Ew," Raph muttered, throwing a balled-up sock in my direction. "Let's leave the daddy talk between you and your woman."

"I'd need to *have* a woman first," Luca quipped.

"Man. Woman," Smitty said, flinging my arms wide. "I'm equal opportunity."

The room reacted to this in the same way they had the first time Smitty had made the declaration. With shrugs, no acknowledgment, and then moving on to the next important subject at hand—namely *not* who Smitty fucked, but rather the fact that his dick was out. Again.

"Christ, man," Raph grumbled. "I don't give a fuck who

you fuck, I'd just like to go one day without accidentally side-eyeing your dick."

Smitty glanced down, but for the record, didn't fix the towel. "It's a nice dick," he said. "I've been told it's a nice dick."

Marcel sighed and shook his head.

Smitty was beaned with several more socks.

"So."

This came from Luca.

I turned to glance at him, deliberately ignoring the spot next to Smitty and his bare ass—since he'd tossed the towel aside and was now slowly tugging on his socks.

Socks before underwear.

What was the man doing?

"Beers?" Luca asked.

I considered that, considered that if I didn't go, what it would mean.

Namely that I was pushing them away again.

I was done doing that.

"Beers," I said by way of agreement. "But then I need your guys' help."

There weren't that many guys left in the room—Smitty, Marcel, Raph, Luca, Theo, and Martin—the rest having gone off to do who knew what, but the guys who remained were those I was close to. They were the ones who'd been there and the ones I'd pushed away.

But I didn't doubt for a second that they'd be all in.

And my instincts proved right because they all nodded or voiced their agreement.

Though Smitty did this by pulling on his underwear.

Thank fuck.

FOURTEEN

PRUDENCE HANSLEY WAS A HOOT.

I was thrilled she was coming to work for the Breakers, especially in Oliver's department.

I knew the man had good taste.

But his hiring of Pru cemented that.

Pru and I had been friends for near on six years now.

I had been finishing up my doctorate and writing a thesis on mental health for collegiate athletes. Pru had been one of the athletes I'd interviewed and worked with at OSU. It had been a bonus to be at such a great school with such great athletes, but it had been a bigger bonus to have one with so many talented female athletes.

The *biggest* bonus?

Meeting Pru.

She was *awesome*.

And now Pru was going to be here for at least part of the

time. Case in point, she was coming in early so she could meet up with me for a drink at our favorite place in town.

CeCe's had the *best* bar food.

Mozzarella sticks. Cheese curds. Nachos topped with five blends of cheese. Jalapeño poppers (with, no surprise, extra cheese).

They had things like wings and fries and chicken strips.

But Pru and I tended to stick to the dairy-based side of the menu. It went better with the girlie cocktails we liked to order.

Tonight?

Cosmos.

Next time?

Maybe hurricanes, but we were laying off those for our current get-together considering that we'd both had too many of the alcohol-laden drinks that went down like juice the last time we were together, and Pru needed to be coherent for her first day on the new job the following day.

So, it was evening.

It was chilly.

The sky was clear, the moon was full, and I was in CeCe's with one of my closest friends who was going to be working *with* me instead of several states away. Halftime because Oliver —and seriously, did he get more awesome?—had offered her a half-remote position so she could keep playing. Even though her playing career was a bit in limbo and she wasn't sure she'd be returning to the NWHL next season because she'd been fending off back injuries for a while and she wasn't sure she'd be able to continue playing. The want was there. Her body being ready for it?

That was to be determined.

But Oliver hadn't made her make that choice—work over playing.

He'd made it so she could do both.

And even if I hadn't already been falling for him—let it be stated clearly that I was obviously falling for him—the care he'd taken for my friend, the support he'd shown, yeah, that would have done it.

"So, are you excited?" I asked Pru when my adrenaline-seeking friend finally stopped chattering about the adventures I was planning for the off-season because Pru only had a few games left—

Let it be noted that I wasn't going shark diving with her off the coast of South Africa.

Though Pru had asked. Several times.

Shark diving was a step too far for my meager daredevil abilities.

Frankly, it was approximately a thousand steps too far.

"For the shark diving that you're going to do with me?" Pru waggled her brows. "Yes, *really* excited since my bestest friend in the whole world is coming with me."

I rolled my eyes. "You mean *Beth* is going with you? I'm sure she'd love that."

A snort, then a grin, albeit chagrined. "You're never going to let me forget that, are you?"

"That you told me in a situation where the lifeboat was sinking that you'd save Beth and throw me overboard?"

"Beth doesn't know how to swim!" Pru protested.

"You love her more. I know how it is."

"I—"

Our server brought our first course of cheese—aka cheese curds—and our first round of cosmos.

"I don't love Beth more," Pru said when the server had gone.

"I'm just teasing," I assured her. "Which you know but are trying to make me feel guilty for."

Mischief on pretty, delicate features that shouldn't be associated with a tough, strong hockey player. It was a hilarious juxtaposition for someone as kickass as Pru to look like a fairy. But she did. And it meant plenty of people hadn't taken her seriously over the years.

But she usually changed their minds in just a few seconds.

On the ice that was.

Off it, that was a different story.

Pru didn't take much seriously.

She lived big and bold and was always getting into adventures that made my already curly hair, go *more* curly, just by proxy. And maybe a little gray.

I'd done Machu Picchu. I'd climbed Kilimanjaro. I'd talked about Everest (though thank fuck had decided against it). Kite surfing, sky diving, river rafting, bungee jumping, cave diving. If there was an adventure in it, Pru was all over it.

And doing it with zeal.

She *lived,* and I thought Pru was amazing.

I still didn't want to go shark diving.

Clogging my arteries with fried cheese?

Yeah, *that* was an adventure I could do.

"Would *I* try to make you feel guilty?" Pru asked, attempting innocence. But she was far from innocent and I knew that, so I just lightly punched her on the arm.

"Um. Yes," I said, "you would definitely try to make me feel guilty."

"Rude." Pru snatched the basket of curds. "Then I'm not sharing."

"*I'm* the rude one?" I snatched them back. "I'm not the friend trying to guilt the other one into *shark diving.*"

"I'm— Holy shit," Pru breathed, and I knew she was truly distracted and not trying to fake me out by pretending there was something behind us so she could steal the fried cheese back only because Pru let go of the basket without a peep. "Who is *that?*"

Still holding on to the basket, because Pru could be sneaky, I shifted and turned to see a trio of *huge* walk into the bar.

And at the front of the trio was Marcel.

Who Pru's eyes seemed to be glued to.

Hmm.

But before I could do more than slant a glance to Pru to see her practically drooling over Marcel, who was trailed by Smitty and Raph, I watched Luca, Theo, and Martin follow them into the room. There was a reason Pru was drooling. Marcel was gorgeous. A jawline that could cut through ice, deep brown eyes. His nose was a little crooked, his cheekbones high, and there was a scar that sliced through his right eyebrow. Maybe those parts didn't sound pretty together.

But he was.

Fucking beautiful.

And his body was...lean strength mixed with bulges in all the right places—arms, ass, pecs, thighs.

So yeah, he was totally drool-able.

But the man who walked in behind the six guys was the only one that made my heart skip a beat. Oliver's eyes seemed to go straight toward mine, warming at the same time that Pru whispered, "Sweet baby Jesus, the man said to get you here, but he didn't say anything about bringing a half-dozen specimens for bean-flicking material."

"Bean-flick—" I blinked, focused on the more important part of that statement. "*Who* said to get me here?"

A hand sliding down my spine. A chest coming close. Warm breath in my ear.

"Babe."

I shuddered as his knuckles drifted across my cheek.

"Hi, Oliver," Pru sing-songed. "Who are your friends?"

I shifted to glance up at the man who'd positioned himself at my spine. "Oliver?" I asked archly, breathing deeply to steady my racing heart. "Did you get Pru to bring me here?"

Half of his mouth curved. I wanted to kiss it. "I might have suggested that she buy you a drink, and"—he paused when the server came over with a full tray of food, of cheesy delight—"apparently the entire kitchen's quantity of fried food?" he finished on a question.

"Oh my God, mozzarella sticks," Smitty murmured, reaching for the basket almost before it hit the table.

"No!" Pru smacked his hand away. "These are for us." She narrowed her eyes when Smitty reached again. "Don't make me break your hand, Connor Smith."

"You need cheese curds, mozzarella sticks, a giant plate of nachos, and jalapeño poppers?"

"Yes," Pru said. "And chili cheese fries *and* a Philly cheesesteak, and those are all for *us*." Her chin came up, and I watched the fairy fade into the badass hockey player. "You want food, you order it, but you don't take ours."

Smitty's mouth opened and closed like a fish.

A *screech* drew everyone's focus. Or at least the six of us that weren't moving chairs. Because apparently, Marcel, Martin, and Raph had skipped the cheese standoff and were bringing stools over. Stools they crammed around the table that was meant for maybe six normal people, but definitely not seven bulky hockey players, one fairy-type hockey player, and one normal woman.

Thus, I was plastered against Oliver.

And frankly, it wasn't a bad place to be.

Though I couldn't let his maneuvering stand without at least pushing back a little bit. Which meant when he tried to snatch a popper, I smacked *his* hand away.

His brows raised.

"No poppers for men who manipulate my friend"—I narrowed my eyes—"who is going to be their employee."

"Oh, there's no manipulation," Pru called from across the table. "I asked that one if he knew you well. He told me he's been trying to get you to agree to a date."

I almost choked on my tongue as six male pairs of hockey player eyes came to me (not seven because Oliver's hadn't left me since he'd perched himself on the stool next to mine and yanked me flush up next to him).

"You won't date my boy?" Smitty asked.

More tongue choking.

Then I lifted my chin and narrowed my eyes. "He says we've already been on five dates." A glare up at him. "But technically, I don't believe you've actually *asked* me—"

"Really?"

I thought back. "No, I don't believe you've ever said, Hazel Reid, would you go out on a date with me?"

He didn't miss a beat. "Hazel Reid, would you go out on a date with me?"

"I—" My mouth opened and closed. How did I answer that?

Easy. Yes! my brain screamed.

But in front of six of the biggest gossips on the team? And a woman who would probably go straight to the top of that gossip list, thus usurping Smitty and the rest of them to become the biggest?

Pru started cackling.

At one with the gossip squad already.

Marcel, who I was starting to realize was the only nice one in the group (hmph!), took pity on me and picked up the menus that were stashed behind a bucket that held condiments, napkins, and silverware at the end of the table. He passed them around and said, "I want nachos. Who's going to share with me?"

"Me!" Pru called, and pushed the plate to the man sitting next to her.

How she'd maneuvered that, I didn't know.

Except that she was Pru, and Pru could manage anything if she put her mind to it.

Smitty, meanwhile, leveled a glare at her. "Seriously? You'll share with him but not with me?"

"Yup." Pru picked up a chip and popped it into her mouth. "Because he's pretty, and you're not."

Smitty gaped, momentarily at a loss for words, which was a freaking miracle in and of itself because Smitty without words wasn't something that *ever* happened. But put him up next to Pru? And apparently miracles *could* happen.

At least for a few moments.

Because he was Smitty, he recovered quickly. "You think Marcel's pretty?"

A nod. Another chip into her mouth. "Uh-huh," she said around the bite.

Let it be noted that Marcel still hadn't taken a single chip.

"But I'm not," Smitty said.

"Nope." There was a pop on the P sound that made Marcel jump, but he tentatively reached for a chip and placed it in his mouth. "You're manly in a way that's very *take-me-to-bed-and-fuck-me-senseless*"—Marcel choked—"but no, sorry, honey, but you're not pretty."

The table was quiet.

I glanced up, saw Oliver's mouth was parted in surprised shock.

I leaned in, whispered in his ear, "Didn't know you were getting that, did you?"

His head slowly turned so he could meet my eyes. His lips

were close, near enough that if I moved the slightest bit, our mouths would touch. "She is—" Mentally, I braced. If he had a problem with Pru, even after he'd hired her, it would be a problem. Not with the job. I knew that Oliver wouldn't be the kind of guy to do something that would affect that, just because Pru was throwing sass. But if he didn't like Pru out in real life, that would be...well, it would make me feel yucky because Pru was my friend. "—*awesome*," he breathed, astonishment in his gaze.

Awesome.

I felt that against my lips.

I wanted to feel it against my tongue.

So...

Fuck it.

I kissed him.

In front of the seven biggest gossips.

I just...kissed the wonderful, sexy man, who'd gotten a date six before he'd even gotten a date one, who touched my cheek gently, who tucked me into his side and held me like I was precious, and who...I wanted.

Just quite simply, *wanted*.

Oliver didn't hesitate. He kissed me back, tongue and teeth and lips, his arms banding around me, his mouth sending me soaring in just seconds.

But before I fully flew off into space, I heard Pru say, "Well, I think that means Oliver is getting a first date."

FIFTEEN

Oliver

I HELD Hazel's hand when we walked out of CeCe's.

I didn't think I'd eaten that much fried food since...well, *ever*.

Where the girls put it, I didn't know.

But Pru had eventually come around and allowed the guys to share, even Smitty, when I promised she could order anything off the menu.

Which she had.

A ridiculous amount of food that I'd balked at.

But...they'd eaten it all.

Down to the tiniest crumb of cheese curd, they ate every bit of fried and cheese-covered morsel. And drank beer. Well, the girls had cosmos and the guys beers, but alcohol had been consumed and food eaten and that was why I leaned close and whispered, "Date six."

She snorted and grinned up at me. "You don't give up, do you?"

"Group date still counts as a date."

A shake of her head. A sigh. "Apparently it counts as date six."

I almost did a fist pump that she was going along with my ridiculousness. "Yup." I brushed my lips over her temple. "So, what do you want to do for date one?"

Her gaze came to me, and it was nearly impossible to not get lost in her gorgeous brown eyes. They swirled with humor, sparked with happiness, danced with mischief. I wanted to kiss her again, but...romance.

So, I tugged her toward her car, waited for her to unlock the doors.

"Oliver?" she asked, once I'd opened the driver's side one and was urging her inside. I flattened my palm on her back, paused my urging.

"Yeah, babe?"

Her body drifted to me, and I got flowers in my nose, soft curves against my hard, a sweet smile aimed in my direction. "Aren't you going to kiss me goodnight?"

My cock twitched, as though she'd reached down and cupped me between my legs.

"We haven't had a first date yet, baby."

A smile that could rival the Mona Lisa. It was full of secrets and confidence and naughtiness. "We've had six."

"Oh, is that how you're playing it, babe?"

She shrugged. "I'm going to play it however it'll get your tongue in my mouth."

More cock-twitching.

And then I tugged her close, slipping an arm around her waist, getting the curves against my body and against my palm —fuck, but if I didn't know which ones were better. Either way, I didn't care. She wanted it. I could give it to her.

It was as simple as that.

I dropped my mouth to hers.

A kiss. It shouldn't be anything extraordinary. But with Hazel it was. One touch of her lips and the universe fell away. I was floating through space, my only anchor her tongue, her body, her hands. They wove into my hair as she went on tiptoe, holding tight, her body weight going against me. I didn't think about my leg or the prosthesis when I took it, how everything had changed, but when it came to Hazel, everything was for the better.

It was touch and sensation.

Her and me.

Pleasure coiling through me, chased rapidly by desire.

I stepped forward, pinning her against the car, rocking into her, stroking my hand along her rib cage, knuckles brushing along the side of her breast. She startled then moaned, the sound vibrating against my tongue, leaning into my touch.

And fuck what I wouldn't give to not be in a parking lot right now.

Just...one more second.

One more touch.

Her hand slid from my hair and down along my side. It slipped beneath the hem of my shirt, dancing over my skin, on my back...and then around to my front.

Oh, that was fucking good.

It was also bad. *Really* bad because it made me hard-pressed to remember that we were in a parking lot, that I was going for romance, that I needed to ignore the urge to spread her over the backseat and fuck her senseless. Or to sit in the driver's seat and have her on top of me, fucking *me* senseless. Or both and—

With a groan, I tore my mouth from hers.

My hips were pressed to hers, the socket of my prosthesis was digging into my thigh, and everything was stiff—but most especially my cock, so really there were worse problems to have when it came down to it. Slowly, I pushed off her, making sure I had my balance before fully straightening and then making sure she had hers.

Having to think about that, about her, making sure she was good, settled my desire, reinforced my control, stopped me from getting her in the back seat and trying to sort out the logistics of fucking her against that leather and doing my best to fog up those windows.

Later.

We would do that later.

Because logistics was also something I needed to think about, something I should have considered...oh, six dates before (okay, almost two weeks ago, during that first session in her office when I realized she was attracted to me and not disgusted by what I had become). But the point was that I hadn't slept with a woman since my injury, and I'd done PT for a lot of different movements and activities, practicing like crazy for anything I might encounter.

Except fucking.

I hadn't practiced fucking.

"What?" Hazel asked, her chest heaving, her mouth kiss-swollen, eyes half-lidded.

I dragged my thumb over that bottom lip, trying to summon the control to not take it again. "I was just thinking."

"Thinking instead of kissing?" she asked lightly. Her hands smoothed over my chest.

Another kiss.

I wanted it.

But...parking lot. Romance.

Still, I could tell her what I was thinking about. "Thinking about fucking instead of kissing."

Her mouth formed an adorable little O, and I forgot about

parking lots and public places. I forgot about romance. Instead, I slanted my lips over hers, tasting that O, tasting the cosmos on her tongue, savoring the lazy strokes we gave each other, the way she clung to me for several long moments before I summoned my control again and released her.

"I like thinking about fucking," she murmured.

I chuckled. "I like it, too," I told her, "and believe me, I'm going to be thinking about it a whole lot between now and date one."

Teeth into a plump, bruised lip.

Fingers clenching my shoulders.

Temptation personified.

I nudged her toward the driver's seat again. "Go home, babe."

She sighed and wrinkled her nose. "I don't wanna."

Amusement trickled through me. "You should, anyway."

"Or..." A breath. "You could get in my car, and I can drive you back to my place and—"

"Gonna stop you right there, baby," I murmured, leaning close and pressing a light kiss to her earlobe. "Candles and music. A nice dinner and flowers. Time together that's not rushed or on a whim or crashed by six nosy hockey players."

"Seven," she murmured. "Pru is maybe the nosiest of the bunch."

I grinned. "I stand corrected. Seven nosy hockey players."

Fingers on my jaw. "I can feel you hard against me."

On a groan, I dropped my head to her shoulder. "Killing me, babe."

"Good," she whispered, her hand sliding over my neck, drifting into the hair on my nape. "Because I'm wet and aching and going to make myself come once, maybe twice when I get home."

It was a wonder I had any blood left in my brain, but I

managed to bite back the groan that was threatening to rumble up my throat. "Get in the car, babe."

She smiled, ran her fingers through my hair one more time.

Then she got in the car.

I closed the door behind her, watched as she drove away.

And then I went home to start planning logistics.

Because I had the feeling that fucking was going to happen sooner rather than later, and I needed to be prepared.

THE NEXT DAY I walked into my office, planning to drop my stuff and then hit the coffee shop on-site to pick up Hazel's drink.

But my office was occupied.

I grinned at the petite, curvy brunette perched on the edge of my desk.

"Giving me ideas, babe."

She held up a to-go cup of coffee for a heartbeat before setting it on my desk. "Desktop sex?"

"And back of the door sex and office chair sex and—"

She squirmed.

I grinned.

I'd spent a long time last night thinking about logistics with my leg, planning and fantasizing in the best way possible. And I thought I had it down.

Or at least, I was game to get in lots and *lots* of practice.

"You know I haven't had sex since the accident," I said softly.

Her expression had been hot, her eyes scorching, but my statement cooled that desire. Which wasn't what I wanted, but partly necessary, I supposed, since she was going to be part of it. "Oliver," she murmured. "We don't have to—"

"Oh," I said, "it's a *have to*. Believe me, I've been dreaming about having you in my bed for ages. It's a *have to*."

She pushed off the desk, crossed to me, resting her palm on my heart.

I liked that, liked when she came close, came to me without hesitation, placed her hand on my chest and seemed to be just taking in the feel of my heart beating. Maybe gauging my reaction by keeping track of my pulse, maybe just enjoying being close.

"It wasn't stopping at a *have to*," she told me, eyes flashing as they met mine, though her smile softened the expression. "It was a we don't have to *rush*. Because there isn't a rush, honey. We can take our time and figure it out and go *slow*."

"So says the woman who's had sex in the last nine months."

"Bad sex," she muttered.

My brows lifted.

"That's not fair." She took a breath. Released it slowly. "It's just that sex with Trevor...well, it wasn't always effortless, and his kisses never made me feel like yours do."

"As much as I don't like to hear you talk about another man, especially one who's a fucking asshole, who clearly didn't appreciate you, I do like that you like my kisses."

"Like is too mild a word."

I grinned. "Like that, too, babe."

A breath. Cheeks going rosy. "I was trying to reassure you that I don't think sex between us is going to be an issue."

"Oh, I know it's not going to be."

Her eyes went wide. "What?"

"I've been planning logistics."

"Lo-logistics?"

"Yup."

Those eyes were so fucking gorgeous going wide like that. "I—"

A knock at the door.

I touched her cheek. "I've got a meeting with Marco and Pru."

She nodded. "Right. I—"

"Give me your number?" I asked, holding up my phone.

Wide, wide eyes, rosy cheeks, a kissable mouth. But she took the phone and plugged in her number. I took it back, made sure to save the contact, then followed her to the door when the knock came again. "I'll call you tonight."

"Okay," she whispered.

"You have Marcel today, right?"

"Yeah."

Another touch of her cheek, brushing along the pale pink blush. "I can't wait to hear about it."

Then I opened the door, ignored the surprised look of Marco, the pleased one of Pru, and watched Hazel with her wide eyes and rosy cheeks walk away from me.

The next stage of my plotting was in play.

SIXTEEN

Hazel

I WAS IN BED, a documentary on a special penguin island playing in the background and thinking that it was time to stop waiting for Oliver to call when my phone rang.

A squee built inside me.

Another when I saw it was a number I didn't have programmed into my cell.

Normally, I didn't pick up any calls from strange numbers—I'd had way too many "We need to reach you about your car's extended warranty" to fall for that trick—but this was Oliver, and though I wanted to pretend that I hadn't been waiting for him to phone, there was an entire TV screen's worth of penguins who would judge my if I tried to lie.

I couldn't handle their little beady eyes on me, mocking my duplicity.

Swiping a finger across the screen as I lifted my phone to my ear, I glared at the tuxedo-wearing birds. Judgy bitches.

"Hello?"

I was so wound up in my face-off with the birds that I hadn't said hello.

Great.

"Oliver?" I pushed out, my voice squeaky.

"You okay?" he murmured, the question rumbling through my speaker, reminding me of his touch, his kiss.

Focused on that and not controlling my filter—which was six shades of useless considering I'd finished nearly a whole bottle of wine while waiting for Oliver's call—I accidentally said, "Yup. Just me and my penguin foes are having a stare down."

It took my a beat to process the silence.

Because wine.

"Penguins?" he eventually asked.

"Yup. The men are sitting on the eggs and the women are going off and hunting like the badass motherfuckers they are, and all the men are sitting at home doing *nothing* while the women are off doing *everything*—like *always*—"

"Aren't the male penguins the ones who ensure that the eggs don't freeze?"

"Don't get off topic, young sir," I rambled.

"Young sir?"

I went on like he hadn't spoken. Because penguins and wine and it was fun talking about nonsense with Oliver. "So, while the women are doing *everything*," I said again, "these male penguins are judging me because I drank an entire bottle of wine while waiting for you to call."

Silence.

Then, "Shit."

Still, high off my penguin rant, I said, "And when I was just going to get under covers, give myself an orgasm because I've had six dates without one, not including last night, of course. Or the night before," I added, because *truth*.

Oliver started chuckling.

"Or the night before that one," I went on, tugging the blankets off my body, exposing my bare legs to the cool air. Oh, that was better, especially since the wine had made me horny, tipsy, and hot.

"What's that?"

"Hmm?"

"The rustling," he said, almost sounding panicked now. "I heard rustling. Almost like—"

I dropped my head back on my pillow. "Don't worry. I'm not touching myself. I just had to get the covers off me. I'm hot."

"You are."

Not missing a beat that one.

"You're in bed?"

I rolled to the side, holding the phone to my ear. "Yup."

"And drunk?"

"Tipsy, maybe." A pause as I considered that. "Well, slightly more than tipsy, a hair away from drunk. Tipsy-drunk, as one will."

Another chuckle.

"You have a sexy laugh," I blurted

"Babe." But I could tell he liked that, even though he changed the subject. "You drank a whole bottle of wine waiting for me to call?"

"Needs must."

A beat, then, "I'm sorry."

I sighed, relaxed into the pillow and mattress. Two of the few things I'd splurged on as top of the line, and it was totally worth it to have a good bed and pillow. It was like sleeping on clouds every night. Though I knew I wouldn't have a problem sleeping tonight, not with the wine running through my veins and dragging me under more every second.

"Should I let you go?" he murmured.

"Uh-uh." I burrowed deeper.

"Want me to help you with that orgasm problem?"

Alertness slid through me. "You'll come over?"

A low groan. "No, babe. I meant what I said about romance."

I frowned and sank back onto the pillow, snuggling into the mattress again.

"Fine," I muttered.

"What are you wearing?"

"Seriously?" It was another mutter.

"Humor me."

I wrinkled my nose.

"I'm sorry I was late calling. Today was Marco's last day, so I took him out to dinner. He wanted to reminisce, and that took longer than I expected."

My nose relaxed.

"So, *now* will you tell me what you're wearing?" he asked.

"No."

He sighed. "Why not?"

"For one, the penguins are still judging me. I can feel their beady little eyes on me."

Laughter, warm and rumbly through the airwaves and into my ear, my brain, sliding down my body as though it were a physical caress. Then, "What's two?"

"Hmm?"

"You said *for one*, so what's the second reason you won't tell me what you're wearing?"

Probably, I should have lied. But I was sleepy and tipsy-drunk and didn't have any control over my filter anymore. "You're not here."

Silence. Then, "Babe."

"Don't *babe* me," I grumbled. "You could come over right now—"

"I don't have your address."

I rattled it off.

A groan tumbled through the speakers. "I'm trying to do the right thing. You deserve care and affection, not a quick fuck because we're both so horny that we can't wait."

"How about a quickie and *then* something longer?"

I could manage that. Tipsy-drunk was already morphing into straight tipsy, and that meant I was sleepy, horny, and wanted this man.

He groaned again. "Hazel."

"I like when you say my name."

Rustling through the speakers, the sound of footsteps and movement. "What are *you* doing?" I whispered, a smirk tugging up the corners of my lips. Maybe I couldn't convince him to come over, but if he was getting naked, then I wasn't opposed to mutual self-satisfaction. Especially, if I could get him to Face-Time. I needed the visual of him wrapping that strong hand around his cock, stroking it slow and hard until he—

"I'm coming over."

My breath caught. "Really?"

"Babe," he said, and his voice was gravel, need in every one of the small stones. "You think I could ever truly deny you anything?"

More catching, as though someone was hugging me so tightly that my lungs couldn't inflate. "Oh."

"Yeah. *Oh.*"

The sound of a car door opening and closing.

"Ten minutes."

"*Oh,*" I breathed again.

I heard his car engine turn on, the background noise growing as he must have reached the street. "Babe?" he said.

"Yeah?"

My heart was galloping in my chest. Tipsy-drunk was just tipsy. Or maybe it was just Oliver-smashed because, holy fucking shit, was this happening?

"Eight minutes. Unlock the front door. Go back to your bed and get naked."

"Eight minutes?" I squeaked, glancing around my bedroom, which was a mess. As was the rest of my house. Oh fuck, he was going to be there in eight minutes, and I had dirty laundry on the floor, and a bathroom that was maybe clean, and—shit!—dishes in the sink and—

What if my hairs were in the sink?

I needed—

"Six minutes," he murmured, voice dark and dangerous, and my pussy liked that, a whole hell of a lot. "Get moving, babe."

"I—"

I stumbled out of bed, scooped clothes into my arms and shoved them in the closet. Then ran into my bathroom and checked the sink, rinsing the hairs down the drain and brushing my teeth for good measure.

"Four minutes," came his husky voice.

Shit.

Oh my God.

But also, *shit*.

I ran for the ground floor, for the front door, knowing there was no time to clean my kitchen, not when he said, "Two minutes."

I flicked the lock. "It's open."

"Upstairs. Naked. One minute."

"I—"

"One minute, babe. I'm hanging up now."

Lights flashed across my lawn. My throat seized with panic, with excitement, with so much fucking need.

A car engine.

A door slamming.

Turning, I sprinted up the stairs, leaving the bedroom light on, so he'd know where to go, and then I was reaching for the hem of my tank top when I heard it.

The front door opening and closing.

Footsteps on the stairs.

Quickly, without thinking about it, without chickening out, I yanked my top over my head, shimmied out of my panties, letting both puddle to the carpet, and turned to face the hall...

Just as Oliver strode through.

He was rumpled and gorgeous and...the sexiest man I'd ever seen.

His gaze went to mine, dropped slowly, and I watched his jaw clench, his hands fist as his eyes traced over my naked body. "Beautiful." One rasped word. Maybe cliché, but the way he said it, every syllable filled with need and reverence and *heat* and...it was the best compliment I'd ever received in my life.

His stare made the slow trail back up and then drifted over my shoulder.

And he smiled.

And...it was a physical assault on my senses.

"You weren't kidding about the penguins."

Silently, I shook my head. Words were failing me. Need had clawed its way up my throat, had the desire inside me churning. My hands shook. My breaths were coming in rapid gusts. My palms were damp, and my pussy...well, that had gone well beyond damp. I could feel myself coating the insides of my thighs.

"Oliver?" I asked, rooted in place.

Just go to him.

Take five steps and launch myself into his arms.

But something about the way he was staring at me made that impossible.

I could only stand there and wait.

And wait.

And—

He moved so quickly that one second, he was five feet away, the next he was in my face, his body flush to mine...and coaxing me backward. Back. Back. My legs collided with my bed, and I tumbled onto the mattress.

"Beautiful," he murmured again.

Then he was on top of me. The movement a little stilted, a bit ungraceful, but I was hardly a ballerina when I scrambled up the bed, trying to make room for him. His mouth met mine, his lips working, his tongue slipping inside.

Then his *fingers* slipped inside.

"Fuck, babe," he groaned, the long, thick digit stroking into my pussy. "So fucking wet."

"I—"

He slid another finger in, not giving me a moment to breathe, to think, to worry that I was naked and he wasn't.

"Fuck," I hissed, thighs falling wide, my mouth going slack.

He flicked his tongue over my lips then dragged his mouth down my throat, nipping at the sensitive skin there, kissing his way down my chest, pausing and nuzzling into my cleavage. One rough palm squeezed my breasts, massaging the flesh, thumbs brushing over my nipples.

I hissed again, in the best way, and he didn't hesitate to take advantage of the sensitive spot, leaning close to suck one deeply into his mouth. I moaned, fingers going to his hair, clenching tight, probably *too* tight, but the man's tongue was a revelation. It needed to be gilded and hung on the wall. Except that would mean I couldn't have it working my nipple, trailing along my skin, dipping down—

He pulled his hair out of my hands, slid down my body.

And then I got that fabulous tongue on my pussy.

The hand that had been on my breasts was braced at my hip, his hot breath was on my folds. His tongue traced through the wet heat of me, delving deep inside me, teasing out every sensitive spot, every place that made me squirm, homing in on the pressure, the movements, the rhythm that had me writhing against his mouth.

"I—" I dropped my head back to the pillows when he sucked my clit hard. "That, please. Do *that* again."

He sucked me harder, added a flick of his tongue.

"Oh."

I shuddered.

He repeated the sucking, the flick, slid another finger inside.

Another shudder. This one because I was on the brink of shattering. His palm slid under my ass, tilting my hips up, bringing his mouth more flush against me, and then he repeated the sucking, the flicking, the keeping me tight and close and—

Pleasure swirled, went taut.

Flooded through me and went on and on and on.

Every muscle was tight, and then every muscle went slack, so loose that my head dropped back onto my pillow, my arms to the mattress.

Oliver was still licking me.

Slow and light, easing me down, avoiding my clit—thank God, that bundle of nerves was so sensitive that even his breath being near it felt like it might be too much. He caught me from where I'd catapulted into the stratosphere, allowed me to slowly drift toward earth.

Then I was back in my own body, could feel the bed

beneath me again, the sheets on my skin, the comforter all bunched up from where I'd just tossed it aside earlier.

He slowly crawled up my body, fully dressed, wiping his chin and mouth on his sleeve.

A kiss to my jaw. A brush of knuckles against my cheek.

Then he nuzzled my throat and whispered, "Why do I feel like the penguins are judging me?"

My eyes flew open, saw the gathering of birds on the screen.

Their beady eyes right on me.

Judging.

Yup. Those fuckers were totally judging.

SEVENTEEN

Oliver

SHE BURST OUT LAUGHING, and it was almost the best sound on earth.

Almost the best because the absolute best was Hazel coming against my tongue.

Hands down.

I would remember her moaning my name until I breathed my last breath.

"Here," she said, grabbing the remote from the nightstand and handing it to me. "Pick something to watch while I suck you off."

The remote tumbled from my fingers.

Mainly because that painted a picture I'd been fantasizing about for a good long while, but also to catch her shoulders when she tried to crawl down my body.

"Babe."

She cupped me, and since I was only wearing sweats and I was harder than I'd been in my entire life and I was holding on to my control by the thinnest of razor-thin margins, I promptly forgot whatever the fuck I'd been about to say, my hands sliding from her shoulders.

Her fingers slipped under the waistband of my sweats, beneath my underwear.

They were cool and soft as they circled my cock. One stroke, and I was ready to explode, but I managed to summon a modicum of strength and started to reach for her wrist, intent on tugging her free. "Babe," I began. "I didn't—"

She kept moving, shifting farther from me. "Don't give me some bullshit line about how you only came here for me, so now I don't get to give you pleasure." She released me, reached for the top of my sweats, and started tugging them down. "It gives me pleasure to give you pleasure, same as the reason you're hard and straining against your pants from licking me senseless, honey."

"I—"

Her hands paused, my cock an inch away from being free. "So, if you don't want me to do this, say so, and that's fine. But make sure it's because you really don't want it or you're not ready, and not because you have this inane thought that you're taking advantage of me when I dragged you out of your house at ten at night, all because I was horny and pushy."

"I like you horny and pushy."

A corner of her mouth curved. "Good, because I tend to be those two things a lot."

"Along with sweet, kind, considerate, and a remarkably good kisser. Though you do watch penguin documentaries, so a perk might be that you're kinky as hell."

The other corner curved. "You already know about my countertop and desktop sex fantasies, should I tell you about my avian ones?"

"*Are* there avian ones?" A ripple of concern slid through

me. Was she into feathers? That wouldn't be too bad. I could do a lot with a feather and her naked skin. But if it went further, like baby birding some food...well, that wasn't going to go on my Fuck List.

"No."

I relaxed. "Good."

"Now, can I suck your cock so deep that my eyes water until you come in the back of my throat?"

I choked, the cock in question jumping with excitement. "Um..."

"Is that no?"

No, it wasn't a *no*. It was a yes, very much a yes.

"Honey?"

"Babe?"

"Is it a yes?"

I nodded.

"Need the word, honey."

"Yes, babe. Fucking please, do that."

Her smile lit up the room—or at least it competed with the documentary playing in the background—but then I wasn't thinking of anything but helping her get my pants down. Though, with a quick tug that had my cock springing free, she proved she didn't need my help to do anything.

Least of which was getting me deep in her mouth.

She sucked me hard enough that my eyes rolled back in my head, but then she paired it by dragging her teeth lightly up and down my shaft, her grip tight and twisting, her lips spread wide, her throat working to take me deep. I gripped the sheets, resisting the urge to thrust up, to bury myself in the back of her throat, not wanting to gag her. She pulled back, the head of my cock resting on her bottom lip.

"Don't hold back." Her mouth moved against me, forming the words.

My back bowed, my cock slipped back between her lips, deep, and she gripped me again, stroking me, using her teeth and tongue and—

Holy fucking shit, this wasn't going to take long.

Orgasm so fucking close I could feel it tingling at the base of my spine, I struggled to slow, to regain control, to—

Then she cupped my balls, tightened her lips and I jerked, hitting the back of her throat. She coughed slightly, pulled back, tears clinging to the edges of her lashes, but before I could retreat, make sure I didn't hurt her, she all but dove on my cock.

Deep strokes.

Lots of suction.

A tight hand.

I exploded.

She swallowed me down, but even if I'd been coherent enough to try to pull away so she didn't have to, her grip tightened, she took me deeper, and...I came so fucking long and hard that I wasn't sure if I still had a body any longer.

Eventually, I came to with Hazel cuddled up next to me, smiling like a Cheshire cat, her hand under my T-shirt, my sweats still around my thighs.

"You have a really nice cock, you know that, right?"

"Considering it's still hanging out," I muttered, summoning the strength to yank up my underwear and pants, "it's good you think that."

Fuck.

I hadn't even taken off my shoes.

"Oliver?"

"Hmm?" Smoothing back her hair, I pressed a kiss to her forehead.

"I liked that." She snuggled closer. "That ticks one box off my fantasy list."

"Good," I managed to say. I'd sit up in a second, leave her to sleep, but…just in a second. Because I didn't feel like I had any bones left in my body.

"I think you might be able to tick off my entire list."

My limbs were weighed down with concrete, I was so relaxed. The semi-constant background noise of pain of my injury had finally silenced, leaving only relaxed muscles and nerves and a brain that was full of haze. "Mmm-hmm."

A giggle then her arm tightened around me. "Oliver?"

"Hmm?" I said again.

"Will you stay?"

I sucked in a breath, some of that relaxation fading.

"Just for a little while?" she added when I didn't immediately respond. "It's okay if you don't want to," she whispered as I was still trying to form words that weren't *hmm* or *mmm.* "I know that you came out of your way and—"

"Babe."

"Yeah?"

I summoned some inhuman strength and managed to say, "I didn't even take my shoes off, I was in such a hurry to get to you. My shoes," I repeated, wrapping an arm around her and tucking her close. "That's how much I wanted to be here. You want me to stay, I'm here. Though," I added gently. "I need to take off my leg to sleep, so if that's something you're not comfortable with…"

She sat up, hand on my chest. "It's you, honey. I'm comfortable with every part of you."

Something inside me relaxed. The last of those supports holding up the wall that kept everyone at a distance, the little bit of fear that *this* would be the moment she rejected me.

"Is there anything you need to make it easier?" she asked.

"I wouldn't turn down a charger for my phone on the nightstand."

She grinned, pushed off me. "I think I can do that." Then

she was out of bed, and I was watching her naked ass head for the door. She stooped to pick up her tank top and panties, pulling both on. Then she disappeared into the hall.

I summoned the energy to get out of bed, dealt with the post-best-orgasm-of-my-life wobble, yanked up my pants and moved to one of the two doors in the corner. One revealed a closet—messy enough to make me smile, apparently my woman was a packrat. The other was the bathroom. I did my thing, washed my hands, and when I came out to the bedroom again, it was to find Hazel plugging in a charger and draping the cord over the wood of the nightstand.

"There's an extra toothbrush in the drawer by the sink."

"Thanks, babe." I turned back, found the drawer and the toothbrush, did my thing again—albeit with my teeth this time, and returned to the bedroom. The penguins were off, but in its place was some cooking show that Hazel paused.

She got up, crossed to me, pressing a kiss to my jaw, and trailing her hand across my stomach.

As though she'd done that a hundred times before.

I liked it.

Liked the way it made me feel like I belonged here.

Smiling and probably having no idea that she had once again rocked me to my core, she moved into the bathroom, closing the door behind her.

The water turned on.

I moved to the bed, dug my wallet and keys out of my pocket, my cell out of the other, plugged it into the charger, and then took care of removing my prosthesis—working off the socket that attached it to the portion of my leg beneath my knee the doctors had been able to save, propping the prosthesis against the nightstand, then scooting back onto the bed and peeling away the liners and socks I wore beneath to cushion the impact on my skin and remaining limb.

Hazel came out of the bathroom, walking straight toward me, her eyes not once going to the stump or the space where my leg should be.

Instead, she crawled into bed, snuggled up next to me, yanked the covers up, and threw an arm over my waist, sighing contentedly.

"Beautiful."

Her head tilted back, eyes hitting my. "What's beautiful?"

"You." I ran my knuckles over her cheek. "And what you've given me. I—" I wrapped my arms around her. "I didn't think I could have that. Not because I didn't deserve it or there was something wrong with me—I battled through those demons long ago, and losing my leg wasn't going to bring me back. I just...I just never thought that being with a woman would bring me this much peace, didn't think I could open up enough to have that peace."

"Because when you found it with Theresa and Alex," she whispered, "and then that peace was taken away."

I nodded, voice cracking when I said, "It took them ages to get in. Then they were..."

Her voice dropped to a whisper. "And then they were gone."

I nodded again, smoothed her curls back, letting them bounce through my fingers. "Yeah, babe. Then they were gone. But"—a breath, needing to tell her this, needing to admit it aloud since it was all up in my heart—"you're here now."

She gripped me tighter, snuggled closer against me, sliding her leg over my thighs so she had me wrapped in a full-body hug. "I'm here," she said, "and I'm not going anywhere."

I was wide open. Vulnerable.

But Hazel had her body wrapped around me. Her promise on the air.

So, I wasn't scared.

"WHAT DO YOU THINK?" I asked, the next night.

Hazel walked through my living room with its gray on gray on gray decor and winced. "It's nice," she began.

But I could see her face and having spent some time at her place the previous morning, I knew that it was as I'd thought. Her house was a home. Warm and lived in, with loads of pictures and knick-knacks and artwork. It wasn't like I wanted my shelves and walls filled with clutter. It was just...I wasn't afraid of the connection now.

I wasn't afraid to have something warm, worried that it might be taken away.

That had already happened, and I'd survived, and I was doing Teresa and Alex a disservice by continuing to hide. And if they were there, they'd kick my ass for daring to live that way. *A big life*, Teresa always said. *We want you to live a big, big life.*

Hazel had helped me remember that.

Because she saw beneath the barriers.

Gave me the courage to move beyond them.

So, I was continuing with my plan to slowly (okay, maybe not so slowly), to reel her in, and that meant getting her to invest in me, in *us*. Which was why I'd invited her over under the guise of "helping" me with a few things.

"You see my problem?" I said.

"That it looks like a very expensive hotel room?" she asked. "Or that fancy living room that you're not allowed to step foot in because you might spill on the white carpet?"

"Yes. That."

She grinned. "I see your problem."

"So, you'll help me?"

"Go boho chic like my place?"

The term boho made me shudder, and chic wasn't much

better, but I put on a brave face and nodded. One, I wanted Hazel to keep coming around and decorating my house as a great excuse to spend time with her. Two, if she managed to give me a bit of what she had at her place, I could build on that, keep making my house a home. "If that's what you think will work best," I said, meaning it. "I want to come home and feel home, not like I can't step on that white carpet."

She smiled at me, wide and open. "I *am* teasing about the boho chic, but I don't think you'd go wrong with a little color."

Color I could do.

Especially if it wasn't more gray.

"So," I said, "if I turn you loose at Target with my credit card, can you give me a little color in here?"

"In here," she said, rolling her earring, as she always seemed to do when she was thinking hard about something, "Target will do. This whole house?" She spread her hands wide. "It's a lot of space, and a designer might be better."

"A designer is what got me into this."

"You and me and Target will take time."

I shrugged. "I have time."

"You and me and Target means multiple trips to Target."

Another shrug. "I like Target."

She placed the back of her hand on my forehead. "Do you have a fever?" she teased. "What man in his right mind likes Target?"

"Will Target be with you?"

One half of her mouth hitched up. "Yes."

"Then I like Target."

She melted, her body going soft against me, and I'd thus resisted kissing her so far, but I couldn't resist then, not with her so close and so soft.

When we broke apart, I dragged my mouth down her neck, nipped the sensitive skin of her collarbone. "Come on," I said, tugging her into the kitchen, "I'll cook, and then we can go shopping."

Hazel sidled up to me. "You know what's great about Target?"

"What?" I murmured, taking another bite out of her—figuratively, not literally, though I did have my teeth on her skin, her taste on my tongue.

"You can get food there," she whispered.

I grinned. "Popcorn and slushies?"

"That." A beat. "And Starbucks."

"My woman needs coffee?"

She beamed up at me. "Your woman always needs coffee." A hand on my waist, her lips on my throat. "And a cake pop."

"You get this place looking and feeling like a home instead of a very luxurious jail, and I'll buy you *two* cake pops."

Fluttering eyelashes, twitching lips. "Oh, you know how to treat a girl."

I cracked up.

Then swatted her on the butt.

Then I took my woman to Target.

And got her *three* cake pops.

EIGHTEEN

Hazel

"UM, WHAT?" Marcel asked.

I'd had my session with him yesterday, visualizing exercises, writing down some goals and things to work toward. Mediation and a bit of yoga.

But I'd saved the big guns for today.

Rage room 2.0.

Or at least, it was 2.0 for me.

For Marcel, he was looking around the room—the same one I and Oliver had gone to town on—and his eyes were wide.

"Break something," I said. "Anything. It's all here for us to destroy."

"I—" His mouth opened and closed, his head jerked back, and I got a sick feeling in my stomach. Had I read this completely wrong? "But," he whispered, picking up a truly ugly olive and turquoise plate from the stack that sat on a table I'd taken my baseball bat to just a few days before. "Why would I want to break this?"

Because it's ugly as hell.

But I didn't say that.

Instead, I smiled encouragingly. "Because it's designed for it. Because sometimes, we need to break things in order to put ourselves back together. Because sometimes, it feels really fucking good to toss a plate instead of beating yourself up because you missed a breakaway."

His eyes, an amber brown, flared with emotion before shifting away.

Damn.

He wasn't going to bite.

He was shutting down.

Which was the worst thing he could do. Marcel in his head wasn't a happy place, not when he rehashed every mistake he made during a game over and over again.

I shouldn't have mentioned the breakaway.

I might as well have poked the wound inside him that was growing every day because he hadn't scored in eighteen games with a stick.

And then rubbed salt in it.

How to salvage this? How to—

He launched the plate at the wall.

It shattered, loudly in the quiet space, making me jump and squeak out a breath.

"Shit," he breathed. "I'm sorry. I—"

I snatched a plate and launched it. It crashed against the wall and broke, not into as many pieces as he'd made his plate break. But it was still in shards on the ground.

Marcel started. "Whoa."

"What?"

"I just threw a plate." He stared at me. "*You* just threw a plate."

I grinned. "We did." A beat. "So, how'd it feel?"

"I—"

When he didn't go on, I just grabbed another plate, shoved it at him. Then snagged one for myself.

"First one to hit that ugly-ass blue teacup on the shelf wins."

"Wh-what?" he sputtered.

I launched my plate, discus style, at the shelf and teacup. Missed, of course. Because I didn't have great aim to begin with, but at a target ten feet away? Hopeless.

Marcel, a sniper on the ice when he was on fire, wouldn't have any trouble.

But he just stared at me.

"That teacup is awful," I said. "I want it gone."

I grabbed another plate, threw it. Missed horribly.

Still watching me, he lobbed the plate he held. It flew across the room like a frisbee and, of course (freaking athletes and their good aim), took out the teacup. Both plate and cup exploded into a ton of pieces.

I handed him another plate.

"Where next?" he asked.

Yes!

I just barely resisted the urge to fist pump. Instead, I glanced around the room.

"The mirror."

He launched it.

It hit the mirror.

Then he asked, "Where next?" again.

I finally breathed easy.

Because we were on.

This was going to work.

It *had* to.

THE NEXT EVENING, I sat in the owner's box, staring down at the ice.

Okay, not staring at the ice so much as watching the players on the ice.

One player.

Marcel.

Who was on a *tear*.

Thank *freaking* God!

We'd gone through those plates, and then the ugly teacups, and then a typewriter, several vases, an old Dell computer, several baskets, decorative plates, and the gold-plated mirror.

By the end, Marcel had been going whole hog, and I'd just sat back as he exorcised some pretty serious demons.

It had been glorious.

He'd been glorious.

Sweat-damp hair sticking to his forehead, amber eyes gleaming, his damp T-shirt clinging to his muscles. Pru was right. He was beautiful.

Even more so with a hockey helmet, I thought, watching him carry the puck up the ice and hand it off on a really nice pass to Raph, who picked it up and drove toward the net. The guys got an excellent chance on goal that the other team's goalie unfortunately stopped.

But more important, Marcel looked like himself.

"I don't know what you did," Luc murmured, using his clip-board to block his mouth, just in case the cameras were on us and someone got it in their mind to lip read. Which had been known to happen on occasion.

Seriously, though, that was why I loved Luc. He thought of those things and knew that with Marcel starting to relax a bit, his confidence coming back—tonight's game play being a much-needed bolster to it—that the last thing he needed was some reporter asking a dumb question about why he needed appointments with a sports psychologist.

Hey dumbass, I always wanted to say when Luc or one of the players got a question about my role with the Breakers. *They're athletes, not robots. Which means they're human, and human shit gets in the way. So, maybe they need to talk to someone to get their head straight every once in a while.*

Or need a break before they're ready to get on the ice.

Especially during a long season with eighty-two games in a physical, dangerous sport.

Oh, and maybe, just maybe, they might not always be mentally on their game.

But fans wanted results. Owners wanted to make money.

So there often wasn't the space to take care of both sides of the athlete. But as far as I was concerned, my job was as important as Tommy Franklin's behind the bench.

Both mental and physical working together was key.

And seriously, I was so glad that Luc felt the same way.

"I don't know what you did," Luc repeated, "but damn, am I glad you did it."

Marcel was off the ice, so I turned to my friend. "Just don't question the line item in my budget for the rage room, and we'll be all good."

"Rage room?"

I grinned. "I bought him a punch card. He can drop into Rage whenever he wants to drown out those voices in his head."

"I don't know where you get these things," he said, still holding the clipboard up, "but you're seriously a miracle worker. First Oliver, now Marcel. I think we need to talk about upping your salary when your contract is up."

I smiled, buffed my knuckles on my shoulder. "You said it, not me."

There was a pause on the ice as the TV feed took a commercial break. Luc stood, a grin on his face, and tilted his head to the back of the suite, where we would be out of view of the cameras who might be filming for later.

"What's up?" I asked.

"All the other sessions going well?" he asked. "The guys are being receptive and not too difficult?"

"My punching bag is getting a workout," I admitted with a smile, "but it's better than last season. The guys are more settled, as you know, since Shelby was traded."

"I was worried with what happened with Oliver, that they'd regress."

"They're not."

But since my boss had mentioned Oliver twice in as many minutes, I knew that I needed to bring up what I'd intended to discuss at his house on Wednesday. I shouldn't have put it off in the first place, but the team had been traveling and then I'd been busy with sessions and Marcel and...Oliver. I'd been busy with Oliver.

"Oliver is doing great," I murmured. "Truly."

"He *is* doing great," Luc said, "but that great is going to end at some point. It's all going to hit him, and then he's going to really struggle. He's happier now that he's seeing you, that's for sure. But he's not going to be great forever."

"I've stopped seeing him as a patient."

Luc blinked then disappointment slid across his face. "Hazel," he murmured.

"I want you to remove that requirement from his contract."

"I can't do that." Luc shook his head. "I *know* what it's like, know how it feels to have the career ripped away from you, how gutting that can be, how much it can fuck with his life. I got a job with the team right afterward, but my head was fucked for too long." Another shake. "I don't want Oliver to fuck around for a decade, struggling when he can talk to someone."

I squeezed his shoulder. "The part you're missing is that talking to someone has to be a choice."

Luc frowned. "Has he been blocking you?"

"No," I said, "if anything, he's been more honest and open than I ever could have expected. He doesn't need me in that way. He's in a good place, Luc, I promise you that."

"And what if he gets to a not good place?" Luc asked, worry on his face. "I don't want him there."

"You care about him," I said. "That's a good thing. But all we can do is give him a referral to someone who specializes in this kind of trauma—which is not me, and I'm sorry I promised to take him on. This is over my pay grade, and I can't help him." I sighed and admitted the other thing that I needed to tell my boss.

Because if he had an issue with it, I'd...

Something.

Figure out a way to deal, a way to make it work.

Because Oliver was too damned important for it not to.

"I can't help him as a therapist," I said and held Luc's eyes, "because I'm seeing him. As a woman," I added when Luc's brows slid together.

It took a second for him to process, probably because despite the naps I and Oliver had arranged for him and Lexi, my boss still had dark, dark circles under his eyes.

"You're seeing Oliver." A beat. "As a woman."

"Yes." I smiled. "According to him, we've been on eight dates." Eight because the previous night I'd gone over to his place, watched a movie in his bed (with popcorn), we'd fooled around (and let me just say that the man seriously liked my oral skills—not that *his* were too shabby), and then he'd given me a toothbrush, plugged a charger in for *my* phone, and had held me all night while I slept.

Glorious.

And easier for him, since he had crutches at his place and a seat in his shower, which made navigating getting ready in the morning a lot smoother.

Not super fun to have to put on a prosthesis for a middle-of-the-night bathroom trip.

Or to skip a shower together because there wasn't room for him to sit in mine.

So his place. And it had been quiet and easy and it was nice to do nothing after I'd spent the night before dragging him around the aisles of Target, teasing him about boho chic, but really just adding some pops of color to make that gray on gray (and it must be said, *gray*) space look a little homier.

Because he'd asked my to help him make it that way.

He'd asked. *Me.*

The trust made my heart full and filled my tummy with *all* the butterflies and just...God, was it possible to be this happy? I felt like I was constantly floating, always smiling, uncertain why Oliver had chosen me of all people to open up to, but damned glad he had.

No.

I knew why he'd picked me.

The same reason I hadn't been able to keep him as a client. I couldn't separate myself from him in the way I needed to in order to keep things strictly professional. Quite simply, he called to me, and I *had* to answer.

"Eight dates?" Luc asked, his brows so high I was surprised they didn't disappear into his hairline.

"Well, according to Oliver, we've had eight." I smiled. "By my tally, we haven't even had one yet. Mostly because he keeps promising me romance in the form of flowers, dinner, and candlelight, and then we end up doing things like going to Target, Rage, and cuddling in his bed watching penguin documentaries."

Luc grinned. "Sounds like he has his priorities straight." He tugged a lock of my hair. "When are you doing romance?"

"Tomorrow night. Supposedly."

His grin widened.

"You're not mad?" I asked. "Or disappointed? Or worried about coworkers co-mingling?"

Humor on his pretty face. "Not mad. It's your life, Haze. Definitely not disappointed that two people I care about have realized that they care about each other, and they're each making the other smile in a way I haven't seen either of them smile in far too long." An arm around my shoulders, a squeeze. "And worried about coworkers co-mingling? That would be a bit hypocritical considering I married the Breakers' general counsel."

That was a good point.

I smiled at him. "Good."

He nudged my shoulder. "Good."

"And you'll take off the therapy requirement for Oliver?"

A nod. "I trust you. If that's what you think is best, then I'll take it off." He dropped his arm as play resumed on the ice. "But I will be watching closely."

Of course, he would. Because he was a good guy.

"I wouldn't expect anything else."

I trailed him back to our seats.

"Haze?" he asked, just as the puck dropped.

"Yeah?"

"I'm happy for you." Another bump of his shoulder against mine. "Truly, I am."

I was happy. It was an effervescent feeling that bubbled

through my tummy, through my veins, danced along my nerve endings and out my fingertips.

Yeah, I didn't think I'd ever been happier.

Not with Trevor.

Not before.

This was all Oliver.

NINETEEN

Oliver

I'M *sorry I promised to take him on. This is over my pay grade, and I can't help me.*

Fuck.

Fuck.

I tried to breathe through that, breathe through the sharp stab of those words. They were part of a larger conversation, I knew that. I understood that. I *heard* that, heard Luc and Hazel continue talking about me, about her, about *us.*

It was just—

I'm sorry I promised to take him on.

This is over my pay grade, and I can't help him.

I. Cant. Help. Him.

Leaning back against the wall, I gripped the flowers tightly, feeling the stems start to break under my hands. Flowers. Romance. Candles. Dinner.

That was the plan.

But all I could hear was, *I'm sorry I promised to take him on. This is over my pay grade, and I can't help him.*

I'd asked her to help.

I was a fucking *lot.*

Maybe even over her pay grade lot, especially if I wasn't a client and wanted to be a boyfriend.

"Breathe, O," I muttered.

She and Luc had been having a conversation about the therapy sessions. She'd told me she was going to do that. She'd also said that she didn't feel qualified to take on something like the trauma of losing a limb.

This wasn't about me.

This was...*not about me.*

But what if I was too much in other ways? I hardly knew how to be vulnerable enough to connect with people. It wasn't instinctual. It was a struggle, and I had to push through the urge to shore up my defenses, keep people at a distance, and to not only give a small sliver of myself.

Right now, it was easy with Hazel.

Because she made me feel something I never had before.

But what if I got used to that?

What if it stopped being new, and I started to close down again? What if I did that, and she decided I wasn't worth the trouble and—

"Mr. James?"

I blinked and glanced down, saw the tiny little girl standing in front of me. My heart was pounding, palms sweating. The flowers were all but mangled in my hands, and my good knee felt like it was about ready to give way.

Panic.

I was panicking.

But there was a little girl staring up at me, her expression filled with excitement and eagerness. So, I sucked in a breath, released it slowly.

"Yeah, kiddo?" I asked, dropping the flowers into the trash can and trying to moderate my tone, when it felt like I'd just swallowed a razor blade.

"I—" She broke off, nibbled at her bottom lip.

I crouched down, and at least I was getting better at that. It still hurt and put pressure on my stump, and I had to take most of my weight in my good leg, but at least I wasn't at risk of falling over. "You good, kiddo?"

She glanced back at her parents, my gaze following, watching as they nodded in encouragement.

A rise and fall of tiny shoulders.

A chin lifted.

Her hair was curly and brown, her skin creamy, her eyes brown, and her face...if I had a daughter with Hazel, this is what she could look like.

I'm sorry I promised to take him on. This is over my pay grade, and I can't help him.

Fuck, that hurt.

Easy. Easy now.

I was at the arena; people were bound to recognize me. That was part of why I hadn't been back until now.

But this little girl had worked up the courage to talk to me, and even though she was faltering now, I could at least make her night a little brighter. If I played this right, maybe I could even just make her night altogether.

So, I stood, held out a hand. "Come with me, and I'll show you the coolest place in the arena."

She unfroze, wrapped her tiny fingers in my, and said, "Really?"

"Really, really."

I nodded at her parents as I started walking, indicating they follow me. The monitors around the concourse said there were two minutes left in the game, and the Breakers were up by three. There would be just enough time for them to get downstairs.

"Mr. James?"

"Yeah, honey?" I asked, her parents trailing.

"Did you lose your leg?"

I smiled gently. "Yes, I did." I lifted my pant leg enough to show her the bottom of my prosthesis. "See?"

"Wow! You have a superhero leg!"

That made my smile turn genuine. "Pretty cool, huh?"

"Super cool!"

I nodded at security then hit the button for the elevator that would take them downstairs. "What's your name?"

"Hannah St. Claire, Mr. James!"

So much enthusiasm.

"Call me Oliver," I told her then glanced over at her parents. "I should have asked. Do you have a few minutes, Mr. and Mrs. St. Claire?"

The mom nodded and put her hand out for me to shake. "Aimie, please. And this is my husband, Chuck." I shook Chuck's hand. "We have plenty of time, but please, we weren't trying to take too much of yours. You don't have to go to any trouble for us."

"It's no trouble," I assured them.

The elevator door opened, and we stepped on.

"You're my favorite player!" Hannah declared, dancing around the elevator, jerking my hand this way and that.

"Well, you're my favorite Hannah," I told her.

She beamed.

And I felt like the sun could rise and fall by that smile, it was so bright and beautiful and innocent.

It would only take a few moments to reach the lower level

of the arena, the concrete halls where the guys would come off the ice. Normally, I would never take someone here. After a game, the guys just wanted to get through whatever Tommy wanted to talk to them about, the required press, and their cooldown routines.

But I knew the guys would love Hannah.

And...it was the best way to get a game-worn jersey.

I'm sorry I promised to take him on. This is over my pay grade, and I can't help him.

I shoved down the words. Again.

But they still rattled around in my brain.

Enough.

Enough.

E—

The elevator doors opened, and we stepped out.

"Stand over here with me," I told them, tugging Hannah toward the corner where she would be able to see the guys come off the ice. The crowd noise rose. The buzzer went.

Everything went quiet. But only for a few moments.

Because then the guys came down the hall.

Sticks hit the racks.

They headed for the locker room. The corner I'd chosen meant that they could bypass my little group, but I knew that most of the guys would stop. Because they were awesome.

And the first one to notice them?

To stop?

Smitty.

Of course, he was.

Who did what Smitty always did—charmed the shit out of everyone around him, including one Hannah St. Claire and her parents. He swept Hannah up into a giant bear hug, lifted her so she could reach the tall ceiling overhead, revealing the not-so-secret secret (at least to anyone who worked down in the bowels of the arena) that he always jumped up and tapped the ceiling for good luck before and after a game.

"Now I'll have *all* the good luck," he said, setting her down.

He reached behind himself to undo the tag that kept players' jerseys in place then whipped it over his head.

A tug and it was dwarfing Hannah.

Who looked like she'd just won the lottery.

At least, until she glanced back at me, her eyes sad. "You're still my favorite."

Fuck. This girl was trying to steal my heart.

I'm sorry I promised to take him on. This is over my pay grade, and I can't help him. A breath, eyes stinging, but I managed to smile, to keep my voice light. "I know. But Smitty's jersey is bigger, so more of the guys can sign it. Then you can take it home and hang it on your wall."

"I can have it?" she asked with wide eyes, glancing from me to Smitty.

We both nodded.

"Will *you* sign it extra big, since you're my favorite?"

I'm sorry I promised to take him on. This is over my pay grade, and I can't help him.

Deep breath. Let it go.

"Of course, Hannah." I started to glance around. Usually there was a bucket of Sharpies for just this reason, but before I could really look hard, Smitty was tossing me a pen, and I was crouching to scrawl my name across the back of the jersey. Smitty went next.

To which Hannah slanted a glance at me and whispered, "You're my favorite, too."

Smitty's bright white grin slashed through his thick black beard. "I won't tell him," he whispered back.

Marcel came up and signed, ruffling Hannah's hair, also getting a, "You're my favorite, too."

Then Raph and Luca, Martin and Theo. Almost the entire team signed her jersey.

And got "You're my favorite."

In the end, the only two players she didn't get signatures from that night were the ones who were stuck in the PT suite, getting some treatment for injuries.

They didn't get "You're my favorite."

Ha.

"Thanks," I murmured to Smitty, who'd hung around to watch the cuteness.

"Any time." A pause. "Beers next week?"

I'm sorry I promised to take him on. This is over my pay grade, and I can't help him.

I closed my eyes, wanting to grab steel plates, to rivet them in place. To block off this feeling.

"Oliver?"

Hannah's little voice penetrated, and I opened my eyes, saw the happiness and joy on her face. I'd given that to her.

I could give that to Hazel.

To my friends.

"Just a second, honey," Aimie said, "he's talking."

Hannah went quiet.

I'm sorry I promised—

E-*fucking*-nough.

"Beers," I said to Smitty, shaking his hand. "I'm in."

A nod. Relief in my friend's eyes. "I'll text you."

I nodded. Then Smitty disappeared into the locker room.

I'm sorry—

No.

No more of that, of that voice and those thoughts.

If I'd stayed in my head, if I'd braced and built those walls back up, if I soldered those heavy steel plates back in place, reinforced them with rebar and concrete, protected them with barbed wire, I would have missed the significance of what happened next.

Namely, my bending down to hear her. "What's up, Hannah girl?" I asked.

I'm—

She smiled, that huge, the-sun-rose-and-fell-by-her smile, and said, "You're my favorite-ist."

And the last of the voice in my head quieted.

Gone.

Done.

Moving forward.

TWENTY

Hazel

HE WAS SITTING on my front porch when I pulled into my garage.

I'd texted.

I'd called.

But we hadn't connected after the game, and I assumed he'd gone home.

Instead, he was here, waiting for me. Smiling, I grabbed my purse and phone and jumped out of the car. Oliver was already there, striding into the garage. "Hey," I said, "I tried to call you —" I caught sight of his drawn face in the lights of the opener. "What's wrong?"

He took my hand, drew me toward the door to the house.

"Honey, what's wrong?" I asked again.

A nod to the knob, a glance that told me he was waiting for me to unlock it.

"Oliver—"

His hand was still in mine, and he held it tightly as he led me to the living room, pulled me down onto the couch.

"You're scaring me," I whispered.

"I heard you."

Three words that drew my brows together. "What?"

"I heard you tonight in the suite. I'd brought flowers to surprise you, was going to try to coax you out to dinner, but then I heard you tell Luc that I was above your pay grade."

My nostrils flared, and I inhaled. "I don't know what you heard—"

"I heard you say that you couldn't help me."

Oh fuck.

Oh fuck.

I turned to face him on the couch. "Oliver, it wasn't—"

"I heard you say other things, too. I know it was you talking to Luc like you said you would, talking to him about the therapy sessions requirement on my contract, advising him to allow me to do them on my terms."

Since that was what I'd been talking about, I didn't know what else to say.

"I heard you talk about us dating. Heard him give you—us—his approval." His chest rose and fell on a breath. His throat worked as he swallowed. "But all I *heard* was that you couldn't help me. All I could think was that I'd be a burden, that I wouldn't be able to hack it, and would close down, and...one day you'd realize that I wouldn't be worth it."

My heart squeezed like it was in a vise, growing tighter and tighter and *tighter*.

How could he think that? How could he not know that I *knew* the precious gift he was giving me by giving himself, by being willing to take the risk, by sharing all that he had shared so far?

It...just felt like the vise clenched even more fiercely.

Because he'd given so much.

"And I know we're moving fast," he said earnestly. "I know we've gone from nothing to *a lot* in not very much time. But never, ever have I met a woman, met *anyone* who I wanted to open up to, who I wanted to let in. Even Teresa and Alex had to battle their way in. You," he said gently, "just had to look at me with those pretty brown eyes, twirling your earring, lines creasing the sides of your mouth while you pretended to be feeling fine, even though you kept rubbing your temples because your head was pounding."

"Oliver," I whispered, throat burning, eyes stinging. I clung to his hand, probably squeezing too tight, but he was here and telling me this, sharing the emotional mountain he'd just climbed—all on his *freaking own!*—and I was barely keeping it all together. This right here was what I'd been desperate for with Trevor.

The connection.

The ability to talk about deep and heavy shit.

To be able to work through it without days of silent treatment and bitter fights, without a man who wouldn't acknowledge that he'd been hurt.

Instead, I had Oliver. Who had been hurt—so hurt—but had processed it, was moving on.

His knuckles brushed my cheek, and okay *now* I was going to cry. Because I loved when he did that. "You made it easy to fall for you. So *damned* easy," he murmured. "You were so open, and you...and... *I* couldn't be anything but open, *don't* want to be anything but open. Not with you. Because you don't see me for what happened to me. You see me as *me.*"

"Honey." It was a croak, but his fingers squeezed my gently, and I knew he understood.

"Part of me thought if I could concoct a plan to tie you to me, to get you to make my house a home, to get my friends involved, that I might bind you to me tight enough so you wouldn't leave." His palm cupped my cheek. "What I didn't realize until tonight was that *I* could tie myself to you, as well. *I* can treat you like you're precious, not just because it would win me your heart, but because you would do the same. *I* can make you a home in my heart, my life, because you haven't hesitated to do the same. *I* can make you happy because you certainly do that for me."

Tears were pouring down my cheeks.

He wiped them away, but they still came.

Because, "That was the most beautiful thing anyone has ever said to me."

His mouth hitched up. "Happy tears?"

A nod. A sniff. My hands brushing his aside so I could wipe my cheeks. "Yes, honey. Happy tears." I took a breath, swallowed a sob. "You have to know that I feel the same about you. I want to make you happy and take away your pain, make you whole. Because you've given me honesty and eight dates. Because you trusted me with your past and thoughts and present. Because I can't imagine *my* present without you."

"You have to know I love you," he murmured.

Fuck.

This man.

He'd totally reached into my chest and seized my heart, with a smile and a few questions and taking ten minutes to fix a fan on my computer that was giving me a headache.

"An I love you before a first date?"

His mouth quirked. "Yeah, babe. An *I love you* before our first date."

I slipped my hand from his, but only so I could toss both of my arms around his shoulders and plaster myself against him. "I guess it's a good thing I love you, too, isn't it?"

His pale blue eyes were filled with humor, but I didn't miss the trickle of relief that crept into the edges when I told him I loved him, too. "A damned good thing," he murmured, dropping his head and pressing a kiss to my jaw.

"Honey?"

His mouth moved to my ear. He touched his lips to the lobe. "Yeah?"

"You think you can put that mouth on mine?"

***

I WAS SO ready for the date.

We'd made out on my couch like teenagers for ages, but then I had started to nod off, and Oliver had gone home.

I'd wanted him to stay, but he'd simply kissed me on the forehead, slipped out the front door, after telling me he'd be over at seven for our date tomorrow.

And to dress nice.

So...I was dressing nice.

Heels. Tight dress. Fancy lingerie beneath. *All* the makeup. My hair was washed and dried, which meant that, for once, I'd skipped dry shampoo.

Perfume on.

Necklaces that draped over the low-cut neckline of my dress, drawing the eye down to what was revealed by my fancy lingerie—and also teasing over the skin there, the cool abrasion reminding me of Oliver's fingers trailing between my breasts.

A tease all night.

I couldn't wait.

Nor could I wait for Oliver to get there. I wanted to see his face. Normally I wore Breakers gear to work—jeans and a team T-shirt and jacket—though sometimes I paired my jeans with a nice blouse (still topped with the team jacket, so the blouse didn't get a lot of air time). Rarer still, I'd wear a pair of slacks with such a blouse (usually when I had an important meeting). But for most of the time, it was jeans and a T-shirt and flats.

The doorbell rang, and I looked at my reflection. Smiled.

Tonight, I'd brought it.

THIS WASN'T what I'd been expecting.

He'd told me to dress nice.

And now we were sitting in the parking lot of a McDonald's.

Sitting in his car, not going in.

Look, I was a woman who could be down with a Big Mac, and don't even get me started on fries and their apple pies. If there was a guilty pleasure of mine to be named, the fries and apple pies were right up there for top contender.

It was just...we were sitting in the car.

Oliver had parked and turned to me and started asking me about my day.

Which was nice. Except, he'd promised romance, and we were outside McDonald's. And I was wearing heels and a dress and expecting white tablecloths, quiet music, and candlelight.

And worst of all, he was still asking me questions about my day. I was reciprocating—because I wasn't a *monster*—and all the while, my stomach was rumbling, and I didn't have salt from the French fries coating my fingers.

Which spoke to who *was* the monster.

Namely, the man who was stopping me from getting my fingers covered in salt and my belly full of fries and apple pie.

Because if our first date was at McDonald's, then that was fine.

I'd rock my dress and heels inside.

But so help me God, the man had better get me *inside*

before I lost my shit. Also—this just in—I'd passed hungry and gone straight to hangry.

"...so Pru went back to finish up her season," he said, holding my hand—which was sweet—and gently stroking my fingers—also sweet. "But she's got a handle on the young guys coming up. A really good handle, actually," he added. "And she's going to do some traveling in between her last few games, and apparently after?" His brows lifted as he met my gaze. "During which you're going *shark diving* with her?"

A sigh.

"Pru's a gift," I told him. "But that gift of my friend still isn't getting me in a cage in cold ass water off the coast of South Africa, swimming in a floating tin can just waiting to be eaten."

Lips twitching, he stroked a finger over my palm. "Not much of a daredevil?"

"Compared to Pru?" A shake of my head as my stomach rumbled. "No. Definitely not."

"What kind of things would you consider daring, *not* Pru-style?"

I tried to come up with something witty, but seriously, all I could think was: *Apple pie. Apple pie. Apple pie. Apple—*

"Trying to complete the Kitchen Sink Challenge at The Creamery?"

Oh God, thinking of ice cream wasn't helping. Why had I worked through lunch? Why hadn't I had a snack?

Oh yeah.

Because I'd been trying to bring my A game for this fancy date at *McDonald's!*

Breathe. Food would be coming soon...and if not, I had a protein bar in my purse. I'd eat that.

He grinned and glanced over at me. "The Kitchen Sink Challenge?"

A nod.

Apple pie. Apple pie. Apple—

"I could get behind a Kitchen Sink Challenge. The ice cream at the Creamery is really good—"

Apple pie. French fries. Apple pie. French—

"So, how'd you and Pru get to be friends?"

French fries. Apple—

Focus.

I sucked in a breath, ignored my stomach, and began, "I—"

"Oh, hold that thought," he said, glancing over my shoulder at what I assumed was the front door leading into the restaurant. "Let's go." He popped his car door, rounded the front of the car, and opened mine.

Fries!

Fucking *finally!*

I got out, started to turn for the restaurant.

Oliver caught my hand, tugged me against his chest. "Did I tell you that you are beautiful tonight?"

"Yes."

He brushed back my hair. "Well, you look extra beautiful in the moonlight."

Yeah, yeah.

I started for the front doors...because fries and apple pie—

He caught my hand, his brows furrowed together. "Did you think we were going inside?"

My heart sank. Were we—*oh God*—were we *not* going inside? After all that dreaming of French fries and apple pies? Seriously?

"I—"

"We're getting in that." He nodded behind me, and I spun to see a limo parked along the curb. His brows furrowed. "Did you—did you think I'd take you for fast food when I told you to dress nice?"

"We're in the lot," I pointed out.

"Because this was the closest place to your house we could meet it." He tugged at a curl. "The limo couldn't navigate the streets near your house. They're too narrow."

"Oh."

"McDonald's in that dress?" he said lightly. "Never, babe."

I looked at the restaurant longingly, stifled a sigh.

His palm cupped my jaw. "What is it?"

My chin dropped to my chest. "I'm hungry," I whined. Yes, it was a whine, sadly. When I could have just told him that ten minutes ago. "I was excited for our date, so I worked through lunch, and then I didn't have a chance to eat because I was getting ready and—"

My stomach growled, loud enough, it seemed, to shatter every window in the vicinity.

"I'm just really freaking hungry," I said miserably, "and I either need to eat the granola bar in my purse or I need a large fries, a Diet Coke, and two apple pies."

Oliver stared at me like he'd never seen me before.

Then he took my hand.

Tugged me forward.

TWENTY-ONE

Oliver

I SAT in the back of the limo next to Hazel and watched her absolutely demolish a large fries.

And then pound two apple pies.

And then drain a large Diet Coke.

I'd nearly lost a finger trying to snag a fry, upon which she'd smacked my hand away, snatched the paper bag closer to her, and huddled in the corner, a la Gollum with my precious.

My woman was a force when she was hungry.

That was good to have confirmed. Not just when she was with Pru.

I also made sure to go back through our conversation, commit to memory the tension in her face, the lines next to her mouth and eyes. I'd thought she'd had another headache and was going to see if I couldn't offer her a massage (oh, such a tough job to put my hands on my woman—yes, I got referring to her as *my woman* was possessive and caveman, but I was as much her man as she was my woman).

But then the limo had pulled up, and her shoulders had drooped, and—

She'd admitted to being hungry.

So, I'd signaled to the limo driver to wait, brought her inside and paid for her food (food I'd thought she might be sharing at the time, clearly that had been wrong, and if I'd wanted fries, I should have ordered some for himself).

A couple of minutes later we were in the limo, she was chowing down, and we were on the way to our date.

"So, this scene is telling me that I should bring fries and pies instead of flowers to our dates."

She shoved the empty soda cup in the bag and crumpled the top, shoving it into the corner of the backseat. "That would be amazing," she said, and I was glad to see all the tension had left her face, and my relaxed and settled Hazel was back.

"Babe."

A shrug, her lips twitching. "I guess I revealed on our first date that I can't skip meals, otherwise I end up as Hangry Hazel, and no one likes that."

"I like Hangry Hazel." The lights from the streetlights flashed on her skin as we drove to the airport. "Next time, I'll just bring snacks."

That made her smile.

Which made me feel about ten feet tall.

"Snacks would be good."

Mouth still tilted up, she turned to glance out the windows, at the streetlights flashing by, the houses and buildings spreading out, more open space between them. "Where are we going?"

"On Date One."

She slanted a glance at me. "Hilarious."

"So now, are you going to tell me about Pru?" I liked the other woman. A lot. But Pru *was* a lot. And seemed like she didn't fit with Hazel, who was definitely outgoing and confident, but Pru crossed the line from outgoing and confident into *outgoing and confident.*

The italics were warranted.

"We met while I was working on my PhD. She was one of the athletes I studied for my thesis, and we hit it off. Pru makes it almost impossible to not like her, and her enthusiasm for life is contagious." A shrug. "We hit it off, stayed in touch, and now we're going to be coworkers." A wink. "You'd better watch out. You've just brought one half of the terrible twos into your department, and considering the other half is me, your life is about to get really interesting."

"If it involves you, then I'll take interesting any day of the week."

She smiled. "You say that now. But"—she leaned close and trailed a hand down my chest—"you haven't dealt with us together for an extended period of time."

Fuck, she was cute.

"Don't make me mess up your lipstick, babe. I know you went to a lot of trouble."

Her head tilted to the side, eyes warm as she studied me. "I already messed it up with the soda."

"Yeah?" I asked, dropping a hand to her waist and drawing her close.

"Yeah," she murmured, winding her arms around my neck.

The car slowed, turning into the airport lot. We had mere moments before we had to get out of the car, but...fuck it.

I lowered my head and kissed her.

She smelled like cinnamon and tasted like apples, and I knew I was messing up any lipstick she still had on. But I didn't give a damn, didn't give a fuck that what was left was probably smeared all over my mouth.

The car stopped.

I couldn't tear myself away, not when her soft curves were under my hands, when her body was pressed to mine, her tongue in my mouth, her quiet moans rumbling up through her throat. The woman could kiss in a way that made me unable to see sense. So instead of pulling away, I pressed closer, drew her tighter against me, and I kissed the fuck out of the woman who'd stolen my heart.

The door opened. A throat was cleared.

I couldn't summon a fuck to care.

The throat was cleared again.

"Sorry, sir," the driver said, her voice regretful, "but you'll miss your takeoff time if you don't get out now."

That was, perhaps, the one thing that could pull me out of the downward spiral of desire, to not tear my lips away and demand that she haul her ass back into the driver's seat and circle the block a hundred times so I could continue kissing and holding Hazel.

But...romance.

And not the kind that began at McDonald's because my girl was two seconds away from losing her shit.

Romance that my woman deserved because I wanted to show her what she meant to me, because I wanted to give her some happy. Because I *could* give her some happy. *That* was what I'd learned from Hannah, from bringing her down into the arena. I wasn't someone who had to put walls up and only give. I also wasn't someone who, when the walls were down, only took and took until the well went dry.

I could do both.

I could accept the happy, the love that Hazel gave.

And I could give it back just as powerfully.

Wanting to give it back was what finally had me pulling away and stifling a groan. I'd planned this night for her, wanted to make it special. That couldn't happen if I fucked her in the back seat of the limo and we missed our takeoff.

"*Now* your lipstick is messed up, babe."

She grinned up at me, wiped the corner of my mouth. "So is yours, honey."

Laughing, Hazel took the driver's hand, accepting the assistance to get out of the car, and giving me a fantastic start to the date—namely a view of her ass in that slinky black dress. I followed and we both hit the tarmac.

Her eyes went wide, surveying the various vehicles on the airstrip. Lots of small planes, some old, most modern, several jets that probably belonged to some of the bigwigs in town, and our destination—a hanger off in the corner that ran night time tours of the city.

"Are we going in one of the planes?" Her eyes were wide. *So* wide.

"I know it's not shark diving," I teased, amusement blipping through me, "and it's not a kitchen sink full of ice cream." I shook my head. "But we *are* going in a helicopter."

Her eyes went somehow wider. Shit. Was she afraid of flying? I hadn't thought to ask.

Before I could, she did a little dance. "That is *so* cool!" She clapped her hands together. "I've always wanted to ride in a helicopter!

Phew.

Her with the food thing.

Me with the copter thing

I made a mental note to make sure we talked about this stuff. Because it was important...and also because I needed to know when to make a pitstop at McDonald's so I could get my woman some fries.

"THIS IS INCREDIBLE," she whispered through the microphone attached to the headset each of us had been given.

A quick safety talk.

Signing our lives away on some waivers.

And then we'd been in the air, a light snack—for Hazel's sake—set in a container between us, and the lights of Baltimore glimmering around us.

We'd been flying for about forty minutes, having flown around the city, the pilot pointing out the sights, and now we were circling the airport and getting ready to land again. Where the limo would be waiting for the next part of our date.

Dinner on the waterfront.

In a place with candles and music and soft lighting.

"You have any room in that stomach of yours?"

"Why?" she asked. "We hitting up the Ice Creamery for dessert?"

I grinned. "Maybe later. We have a reservation at Lana's."

"Lana's?" she gasped, her eyes sparkling with excitement. "I've always wanted to go there."

"I know," I said.

"How?" she began to ask before clarity dawned and she shrugged ruefully. "Pru."

I nodded. "Pru might have dished on a few things. Though," I said, teasing entering my tone, "she didn't tell me that her best friend is a nervous flier."

"I am *not!*" she gasped.

"Babe, you're clutching my hand as we go down, and you practically broke my fingers when we went up."

Katie, our pilot, laughed quietly. "You did look a little gray when we first went up."

"Rude," Hazel muttered, but her lips were twitching and *her* tone said that she found us anything but rude. "Just because

I'm not a helicopter pilot and super chill while I'm wielding a death machine."

Katie laughed a little louder. I joined in.

"I like the going straight and smooth part," Hazel went on, "and I like the lights. Those are beautiful. But the going up and down freaks me out a bit." Her eyes hit mine. "For the record, I'm the same way on planes, so if that's an issue, speak now or forever hold your peace."

I flexed my fingers against her grip. "I don't mind you holding my hand, babe."

She grinned up at me.

"Even if you tried to break it."

That grin turned glare and she huffed. "Because I was *excited*," she grumbled, reaching up with her free hand like she was going to twist her earring, but since it was covered by the headphones, she dropped it back into her lap, her lips pressing flat. "And a little nervous, okay? Is that a crime?"

My knuckles on her cheek, because I loved the feel of her skin, because I loved what her eyes did when I touched her like that. "No." I kissed the tip of her nose, bumping both of our mics together in a way that probably wasn't smooth in the least, but since it involved my mouth on her body, I couldn't be *too* hard on myself. "So long as you keep holding my hand."

Her mouth twitched. "That I can do."

Our eyes locked. "Even if the ride gets bumpy, babe."

Now her smile softened, and her hand found my thigh, squeezed lightly.

"That I can do."

TWENTY-TWO

NEVER IN MY life had I been so full.

And turned on.

And...*full.*

French fries and apple pies. Cheese and fruit and salami. Champagne. Soda. And then a huge steak, mashed potatoes, a side of summer squash (me trying to pretend I was healthy), and a slab of chocolate cake that had so many layers it could rival the Empire State building.

I'd consumed many times my body weight in calories.

I'd need to do a million pilates classes (this was a slight exaggeration) to make up for the food I'd eaten.

And yet, even though I felt so deep in a food coma that I could hardly move, I was also so turned on that I could barely think straight.

Probably that was because Oliver had cozied up to me in the booth, his side pressed to mine.

He'd touched me the entire meal—fingers on my cheek,

trailing down my arm, a kiss to my jaw, my throat, a palm resting on my thigh. *That* was the worst. Because it had been resting on the bare skin of my thigh, just below the hem of my dress, and I'd spent no less than five minutes warring with myself over asking—okay, *begging*—him to just slide that hand north.

Dripping.

I was absolutely dripping.

It was a wonder I'd been able to eat at all. But then again, I hadn't earned my ass and thighs and breasts by being unable to eat under stressful circumstances.

If trying to not jump Oliver could be considered stressful.

I paused, considered that.

Okay.

Not jumping Oliver when I really wanted to could be considered majorly stressful.

"Can we walk around the block?" I asked, as he helped my into my coat by the front door of the restaurant. His fingers smoothed down the wool collar of the plain black peacoat.

His brows drew down as he shrugged into his own jacket. "It's cold out."

I rubbed my tummy. "My stomach needs to be vertical for a bit."

Dark brows drawing together, confusion on his pretty face. "Isn't it pretty much always vertical?" he asked, buttoning the front of his coat.

Yes, I supposed, except when one was lying down.

But that wasn't what I'd meant.

"Translation," I told him, "I ate too much, so I need to walk it off so I can stop feeling like a bloated walrus."

A flash of white teeth. "Got it."

He tugged open the door for me, holding it so I could walk through, his fingertips brushing the side of my neck as I stepped out into the cool—okay, *cold* evening air. Spring was coming, and we'd had a few decent nights lately, including the few hours we'd spent together with Noah on Luc and Lexi's back porch, but tonight wasn't one of them.

In a word: brisk.

And another: wind chill.

Or that was two, I supposed. Either way, he found the limo driver (not far from the restaurant), told her we'd be taking a loop and would meet her back there, and then took my hand, lacing our fingers together.

Since it was almost spring, I didn't have gloves, and though the air was frosty, I was glad to be without them.

Otherwise, how would I feel Oliver's warm, rough fingers against mine?

I wouldn't have. That's how.

Yes, I was being silly. No, I didn't care. I was happy and fulfilled and couldn't think of a time in my life that I'd felt this giddy just being with another human being.

Oliver was...*mine*.

He tugged me toward the right, walking with purpose, though I knew there wasn't really anything in the direction he was taking me—aside from a few closed shops and darkened streets that were busier for lunch than they were for dinner.

Um...

Oliver was mine who was taking me down a scary, dark road? "Where are we—"

I hadn't finished the question before he turned and yanked my down an alley—dimly lit, shaded from the wind, and not filled with the normal funk one might expect of alleys in general.

One moment the query was on my tongue.

The next minute it was Oliver's tongue on mine.

Oh, that's where he was taking me.

And that was pretty much the last thought—as simple as it was—that slid through my brain before my back was against the brick wall and Oliver's mouth was on mine. Soft lips, a firm tongue, and hands, rough, calloused palms that finally—*finally!*—slipped beneath the hem of my skirt. After a scorching kiss, he released my mouth, dragged his down my throat, nipping where my neck met my shoulder, his hands continuing to move north.

Cold air on my thighs.

But that wasn't why I was shivering.

Nope. The shiver was because he'd cupped my ass, and in cupping my flesh, his fingers were spreading my cheeks, sliding in...dancing lightly over the soaked scrap of silk covering my pussy. His grip tightened, the lace felt like the best sort of roughness, dragging over my clit, pulling taut over my folds, rubbing over my crack, pressing over my hole there, making my want more than just my pussy filled.

So not first date desire.

This was date one million desire. This was having explored everything with Oliver and wanting so much more.

And not just in my vagina.

He slipped one hand out from my dress, tilted my head, and kissed me.

Then he broke away, breaths coming rapidly, his forehead to mine, his eyes on mine. "Don't think I didn't just add wall sex to my Fuck List."

My lungs were working just as hard, and it was supremely difficult to focus when his hand was still on my ass, his fingertips still trailing over the lace—clit, labia, anus, clit, labia, anus. I wanted him everywhere down there, all at once, and all the dirty books I read weren't helping. Which was probably why I rose on tiptoe and whispered, "I've got a few more things to add to your list, baby."

Wickedness in pale blue eyes. "Yeah? How's your stomach?"

I drew my brows together, trying to process the change in topic—sex to stomachs. "Fine."

"Good." He took my hand, started tugging me toward the street. "Tell me about your list in the car."

Spinning. I was spinning.

Then I processed the train of his thoughts—walking to ease my fullness (not that we'd walked far, but apparently kissing could also be a cure for overeating) to sexual fantasies to getting back to one of our places as quickly as possible in order to tick off some of those sexual fantasies. Namely—at least on my part —having his cock inside me as quickly as possible, hopefully as *deep* as possible.

And maybe as fast as possible.

"How do you feel about car sex?" I asked.

A groan.

His fingers clenching on mine.

We reached the limo a few moments later, and he opened the door before the driver could get out, shoving me inside and slamming the door behind us. The divider went up, the car started moving, and Oliver had me in his lap a moment after that. "You're killing me, babe," he growled. "I'm trying to do right by you, to make it special and mean something and you're fucking temptation personified."

My hands went to his cheeks, cupped them as I stared into his pale blue eyes. "Honey," I said gently, "it's already going to mean *everything* because it's with you."

He went still.

His hand clenched on my ass, drew me nearer for a kiss that blazed through my veins and threatened to turn my blood to steam, my organs to ash.

"I love you."

Not said gently, his voice gravel, his hands still on my ass, his cock hard against my, his eyes blazing, and breaths—smelling like chocolate—dancing over my skin.

My heart squeezed. "I love you, too."

Those blazing eyes held mine, delving deep, searching for something I didn't understand, couldn't pinpoint, because I wasn't the one in his mind. Though I knew it probably had something to do with him wanting to show me how much I meant to him. But the thing was, I already knew that. He'd shown it to me, not just tonight, but many times over the last couple of weeks.

Which was why I wouldn't push him.

Because though he wanted me—I could feel that with crystal certainty between my thighs—this was important to him.

But I wanted to make one thing clear, just in case the opportunity presented itself in the future.

Never let it be said that I didn't ask for what I wanted—at least with Oliver.

Something he'd given me the courage to do.

Something Trevor never had.

Yet another reason my broken engagement was for the best.

Pushing that out of my mind, I spoke against his lips. "For the record, I love car sex. But I *especially* love limo sex."

He growled, pulled back, hands going to the hem of my skirt. "You've had limo sex?" He sounded jealous, and some part of me took great pleasure in that.

"Not yet"—a gasp as he yanked up my dress—"but I'm game to try." Hot eyes. A hard body beneath mine, and I couldn't stop myself from nibbling at his lips. "Same goes for car sex of any type. I've read about it. I've fantasized about doing it. I just...haven't gotten there."

"Hmm."

"What?"

Fingers biting into my ass. "Another item for my Fuck List." Sin. His smile was pure sin, and his hands tightened further, drew me closer. "I'm game for limo sex."

"Wh-what?"

He kissed me, so long and hard that I forgot my train of thought.

"I'm going to fuck you on this seat, babe," he said when we broke away, both gasping for air.

I inhaled, so sharply, it was a miracle I didn't choke on my own spit.

Fingers on my cheek. "See, you like that," he murmured, all hot silk.

A nod. How could I *not* like it? The man smiling at me like he was the dark hero in one of my books, as though he were going to use and abuse my body until I still felt him the next day? Yeah. I really fucking liked that.

His hips moved against mine, rubbing his cock against me, making me desperate to have all the layers between us gone. "I'm going to fuck you hard, babe."

My breath slid out of me on a rasping exhale, as I nodded again. Yes. I wanted that. Especially when my heart had already felt like it would pound out of my chest, as though it would explode because it was pumping so hard, but Oliver saying he was going to fuck me and do it hard, sent my pulse into the stratosphere. My heart absolutely thudded against my rib cage, and I felt like I'd been dunked in a vat of lava, my skin went so hot and tight. Liquid heat drenched my panties. My clit pulsed, and my nipples went hard and sensitive, chafing against the lace of my bra in the best way.

But...

He'd been so determined to make our first time romantic and sweet, and I'd thought that he would unequivocally turn me down and make me wait until he drove us home, after the limo dropped us at McDonald's, of course.

For him to give in, to say he was *game,* that he was going to fuck me hard, and...I couldn't lie and say the only thing I felt was arousal.

That was a solid eighty-six percent of it, for sure.

But the other fourteen percent got a little nervous.

Would the driver hear? Were the windows tinted enough so that the people in the other cars couldn't see us? Did it matter? Was that fear wrapped up with my arousal and threatening to send me flying?

The answer to the last one was yes.

Which meant, ultimately, the answer to the first three questions didn't matter.

"You sure, honey?" I asked.

Because even though I felt seconds away from an orgasm, I didn't want to take away from what Oliver was imagining, planning, *wanting.*

So, I resisted the urge to yank out his cock and sit on it, and instead waited for him to answer.

His answer was to work at the buttons on my coat, and to do it fast, his words gruff on my skin as he leaned forward to nip at my throat. "Gonna get it hard, babe, so you'd better get ready."

Ho, Mama.

My pussy clenched. My nipples went harder.

And suddenly, I was burning up, in a frenzy, my fingers moving to help him, trying to yank the heavy garment down my arms. It bunched on my elbows, mostly because I stopped fighting with the fastenings on my coat and began to work at his. I'd been dreaming of undoing the buttons on his dress shirt all night, of kissing a path along the skin I revealed inch by inch by inch.

But the damned wool of his jacket was in the way, and then he was yanking *my* coat off, distracting me from my task, and tossing it to the floor of the limo.

Cool air kissed the backs of my thighs then my spine as his fingers went to the tab of my zipper and yanked it down.

"Fuck if I haven't been dreaming of doing that all night," he muttered, echoing my thoughts as he tugged at the fabric, yanking it down over my arms and revealing the lace of my bra.

Which was virtually sheer, offered absolutely no support, and the clasp was always a bit uncomfortable in the back, digging into my skin. But that small amount of discomfort was absolutely worth it when it made Oliver look at my body like *that*.

Like I was a goddess, and he was going to fall prostrate at my feet.

Or, like I was going to be fucked within an inch of my life.

Ho, Mama again.

Because I really liked the second one.

I heard stitches rip as he bunched my dress around my waist, exposing my pussy, and even in the dim light of the limo, I could see that the pale red lace was so wet it had darkened to crimson.

"Fuck," he groaned, reaching behind me to flick open my bra, dragging it down just enough that my nipples were exposed...to his mouth.

He sucked and tongued me, rolled the sensitive bud over the roof of his mouth.

"Oh God," I breathed, yanking his coat wide, fumbling with the buttons on his shirt, and finally getting them open. Yes, thank sweet baby Jesus, that was exactly what I needed.

Skin.

Bare skin.

And my mouth on that bare skin.

The car turned and his arms tightened on me before I could fall out of his lap. I lost my connection with his fabulous chest, but I wasn't worse for wear, not in the least. The arm he wound around my waist so I wouldn't fall happened to have a hand attached to it.

And that hand...

It slid right between my thighs.

TWENTY-THREE

Oliver

SHE WAS WET AND HOT, and I was desperate to get inside her.

Fuck, but her tits were there, nipples calling to my tongue.

I had my fingers in her pussy, but it wasn't enough. I wanted more. Needed—

She pushed my hand away, my fingers sliding out of her on a wet sound, and moved down my body as she reached for the button of my slacks, flicking it open, tugging the zipper, yanking the material of my pants wide enough to free my cock.

And then her mouth was on me.

Sucking me deep, bobbing until I hit the back of her throat, her moans vibrating through my dick.

Two strokes and I was ready to explode.

With red creeping into the edges of my vision, my control shattered, my orgasm dangerously close, I tangled my fingers in her hair, lifted her head off me. She didn't come easy, her lips tight, suction intense enough to push me even closer to the edge.

An edge I wasn't going to reach alone.

Fingers tightening, I tugged her off, ignoring the *pop* of sound, how her reluctance to stop sucking me brought me so near coming that my toes were hanging off the cliff, threatening to drag me down into the abyss below.

Her body was still bent over mine, her hot breath on my cock.

So easy.

It would be so easy to grab on to those curls again, to yank her back down.

But I needed inside her more than I needed her mouth on my cock.

Using one arm to steady her, I brought my other up, used my fingers to rip the scrap of lace she called panties down her thighs, off one foot. Not bothering with the other, I coaxed her back on top of me, felt the brush of her wet heat against me, started to tug her down.

Then remembered I needed to use a condom.

Fuck.

A bucking movement to extract my wallet, arm tight to keep her to me, fingers trembling as I tore through it, found the plastic square. I tossed my wallet on the seat, tore the condom open with my teeth, and it took me too fucking long to roll it down my length.

And by too long, it was approximately zero-point-six milliseconds.

Okay, so I was less focused on time than on the fact that Hazel was close and so wet I could see her pussy glistening in the streetlights that shone through the windows as we drove by. My fingers tightened, tugging her forward, trying to drag her down.

"On my cock, babe," I ordered when she didn't do anything but move forward, drag her pussy over me.

"Okay," she murmured. And smiled.

And...sank down.

"Oh fuck," I hissed.

Tight. Hot. So wet I was immediately balls deep.

"Oh," she breathed, head falling back, her breasts bouncing as she ground down on me. Deep, so fucking deep. Forward and back. Up and down. Hips rocking, tits jiggling, hands gripping my shoulders tight.

My slacks were still on, and I could feel them growing wetter every time she moved against me. Everyone would know exactly what we had been doing the moment they saw me, but I didn't give a fuck.

Because Hazel on me, my cock buried deep, my hands on her ass, holding her tight as we found our rhythm was the best fucking thing on the planet.

Her hands found my face, and she kissed me until my lungs felt like they were going to explode, rocking against me, thrusting faster by the second, the car's movement bouncing her against me in a way that would have me hard-pressed to disagree with anyone who said car sex was the best sex.

She broke away from me, head dropping back, hips still moving, and I felt my orgasm cross that imaginary line in my mind, my body. The one that told me it was coming, there would be no stopping it, and I'd better hope to fuck that I got her there and soon because I'd be exploding, and there was no way to head it off.

I wasn't going to come alone.

Luckily, the universe decided to throw me a bone, because just as I was thinking that, the car went over a bump and she jolted against me, voice breaking, "O-Oliver."

Fingers into the flesh of her ass, thumb to her clit. "Keep going, babe."

"I—"

I thrust up into her, orgasm coiling at the base of my spine, threatening to explode outward. "Keep *going*, babe."

Please, for fuck's sake, she had to keep going.

She did. Thank fuck, but she did.

And the universe threw me another solid because the car jolted again. Her breath caught. Her fingers clenched tight on my shoulders, her hips jerked, moans began tumbling out of her throat in rapid succession.

I came.

But even as pleasure shot through me, I dropped my head, my mouth going to her nipple, sucking hard, grazing my teeth over the rosy peak.

"Oh *God*."

I pressed hard. Sucked harder.

She bucked.

And she was there.

Tightening around me, squeezing tight, milking every last bit of pleasure out of me. Somehow, distantly, I managed to keep my grip on her hips, to continue thrusting into her, to keep moving her against me.

Up. Down. Front. Back.

She clenched hard.

And came and came and *came*.

It was the best fucking thing I'd ever seen, ever *felt*.

Then she collapsed against me, arms wrapping tightly around me, and even though I was fucking wrecked from the best orgasm of my life, my body feeling like it had been surrounded in concrete and dropped into the ocean—sinking, sinking, *sinking*—I still managed to bring her close, to hold her tight.

To whisper in her ear, "I love you."

A squeeze of her arms. Her body.

We held on to each other as we tried to catch our breath (at least on my part) and summon the strength to move our limbs (also on my part), and to say something, *anything* that could capture what I was feeling in that moment.

Complete.

Whole.

Totally fucking in love with this woman.

But all I could do was hold her close, breathe in the smell of her until it was imprinted on my soul, and thank the universe for bringing her into my life.

TWENTY-FOUR

Hazel

"I'M SORRY," I murmured as we drove to his house.

He slowed at a stoplight, turned his head to gape at me. "For *what?*"

"I know you wanted our first time to be romantic," I said, on a wince. We'd been driving about five minutes, plus the ten minutes after we'd fucked like rabbits in the back of the limo (gloriously), and for the last fourteen minutes, guilt had been eating away at my post-orgasm bliss.

"I wanted our first time to mean something."

I winced again.

I was sitting in the passenger's seat of his car, my bag in the trunk, silence in the cab. My dress was unzipped, my coat half-buttoned, my panties having disappeared somewhere that I didn't know for certain but suspected was in Oliver's pocket, since he'd tugged them off when they'd been tangled on one high heel after the limo had stopped and we'd both roused ourselves enough to realize we were back in the McDonald's parking lot.

French fries.

Apple pies.

Suddenly, I had another craving.

Luckily for me, we hadn't gone inside and added to my calorie count, nor had the driver opened the door. She had just parked along the curb and waited...

For a *while*.

Because it had taken us a while to separate, to deal with the condom and wrestle my dress so it wasn't a tourniquet around my middle (but not zipped, because apparently the ripping sound I'd heard earlier had been my zipper being made non-functional—which, okay was hot as hell that he'd been so lost in me and what we were doing that he hadn't been able to moderate his strength). So needless to say, it took us some time to restore our clothing into some semblance of decency.

Or at least so we wouldn't get arrested for public nudity.

Only when we had our coats on—mine a requirement to keep me from being cited, his because he needed to cover a wet stain on his slacks (and maybe I should be embarrassed by that, but while I might feel guilty for hijacking his romance, I wasn't embarrassed by the hottest sexual experience of my life—not in the least).

"I wanted our first time to mean something," he said again, picking up my hand and pressing a kiss to my palm. "And it did. Because it was with you."

My breath caught. "But it wasn't romantic."

"You're right," he said softly, as he navigated his car to his place. "It wasn't."

My heart squeezed. "I'm sorry," I whispered.

He'd had it all planned, and I ruined that by jumping him

and suggesting car sex—though it was his fault, too, I supposed. He'd jumped me in that alley and—

"I'm not."

He dropped his palm to his thigh, lightly squeezed his fingers around mine so I kept it there.

"I made it this big thing in my head because you deserve everything perfect, everything wonderful. I wanted this night with you to be that." Another squeeze. "And it was, babe. Because it was you and me and *us*. So no, it wasn't candles and flowers and me kissing every inch of your body, but that doesn't mean it wasn't perfect."

I sniffed.

He did his thing—brushed his knuckles over my cheek. "But I do hope you're still not too full."

My brows drew together. "Why?"

"Because there is absolutely no way that I'm done with you tonight."

Heat slicking down my spine, coiling between my thighs. I'd just come, and done it hard, but one rasp of his voice, that heat in his eyes, and I was ready all over again.

"Good," I said, squeezing his thigh, "because I have more items to add to your Fuck List."

His leg went taut below my hand.

And then he was laughing as he drove the rest of the way to his place.

I joined in.

But neither of us were laughing when we got up to his bedroom.

Because Oliver had made it his mission to tick those boxes of my fantasies, and he did it all night long.

"THAT'S OKAY, MOM," I said into the phone. "But are you sure I can't bring you anything? Soup? I'd be happy to drop by the egg flower soup from Golden Panda. I know it makes you feel better."

My mother's voice was raspy, the bug that had her canceling Sunday dinner that evening evident.

"Your father already picked some up for me, Spiced Pecan. I'm going to rest up, and I'll see you and Oliver in a couple of weeks."

Twice a month we tried to get together for dinner.

Sometimes it was every Sunday.

Sometimes we went a whole month.

But the goal was every other week.

And this was that week. My mom had been talking about the dinner she'd been planning for Oliver every day, texting questions about what he would and wouldn't eat, what his favorites were, whether or not he'd gotten a date six through eight.

Which obviously he had.

Along with that fabulous date one.

And what seemed like a million dates in between, though really, we'd just spent the weekend together. In bed and cuddled close, ordering takeout in, and watching movies (albeit not documentaries about penguins).

Now it was Sunday at four. I was getting ready to make the half hour drive to my parents' place.

And my mom had the sickies.

"I'm sorry, Sugar Snap," my mom said. "I thought it was allergies with the season change, but now I've got a fever. Please, tell Oliver that I'm sorry."

"Of course, Mom. But seriously, don't worry about us. Just feel better. I'm not here next Sunday"—I had a conference I would be flying home from—"and I know you're visiting your grandbabies the following weekend, so Oliver and I will be there in three weeks, okay?"

"He'd better bring an empty stomach. You, too. Because I'm going to bring my A game."

I smiled, even as I felt obligated to say, "Don't go to any trouble."

My mom hissed out a breath. "By then the man will have probably gotten twenty dates, and I still won't have met him. I'm bringing my A game, Lovely Lemon Meringue, and he'd better bring those abs and an empty stomach."

I chuckled. "Okay, Mom. Rest up. I love you."

"Love you, too, my Heavenly Éclair."

I smothered a giggle because seriously, where did she get this stuff? Did she have a list? Because I, for the life of me, couldn't remember a time when my mother had missed an opportunity for a baked-good-themed endearment. Maybe *I* should start making a list, just to document the brilliance.

With goodbyes exchanged, we hung up, and I turned to see Oliver leaning against the door to his bathroom, arms crossed, expression relaxed, though his eyes held a trace of concern.

Such a good man.

"Everything okay?" he asked.

"All's good. My mom has a bug, so she needs to cancel dinner."

Oliver frowned and stepped closer. "Does she want us to bring her anything? Sprite, soup, crackers?" His frown deepened. "Or is it more serious? Should we take my to urgent care? The ER?"

Such a good man.

He'd had one conversation with my mother, hadn't even laid eyes on her yet, and he was already trying to step in and take care of her.

The way he was raised should have made that difficult, the

trauma of his injury should have increased the urge to close down and protect himself. But he'd opened up to me, to my life, and he was all in—including caring about my mother. I knew part of it was because he'd had Alex and Teresa, that they'd laid the groundwork for him to know how *good* it could be to put trust in someone, to open up and accept love freely given.

But he'd lost them, too.

So, I understood the gift he was giving me.

He'd made a conscious choice to be vulnerable and invested, to allow me into his life and him into mine.

Which was why I was wrapping the precious gift he'd given me in bubble wrap and stowing it safely in a velvet lined box. I wouldn't *ever* forget that he'd trusted me with it.

Wouldn't *ever* forget to keep it safe.

TWENTY-FIVE

Oliver

JUST SHY OF two weeks later, Hazel woke me up with a soft kiss and stroking her fingers through my hair.

"Morning, honey," she said against my lips.

I groaned and stretched, glancing at the clock that said it was six in the morning. On a Saturday. Gods, why?

"Sleep," I muttered, tugging the blanket up and over us. It had been a long couple of weeks. A *great* couple of weeks, in fact. But still long and tiring. I'd decided to take an additional coaching class, and that on top of going through the files Marco had left for me meant that I had ended the days bleary-eyed and exhausted more often than not.

Thank God for Hazel.

She seemed to never run out of energy, even though she'd worked just as hard. Aside from the weekend Hazel had gone to her conference, we'd spent every evening together, ate most meals together, gone to sleep together.

And woke up every morning cuddling close.

And just like during the rest of the time, she was the Energizer Bunny. Never stopping. Never acting tired.

Including right now.

Because she was lying on me, all bright-eyed and bushy-tailed with her arms crossed over my chest, her chin resting on top of them.

And bouncing lightly.

So I couldn't drift back to sleep.

Stretching forward, she brushed her lips over me again. Since I didn't hate that, even though I hated getting up this early, I slid my fingers into her hair and kissed her a little harder, a little longer.

"I forgot to tell you something," she sing-songed.

I stifled a groan, blinked sleep from my eyes. "What's up, babe?"

"I..." Her lips pressed flat. I was suddenly wide awake. Because there was worry in her eyes. She went on before I could ask again. "I have a surprise for you, and I'm scared you might hate it and be mad at me."

I pushed myself up, wrapping my arms around her as she mirrored my movements, sitting up next to me.

"What is it, baby?"

"I—" Teeth into her bottom lip, her gaze darting away. Then a sigh. "I almost let you sleep through it because it would be easier."

Now I was getting worried.

Tension lanced through my body.

"But I arranged this because I love you, and...um...I was hoping it might bring something back for you that you haven't had since you got injured. So"—she swallowed—"will you get dressed and trust me?"

Trust her?

That was the easy part.

It was what she might be bringing me to face that had tension clawing at my insides.

TWENTY-SIX

Hazel

"SO," I said, forcing my tone to be even, "what do you think?"

He stood in the lobby of the rink—not the one that the Breakers used as a practice facility, but one that was an hour away and had been modified...

For the sleds that were flying on and off the ice.

"I—um—stumbled on this league and reached out to them. They said they have extra equipment for new guys to use and invited me to come." He was still and pale and *silent*. "I didn't tell them it was you or that you'd play. Just that maybe you might be interested."

Oliver didn't reply.

In fact, he hadn't said a word since I asked him to trust me.

Just had gotten out of bed and dressed, trailed me to my car, sat quietly on the ride, and followed me into the rink.

All silently.

Now he was staring at the ice, a muscle clenching in his jaw, and I realized I'd made a mistake.

A huge one.

I grabbed his arm, squeezed lightly. "Let's just go—"

"Oliver!"

We both jumped, and I whirled to see a little girl come tearing up to Oliver, brown curls bouncing. She was wearing a hoodie with the logo of a local youth team on the front and a pair of leggings with Velcro rectangles that I recognized as the undergarments that held hockey players' socks up, though most of the players on the Breakers wore the shorts version.

"Hannah," he said, finally unfreezing when the little girl launched herself at him and threw her arms around his waist. "What's up, buttercup?"

"I've got a game!" she yelled.

He smiled. "That's great."

"Want to come watch?" she asked.

Oliver's eyes flicked to mine, and I held perfectly still, trying to read his expression. An older woman came up then and smiled. "I think they're busy, Hannah. We should go get you dressed for your game."

"Okay," Hannah said, then her eyes drifted to the ice behind us. "Is that *your* game, Oliver?" She didn't wait for him to answer, just kept chattering. "Oh, it is! That's the game for people with superhero parts, and your leg is a superhero part! You'd better get dressed or you'll be late. Coach doesn't like it when I'm late, and I'm sure yours wouldn't either."

The older woman spoke, voice cautious, probably because the only one who didn't see the pain in Oliver's eyes was the little girl. "Honey, I think we should see Oliver another time."

"But—"

Hannah's face dropped, her brows drawing together. "Why are you sad?"

Fuck.

Fuck.

I clenched my teeth so tightly together that I felt a sharp bite of pain in my jaw.

Oliver squatted. "I'm not sad, sweetheart." He paused, seemed to be considering something, and I braced because his pale blue eyes were swirling with some pretty heavy emotions as they came to mine and held. "I'm scared."

"Do you want me to hold your hand when you go in?" Hannah's voice had dropped to a whisper that was almost as loud as her normal voice. "When my mom holds my hand, it makes me feel better."

The air went taut.

I held my breath.

If it looked like he was going to lose his cool, I'd step in because he wouldn't forgive himself for hurting the little girl's feelings later. I knew that because he was a good man, because this little girl obviously loved him.

I knew that because I knew *him*.

Oliver's face gentled and he slowly shook his head. "I don't want to make you late, honey."

Hannah shook her head, sending her ponytail flying. "Coach won't be mad if I'm late because I'm helping someone. She always says that's the most important thing. Aside from being kind."

My heart squeezed.

And yeah, there were tears in my eyes.

Because this little girl was...beautiful. A beautiful soul who was waiting for a grown man to decide if he'd take her hand and gain the courage to step into the rink.

Because the tumult of emotions rippling across Oliver's face included longing.

He wanted to be in there.

He was just...scared.

But he once again proved how amazing he was when he

said, "Then I would love for you to hold my hand."

Hannah smiled and didn't hesitate, just slipped her tiny hand into Oliver's much larger one and started tugging him to the door that led to the ice.

"I hope this is okay," the older woman said quietly to me. "My daughter is a force of nature, and—"

I squeezed her arm. "I think it's perfect. I—I'm worried this wasn't one of my better plans."

The woman had brown curls and eyes that signaled her to be Hannah's mother, but more than the outside, it was the kindness on her face that marked her to be the mom of the sweet little girl who was currently towing Oliver toward a group of men organizing equipment. "I'm Aimie," the mom said.

"Hazel."

"You love him," Aimie went on, "and that means sometimes you have to make tough decisions. One of those is pushing when you think they need it. Another is"—her eyes went back to Oliver and Hannah, who were now talking with the men—"giving them the world, or as much of it as you can."

I sucked in a breath.

"I don't know you, or him very well, but I know enough to understand that *this*"—a nod to where they were pulling out a sled and a pair of short sticks with metal spikes on the shaft, a helmet with a cage, shoulder pads, shin guards, and elbow pads —"*this*," she said again, "is both of those."

Hannah had gotten into the action, was scrounging through the gear, lining it up as though Oliver wouldn't know what went where, bouncing around as the men fitted Oliver into the sled.

She only backed off when he disappeared into a locker room to change, one of the guys at his side, but returned to him the moment he came back out, his prosthesis gone, his body strapped into the sled. The men who'd fitted him stood on the smooth plastic, showing him how to use the shorter sticks, all while Hannah watched, still bouncing but quiet.

And I couldn't take it anymore.

Slipping into the rink, Aimie behind her, I clung to the wall, wanting to go over and make sure Oliver was good but worried it might make him lash out.

Because amongst the fear and longing in his expression, there had also been anger.

I'd overstepped.

Now he was on a ride he might not want, with a little girl watching over and making him go through it because he was too nice of a guy to turn down a child's offer of help.

My insides rippled and twisted, worry knotting my intestines.

Then...he was on the ice.

Oh God, he was doing it. Propelling himself around the cold, hard surface, using the metal spikes on the pair of sticks to shoot forward, moving faster than should be possible, especially considering he'd never done this before.

He was flying, skidding this way and that, a little wobbly, the occasional near miss of a collision—though from my research, collisions in sled hockey were common and brutal, as brutal as those in the NHL—but I could tell that Oliver was just getting a feel for the sled, the long blades that held it aloft, the movements.

He didn't even touch the puck at first.

Just skated.

A quick turn had him compensating too quickly, weight flying back, and he wiped out hard.

I gasped.

"He's okay," Hannah said sagely, "Oliver is tough."

I blinked, not having heard the little girl come over, but I swallowed another gasp when Oliver picked himself up and continued skating, only this time to try the same turn that had made him fall the first time. And made him crash a second time.

Aimie squeezed my shoulder. "He'll be okay."

"I know," I whispered, though tears burned the back of my eyes when I added, "Thank you."

A nod. "We should go, honey," Aimie told Hannah.

"I want to see him score a goal," Hannah said as she bounced around, her curls flying behind her like a cape. "Please, Mom?"

"I think he's just getting comfortable skating—"

"Score a goal, Oliver!" Hannah shouted.

Oliver's head whipped in our direction, and I saw a flash of white—a smile—before he began propelling himself forward, flipping the stick in a movement that seemed to be natural even though he'd never done it before, scooping up a puck, and carrying it forward. He fumbled a bit, finding a rhythm of skating and pushing, figuring out the right speed, but then it seemed to click, and he brought the puck with him as he closed in on the goalie, and fired a shot at the net.

I held my breath.

Unnecessary.

It flew into the goal, and Hannah cheered like a loon, me and Aimie joining in. I saw another flash of white, and Oliver continued working, weaving through and mixing with the players, who were all warming up, shooting and skating, getting ready for whenever they would put teams for a scrimmage together.

"Okay, baby," Aimie said, "now we've really got to go get ready."

Hannah nodded.

"Thank you," I said, squatting down so I could give Hannah a squeeze, and then rose to do the same to Aimie.

"Can I—can I get your number? I'd like to take you out for lunch as a thank you. Both of you. I don't think I would have—" A shake of my head. "I don't think I would have gotten this far without—"

"Nonsense," Aimie said as Hannah took off for the doors. "But I will gladly exchange numbers, and we owe Oliver—and you—lunch, not the other way around. Hannah has slept in the jersey he got for her every night. He made her year"—Aimie's eyes held mine—"and you did, as well. She loves Oliver, and she loves helping people. Missing five minutes of an 8U game isn't a sacrifice in the least."

"I—"

Aimie nudged me with her shoulder. "No arguments."

It was official. I was adopting this woman and her adorable daughter, and I was doing it *today*.

"Okay," I said, handing Aimie my phone. "We'll split lunch." A beat. "And then we'll argue over who's paying the next one."

Aimie laughed as I plugged in my number, handing me her cell so I could do the same. "It's a deal."

TWENTY-SEVEN

Oliver

BY THE TIME I showered and dressed and made my way out of the locker, my entire body was a mess of tired muscles and over-sensitized nerves.

Hell, it felt like my heart was still pounding, even though I'd been off the ice for a half hour.

But that was hockey.

It was exhausting in a way that was nearly impossible to train for.

Intervals. High impact action. Strength. Speed. Finesse.

And with the sled strapped to my hips and leg, learning a different kind of balance, using a different type of strength.

Nothing was instinctual.

It all took extra brainpower to move, to turn, to sprint, to shoot.

Which meant I was exhausted in a way I hadn't been since I first started playing. But...I'd played.

Holy shit.

It hadn't felt like before. It was different. Frustrating in a way. But it was hockey and on the ice and feeling the breeze on my face and shooting and scoring—even if it was with one hand and my angles were off because I was lower to the ice.

It was hockey.

It was amazing.

And Hazel had given that to me.

I pushed through the doors after I'd thanked Zack and Shelly—the two men who'd loaned me the equipment and had helped me gear up and navigate—promising to be back soon and stepped out of the rink and into the lobby.

My upper body was tired, but I was surprised at how wiped my thighs were, my hips, my calf. Every muscle overcompensating, I supposed, but I'd also figured my back and core, shoulders and arms would be wrecked. Instead, they were tired but okay, and my lower body was like Jell-O. I was ready for a rubdown, a soak in the cool and hot tubs, and then to sleep for a hundred years.

Unfortunately, the best I might do is some IcyHot, coaxing Hazel into bed (for that rubdown...not of my thighs, ha), and then passing out and vegging for the rest of the day.

But I had to find her first.

I'd looked up frequently, had seen her watching me in the stands, but when I came out of the locker room, I didn't see her there. Nor was she against the wall of windows where she, Hannah, and Aimie had cheered for me when I'd chipped a puck into the net.

Not really a goal because we were all just messing around on the ice.

But sort of one because it was in the net and Hannah had called for me to score and I had, even if it had been just in a skate and shoot.

So, not in the stands or by the windows or hiding in the shadows. I tugged out my phone, checked the screen. Nothing.

Weird.

Maybe she was in the bathroom.

I glanced around the lobby, but it was empty.

Or at least, empty of anyone but a few siblings keeping themselves busy by tearing through the space, empty of Hazel. A whistle drew my attention, and I headed toward the next set of doors, to the second rink. It was divided into thirds and there were several games happening at once.

Girls. Tiny little girls who looked more like marshmallow men than hockey players skated around the space.

And one *flew* on the ice.

Snagging the puck off a teammate's stick (not ideal, but I appreciated her spunk and desire to take the puck), skating it up, scoring the goal, and then immediately going to the halfway point of the sectioned-off rink and waiting for the face-off.

While the other girls slowly made their way back—some with a little encouragement from their coach.

The puck dropped.

The girl got it.

Goal.

Again.

A whoop from the stands.

I turned to look, saw Hazel and Aimie cheering loudly, Chuck beside them.

The girl skated back to the middle, and I looked closer, saw that it was Hannah. *Of course* it was Hannah, I thought, grinning like a fool. My little Hannah had spunk for days and was a killer on the ice. Though...

I watched as play continued and Hannah scored three more times, each time scooping up the puck with a definitive confidence I loved but also knew wasn't exactly ideal (or at least the times she took it off her teammates' sticks—which was well more than a half-dozen occurrences). When the coach blew the whistle for a water break, I moved to the bench.

"Okay if I talk to Hannah for a second?" I asked the slender woman with dark brown hair.

Her eyes widened when she recognized me. "Sure," she murmured. "But we're back on in two minutes."

"Got it." I tapped Hannah lightly on the helmet, soaked in the smile that spread on her face.

"Oliver!"

"Hannah!" I winked when the coach chuckled, earned a smile from the cute brunette. "Can you come over here for a sec?"

"Yup!" She jumped down the two stairs that led up to the player's bench and raced over, barely able to contain herself when she asked, "Did you see my goal?"

"Your goal?" I teased. "I saw four of them. You're doing awesome." I held my hand up for a fist bump.

"Did you do awesome, too?"

"I had fun." Another fist bump. "Thanks to you."

She bounced, smile still wide.

"I thought I'd tell you a special secret that makes hockey extra fun for me. Do you want to hear it?"

"Yes!"

"You know what can be better than scoring?" I asked.

Her brows drew together in a way that told me she couldn't imagine anything being better than scoring. Which was kind of true. Putting a goal in was awesome. But, "Passing to your teammates or waiting for them to pass to you can be even more fun."

Her face screwed up. "Why?"

Definitely not convinced.

"Because it takes more skill sometimes," I said. "You know

out there that you can skate straight up and score—you did it four times that I saw—but doesn't doing the same thing get a little boring after a while?" Her brow was still furrowed, though maybe slightly less. "You can do something different—make a move, try to shoot on your backhand, *or* see if you can get your teammate a goal, too."

Her face relaxed.

"Because it feels good to score, right?" I asked.

She nodded.

"And it's fun to make our teammates feel good, too."

Another nod.

"But it also makes you a better hockey player when you can pass *and* shoot *and* make a move." I patted her helmet. "You get good at all three of those, and you'll be unstoppable."

That she liked, as evidenced by her raising her stick in the air and yelling, "Unstoppable!"

"Damn right," I said.

She giggled. "Damn is a bad word."

Shit. I glanced toward the stands. "Don't tell your mom."

A shrug. "Okay!" The whistle blew. "Gotta go!" She was gone before I could say goodbye, but my eyes stayed on her as she went back onto the ice, took the face-off, and started for the goal. *Straight* for the goal, forgetting everything I had just told her.

Until, in almost comical fashion, she skidded to a stop, the pieces seeming to click into place.

And...then she looked up.

She saw a teammate.

And she passed. A damned good pass, too. Slightly in front of the little girl—so she could skate to it without having to slow down. Hannah's teammate fumbled a bit, but then got the puck under control and skated to the net.

A shot.

A block.

The girl got another try, jamming it at the goalie, and...

Goal!

The girl squealed, Hannah bounced on her skates, and they both skated back to center ice.

"You want a job?" the brunette coaching Hannah and company said, her eyes warm. "I've been trying to make that happen for almost six months now."

"You're doing a great job with them."

A shrug. "I'm just a mom, not a former player. My limited skating experience doesn't mean I'm a good coach."

"The smiles on their faces tell me you're a good coach." I stuck out my hand. "Oliver."

"I know." She shook it. "Flo." A beat. "And I'm kidding about the job. Sort of."

I grinned. "I'll see what I can work out for next season," I said. "You guys are almost done now, right?"

A nod.

"I might be more comfortable being back on the ice then."

Her brows drew together, and then it dawned on her. I wasn't the player I'd been. I couldn't just jump onto the rink and be what I was. "Shit, I'm so—"

"Nothing to be sorry about," I murmured. "Shit happens."

Her face gentled, regret in her eyes. "It does. But I'm still sorry it happened to you."

Maybe once that apology would have derailed me, would have made me feel like shit, or less than a whole person. Would have made me think this woman saw me as an injury and nothing more. But Hazel had shown me differently. *I'd* shown myself that I was different. *More.* Which was why I touched her arm and said, "But I meant what I said about next season. I'll give you my number. You call me when it's set, and I'll try to come out and help as much as I can."

"Really?" she exclaimed.

"Really," I said.

"Wow. I—" Her mouth opened and closed. "You are *amazing.*"

My cheeks felt hot. "No," I said quickly. "Hannah is. These girls are. And *you* are because you're a coach who told her players that the most important thing is to help others and to be kind."

Flo sniffed. "Now you're going to make me cry."

"Then you'd better put my number into your phone before you can't see the screen."

A laugh, albeit one that was watery. But she plugged my number into her phone.

Then went to corral the masses.

"Charmer," came a soft voice.

I spun, saw Hazel had come up behind me. She was smiling, but it was tentative. Probably worried she'd pushed me when I wasn't ready, that I would take it out on her because I was upset.

But...how could I be upset?

She'd given me *everything.*

Instead of telling her that, of trying to convince her that I wasn't mad, I tugged her close and wrapped my arms around her. I couldn't lie. I'd been terrified I'd embarrass myself, scared I would look like an idiot who didn't know what to do, upset that it wouldn't feel the same.

And it was all those things.

In a way, I'd felt like a rookie. I had fallen more than was good for my pride. I hadn't known exactly what to do.

But I'd figured it out.

I'd managed.

I'd moved forward while part of me had still been looking back, blending the joy of the past with the excitement of the future, of a new challenge with threads of something I'd loved beyond reason.

Because of Hazel.

So, hell no, I wasn't upset.

I was so fucking in love with this woman.

So, I told her. So, I kissed her.

Then with our fingers laced together, we walked out to her car.

TWENTY-EIGHT

Hazel

IT HAD BEEN ALMOST three weeks since my mom had canceled Sunday dinner. The rescheduled meal was just two days away, and it was Thursday.

The Breakers had been traveling on a long road stretch, so I hadn't had a chance to check back in with Marcel since we'd had our breakthrough. Though we had a session today, and he had sent me a text a couple of days ago while on that road trip, letting me know that he'd found a rage room in San Francisco during their time there and had taken several of the guys there to work off steam from their loss.

Heaven help me if one of them pulled a muscle destroying some old shit.

Sam would kill me if one of the guys got injured, and I did not want to get on the head trainer's bad side.

She was *scary*.

With italics.

Sam took the guys' health and safety very seriously, and

though she was fully on board with my assertion that physical and mental health were equally as important, she wouldn't take kindly to one of "her" (yes, "her" with the quotes because she let everyone know they were her players, and they were to be protected) players getting injured at a rage room. I agreed completely. Still, if destroying some stuff in a safe space meant they received some mental clarity in return—without getting injured—then I knew Sam would be all over it too.

I was just glad Marcel was sharing.

I just prayed that if the guys continued to go, they wore their safety goggles, no one slipped on the mess on the floor, none of the players were impaled with flying shards of porcelain.

A girl could hope.

I just hoped that my *hope* was powerful enough to keep Sam away.

Because things were good.

Really good.

Such a weak description, but it was an apt one.

Oliver and I had fallen into a pattern, waking together, sleeping together, eating together. *Being* together. And it was easy, effortless, as though I'd been waiting my whole life for this man, and we were meant to be together.

Peace.

That was what I'd found.

But this morning, I only had pain.

I should have known better. My headache had been brewing the night before, throughout dinner with Lexi and Luc, during which Luc had told me he'd hired a night nurse—about freaking time, even if Lexi had protested at first. They were both human again. Baby Noah was fine. And we'd all decided to have a couple of drinks to celebrate Luc and Lexi's descent from zombie-dom into humanoids again. The night had gotten a little weird when they gave Oliver a creepy blue stuffed toy called a Fuggler—apparently his prize for winning a plant-growing competition, of all things, the players had competed in last season—named Mac. It had plastic, human-looking teeth, maniacal eyes, and was wearing tighty whities.

Luc had been so excited to give it.

Lexi had been, rightfully, horrified he'd followed through with the giving.

I had shuddered.

Oliver had busted a gut and then started plotting whom he was going to give it to next.

It was late when Oliver and I had made it back to his place, and he'd gone up to bed after showing me KiKi, the plant he had still managed to keep alive. He'd tucked Mac next to the pot, kissed me on the cheek, and headed to the bedroom. I'd stayed downstairs, a documentary (about meerkats) on TV and my laptop open.

A friend from college was working on a paper and had asked me to read through it for her.

The pain had begun in my temples, and it had taken me a bit to realize the fan on my laptop was whirring again and that the alcohol at Luc and Lexi's had left my brain primed for a headache. By then, my temples had begun pounding and the ache had crawled its way through my scalp, squeezing my brain, making the backs of my eyes hurt until I could barely concentrate on the words.

Which was when I'd given up, blearily typing an email to my friend to explain, and had headed to bed, to Oliver, who was already sleeping.

A couple of migraine pills.

A glass of water.

And hoping I'd staved off the worst of it—or at least *slept* through the worst of it.

But...

Now it was morning, and my head was pounding even worse than the night before. I wanted to do nothing but stay in bed, take more medicine, and go back to sleep, hoping that when I eventually woke, it would be gone. But I had a session with Marcel that morning, so I was doing my best to get ready for work while protecting my eyes from the sunlight streaming in through the windows.

Which meant that I was wearing sunglasses inside.

I wasn't a cool celebrity or musician, and I didn't look the least bit cool with my giant sunnies and dim lights, but I had clothes on, had managed to shower, and was slapping some makeup on my face.

The scent of coffee wafted up the hallway, and normally Oliver making coffee for me in the morning was perfection.

This morning, with my migraine fully upon me, it was torture.

My stomach churned.

My tube of lipstick was forgotten, and I barely made it to the toilet in time.

"Babe?"

Oliver's voice was too loud. So was the sound of my own heaving, for that matter.

God, it was all an echo through my brain, making everything worse.

The pounding increased; nausea flared.

I puked again.

Not that anything came up. I was full-on empty.

"Babe?" Oliver asked again.

"Shh," I murmured weakly. I just needed a minute, just needed to settle my stomach, breathe through my pain. I would be okay. I wouldn't miss my time to check in with Marcel. He was in a good place. I needed to make sure that he stayed that way. But even my sunglasses were adding to my agony, squeezing on the sides of my head. I yanked them off, dropped them to the bathmat, and kept my eyes firmly closed.

The coffee cup clinked down on the counter, and I knew Oliver had set it down quietly, but it was still gunshot loud in his bathroom, making the nausea flare again.

Then the noise of my retching once more had the cycle starting over again.

"Coffee," I breathed, when I got myself under a semblance of control.

"You want it?" he whispered, so quietly I could barely hear it.

A shudder "No."

I felt him move away on quiet feet, and then the smell disappeared.

Thank God.

Now, if I only could summon the strength for a cool towel and to brush my teeth. But I didn't have it, so I just sat there, eyes closed, hugging the toilet.

Fun times.

Oliver didn't immediately come back, and I lay there for a while, breathing, *breathing* as the pain ramped up. Then soft footsteps. A crinkle.

"Gum," he murmured.

A good man. I didn't have to summon the energy for brushing my teeth right at that moment. I could just open my mouth, chew for a few heartbeats, and everything would be peppermint and good and—

He slipped the piece of gum into my mouth.

I chewed.

The bitter taste faded.

Then he laid a cool cloth on the back of my neck, and—oh

fuck—that was heaven, cooling my clammy skin, settling my stomach further.

"Can you stand, babe?" Another whisper, still so quiet it barely penetrated.

"In a minute," I whispered back and winced because, God, that was loud in my own brain.

His hand settled on my shoulder, rubbed lightly up and down.

Up and down.

And then his arms were around me, lifting me with a slow, deliberate curl I knew couldn't be easy with his prosthesis and me changing his center of gravity.

Before I could protest, I was cradled against his chest, the towel had been slid to cover my eyes—thank the blessed darkness—and we were moving. Something soft—the bed—beneath my back, cool sheets tugged up and over me.

Quiet.

An empty room.

Then a slight rattle, a pillow under my shoulders. "Meds, babe."

I hadn't told him where they were, he didn't know the dosage—though, I supposed he could easily look in the obvious place (my purse) and read the label—and anyway, I was in too much pain to worry.

Oliver would take care of me.

"Says with food first, you think you can keep crackers down?"

Probably crackers were the only thing I'd be able to keep down.

"Yeah," I whispered.

He adjusted the cloth, keeping it over my eyes and forehead and spent the next few minutes feeding me a couple of crackers and then a few sips of water. Then just holding me, lightly stroking my arm as we waited to see if I would keep that down.

When I did, he put the pills on my tongue—two of them (the right dose)—and let me sip some more water.

We waited a couple of more minutes.

No puking commenced.

He coaxed my back down, flipped the towel so the cool side was against my skin. "Rest, babe," he murmured. The bed dipped like he was going to get up, and I found myself reaching for his arm, halting him.

"I have a session with Marcel today. I can't miss—"

"I'll call him."

"But—"

"Rest. You're not working. I'll call him." The last was said so firmly, even in a whisper, that I didn't argue.

Plus, I was finally accepting that he was right. There was no way I'd be able to get myself into any sort of shape for work. Even opening my eyes seemed like it would be impossible, not when they felt as though they'd been weighed down by concrete, when my mind was fuzzy and swirling from the meds.

A brush of his fingers over my cheekbone.

"Rest, babe."

I gave in.

And let the blackness come.

TWENTY-NINE

Oliver

I'D DONE my best to work but knew I hadn't made much progress.

Even though Kailey had sent me a beta version of the program I'd asked her to create for tracking player development. Even though it looked awesome, and I wanted to dive deep into it. I couldn't concentrate when I tried to.

Because I was sitting on a chair I'd carried into the hall, staring into the darkened room while Hazel slept.

As she'd been sleeping all day.

In the hall because I knew light was a trigger, and I didn't want to add to her pain with the glare from my laptop screen.

I'd called Marcel, let him know about Hazel's headache, and I'd been periodically checking in on her all day as she slept, making sure she was sleeping—she was—and that she wasn't in pain—the lines creasing her face even as she slept told me enough about her pain level, even unconscious, that I was ready to punch a hole in the wall.

But that would make noise. Another trigger.

And I wasn't going to do anything else to hurt her.

Now the sun had gone down, I still hadn't turned on lights, and I was considering making another quiet trek to her side just to ensure that she was still breathing.

Nearly twelve hours she'd been out.

Part of me was glad of that. I knew my fair share about pain, both from the normal wear and tear on my body that came from being a professional athlete before I'd lost my leg, and in the time afterward with all the surgeries, the rehab, the phantom pain.

Her sleeping through this was a gift.

On that thought, I saw her body shift, the sheets sliding over her legs as she rolled. I shut the laptop and quietly made my way to her, studying her face, seeing the towel had slipped and her eyes were open.

"Babe?" I whispered.

"I'm okay," she whispered back.

I took in the tired eyes, the skin that appeared pale with only a sliver of moonlight illuminating the space through the narrow strip of curtains I'd opened once the sun had gone down. But the grooves lining her mouth, digging into her forehead, creasing the skin next to her eyes were gone. "Need more meds?" I asked almost silently.

"No," she said, starting to sit up. Her voice approaching normal. "I'm really okay. It's gone. I just...need to eat something, stay away from screens, go back to sleep, and I'll be good."

"Okay. I'll make you something to eat. Any requests?"

"Cereal?" she asked. "I—it always makes me feel better," she added when my brows rose.

"Got it."

She moved to adjust the pillows behind her, but I reached

in and helped her. Then tugged the covers up for good measure. Then went back into the bathroom and wet the towel for an additional good measure. Then placed it on her head. Then tucked in the covers a little tighter. Then—

"Honey," she said, her voice a little rough, though her fingers were gentle on my arm. "I'm really okay."

I nodded.

"And I'm sorry I ruined your day. I—I should have known better than to try to keep working when I felt it come on, but then I didn't realize the fan was whirring on my computer, and I shouldn't have had those last drinks with Luc and Lexi, and..." She swallowed. "I'm just really sorry I inconvenienced you."

Fuck.

One, I needed to sort out that fan.

Two, I needed to understand why she thought that she was inconveniencing me because she got a headache. Even if it was because she'd had too many drinks—which wasn't too many from my experience with her. We had drank that and more many times without issue. If anything, it was *my* fault because my fix for the fan didn't stick, and that I'd let her work when I knew she was tired.

Yes, I knew *letting* her do anything sounded douchey, but also, I'd known she was tired, so I could have found a way to "encourage" her into bed.

Barring that, I could have stayed up with her.

Upon which, I would have noticed the fan, or at least noticed that she wasn't feeling well.

So, this was on me, too.

And her being sick wasn't an inconvenience. God knew she'd gone out of her way for me many times, too. We mostly stayed at my home because everything that made it easier for me to get around was here. But she'd also bought an extra pair of crutches and a seat for her shower for her place. Without a word, without commenting.

I'd just gone over one evening and it was there.

Along with my brand of coffee in the cupboards, extra apples and oatmeal, since that was my preferred breakfast of choice.

I'd done the same here—and was why I now had a box of Lucky Charms in my pantry when I hadn't eaten them since I was fifteen, why she had makeup at my place, clothes in my closet, a blow dryer beneath my sink, and a towel thing she wrapped around her head to properly dry her curls.

That was just part of being in a relationship.

Taking care of each other.

So why she had to apologize for getting a headache made me wonder, made me make a mental note to discuss it with her. Because if her ex was an asshole who made her feel bad for getting sick, I was going to make damned sure she knew that I would *never* be inconvenienced by her in that way.

She saw me as more than a man who'd lost my leg.

So, she needed to understand that she was more than a fucking headache.

But she had just slept twelve hours after that headache had knocked her on her ass, her eyes were tired, her skin pale. She needed rest and food, not an emotionally heavy conversation.

"You're not an inconvenience," I told her, patting her leg and standing, knowing from the short conversation I'd had with her mother, the ones I'd overheard in the weeks since, that it wasn't her parents making her feel like an inconvenience.

Which meant I had a solid idea of precisely who'd done that.

And his name was Trevor.

The *fucking* ex.

The one who hadn't given her romance or candles or music, who'd left her after a bachelor party because he wanted variety.

I repeated, the *fucking* ex.

"Baby?" Concern in those pretty brown eyes.

I bent and kissed her forehead. "Not an inconvenience when you love someone, babe."

And then I walked from the room to get her some cereal.

Because she wanted it, and it was within my power to give it.

Simple as that.

THIRTY

Oliver

"OLIVER?"

"Yeah?"

My eyes were closed, Hazel was driving us home, and I was about two minutes from passing out. We'd spent the day at the practice facility. Me slogging through paperwork and Hazel in back-to-back sessions with the guys.

"I...um...have another surprise for you."

"Does it involve me having to do anything physical?" I groaned. I wasn't joking about being ready to pass out.

"That I'm not sure about."

I peeled open my eyes. "Not inspiring confidence, babe."

"You said you needed to keep working on your abs," she teased.

I groaned.

Her lips twitched. "It's not going to make you as tired as sled hockey did the other day."

I reached over, squeezed her thigh. "That was exhausting

but awesome, honey. Although, I'm definitely out of hockey shape," I added when she smiled at me, "but it was also one of the most amazing things anyone has ever done for me."

"I'm glad you're not mad. I was..." A breath. "Worried I'd pushed when I shouldn't have."

"I told you I loved it."

"I know." She worried that bottom lip with her teeth. "But we haven't talked about it much, especially with work being so busy for both of us, and I guess part of me was still..."

"Not mad," I told her. "I was scared out of my mind, but luckily I had a seven-year-old who held my hand the whole time."

Hazel giggled. "Just so you know, I've officially adopted Aimie and Hannah." A grin. "And Chuck isn't so bad, though I think I only heard him say one thing the entire time."

"A man of few words is the only way to survive with those two."

Another giggle.

"And I'm glad you adopted them, because it seems that I've volunteered to help coach Hannah's team next season."

"Oliver."

Her voice sounded strangled, and I sat up, glanced over at her. "What?"

She looked to be very close to tears. "That's"—a shake of her head—"you're a really good man, you know that?"

My eyes stung.

I hadn't felt good.

For a long, long time, I hadn't felt worthy of that.

Now I knew I deserved it.

"You make it easy to be a better one," I said and squeezed her thigh. "You're my heart."

She sniffed, dashed a finger beneath both eyes then covered my hand with her own. "Now that you're trying to make me cry, I'm going to distract you because…" She turned into a nondescript parking lot, a nondescript brown building sitting squatly in the corner. "…we're here. Surprise!"

"What?" I squinted, trying to see where we were. "Have you decided this is the place you'll murder me?"

A snort.

A deep breath.

"No, baby." Another breath. "This is Dr. Francisca's practice."

My eyes widened. I sat back in the seat.

Amanda Francisca was famous for her work with amputees. In particular, she worked with athletes who participated in the Paralympics, Iron Man competitions, Spartan Races, and CrossFit. If there was an elite athlete who needed a prothesis, they went to her.

And she'd reached out to me, months ago.

But…I hadn't been ready.

"She says she can get you back on the ice. Not with sled hockey. Not in the NHL. But something that felt like it was." Hazel spun in her seat and faced me. "It'll take time, months to a year, she said. And in the meantime, you can still play sled hockey, and maybe when you're done with her, you can coach or play in a league or just know that there isn't anything stopping you from getting on the rink."

My chest was so tight that I couldn't squeeze out words.

I was absolutely going to lose it.

Because…Hazel.

"Hey," she breathed, cupping my jaw, one thumb wiping the tears that had escaped my eyes. "I'm sorry. We don't have to do this today. I know it's been a long week and—"

I kissed her.

Hard and deep and long.

And when I broke away, both of our chests heaving, our breaths in rapid succession, I said, "I'm going to marry you."

Her jaw fell open.

Her eyes filled with tears, tears that spilled over.

I wiped them away, kissed her again, and then I got out of the car.

For the record, Dr. Francisa was the shit.

THIRTY-ONE

"MY LITTLE BRAN BISCUIT!" my mom cried as she flew down the front steps and ran across the driveway, hugging me tight almost before I got fully out of the car.

Warm arms. A tight squeeze. The soft baby powder scent I'd always associated with her.

Home.

"Hi, Mom," I said, squeezing her back.

"I've missed you."

"It's been a month."

"And that's thirty-one days too long, my Little Apple Turnover," my mom said, slowly releasing me. "Your hair looks good, but you're pale. When did you have the headache?"

I was good.

"I'm fine, Mom."

"When, Sugar Cakes?"

A sigh. "Thursday. Though it came on Wednesday late. I

tried to sleep through it, but I woke up in a bad way Thursday. Luckily, Oliver was there and took care of me."

My mom's eyes finally drifted over my shoulder, locking onto Oliver, a wide smile spreading over her face. "He's pretty," she whispered.

I started laughing, whispered back, "He's got great abs."

Somehow my mom's smile went wider. "Oh, baby. You did good."

"Nice to meet you, Mr. Reid," I heard Oliver say behind me and turned to see him shaking my dad's hand. "And you, Mrs. Reid," he said, stepping forward and producing a bouquet of flowers he'd picked up...somewhere?

The man was a freaking flower magician.

"Hazel said I wasn't allowed to bring anything," he said, "but my mom always told me to never go to a house empty-handed."

My mom melted as he handed the spring bouquet—a mix of tulips, daffodils, sunflowers, and daisies—over. She glanced at me again, mouthed, "You did good," again, and then wrapped Oliver in a hug I knew would win my man over. Because it was the best kind of hug. A mom hug—tight and long and filled with the scent of baby powder. And she never let go until the person she was hugging did.

Which was seriously the key to a good hug.

"Come in, come in," she told him when he'd dropped his arms and she'd released him. She slipped her arm through his, led him to the house, one hand gripping the bouquet. "I hope you're hungry. I made..." And then she began naming a truly obscene amount of food as I all but dragged him up the front porch and inside.

"Hey, peanut," my dad said.

"Hi, Daddy." I hugged him—and for the record, he gave good hugs, too. Not Mom Hugs, but they were top quality Dad

Hugs, and they made me feel like a little girl again. "How's work?"

A sigh. "They convinced me to stay on another six months."

I stifled a giggle. This was a running joke in our family. My dad constantly complained about wanting to retire from his job as CEO of a local tech firm, saying he wanted to do nothing but sleep, eat, and go fishing, but every time the retirement date approached, he suddenly had another contract for another year or six more months, and I was half-convinced he'd work until he died.

God knew he had enough days off so he and my mom could take vacations.

"When are you going to retire, Dad?"

He tugged a lock of my hair and slid an arm around my shoulders. "Not until you give me grandbabies."

My brows lifted as I glanced up at him. "You already have grandbabies."

A shrug. "Not from you." He squeezed me lightly. "Plus, you'd make beautiful babies with that man."

My heart stuttered. "Not you, too."

"He looks at you right, peanut."

"Dad, it's a little early to start thinking about babies."

"Maybe." A nudge. "But I've got six months at work, so there's a grace period."

I started laughing. "Six months is a grace period?"

"He looks at you right, baby girl." Emphasis on the right. Hell, emphasis on the whole statement, and I felt my belly fill with butterflies, or maybe with a whole herd of kittens playing with tiny balls of yarn.

"He said he's going to marry me," I admitted.

"Smart man." My dad kissed my forehead.

"Dad," I breathed.

"You get a good thing, you don't let it go," he murmured. "We taught you that, and I like this man already because he looks at you right, because *you* look at *him* right. I like him because he brings your mother flowers, so he doesn't show up empty-handed and because he took care of you when you were sick." He cupped my cheek. "But, peanut, most of all, I like the man already because there's happy written all over the lines of your face. You deserve that."

My throat went tight. "Dad," I said again, though it was more like a rasp. "I love him."

"Good, baby," he said.

Then he walked me into the house and into the kitchen where my mom was fussing over arranging the flowers in a vase, and Oliver was washing some dirty dishes that were in the sink from my mom's massive food-prepping.

Another squeeze before my dad released my, his voice quiet enough for my ears only. "Because I can see he deserves that, too."

Tears threatened.

But then my mom started pulling food out and demanding I set the table and calling me Queen Croissantia (which was a personal favorite), and then it was just happy and teasing and my tears (even though they were tears of happy) dried up.

Because I had food to put on the table.

Because I knew it was going to be the best night ever.

"Have another slice, honey," my mom told Oliver, trying to put the last piece of apple pie onto his plate.

"Oh, no, Mrs. Reid, I couldn't. I'm about to burst. But I'd love to take it home and have it tomorrow, if you don't mind," he added quickly when my mom looked ready to protest.

I hid a smile.

Because that was the perfect answer for my mom.

"Toni, please, Oliver," she said for about the millionth time, even though he kept calling her Mrs. Reid, saying that it felt strange to call my parents by their first names. My mom would win him over eventually, but in the meantime, I knew my parents liked that he'd been so polite. Flowers. Dishes. Mr. and Mrs. The man was a charmer. "And I'd be happy to wrap something up for you."

Code for not just pie.

Because the only thing my mom loved more than feeding her family for Sunday dinner, was to feed us during the week as well.

We would be taking home enough food for an army.

Fine with me.

That meant I wouldn't need to cook all week—just slop some stuff on plates and nuke it for dinner or slop some stuff into a Tupperware and nuke it for lunch. And, yeah, yeah, I knew I wasn't supposed to do that with plastic, but sometimes a girl got lazy.

So, nuke *that*.

The night had been perfect. Literally perfect, and I was so happy I could burst. Oliver fit right in, had been his usual awesome self, my parents were *their* usual awesome selves, and it had been so effortless that it felt like he'd been coming over for years.

Even when my mom had asked him about his parents and he'd shared about Alex and Teresa and given the briefest explanation about his bio ones and his time in the system, he hadn't closed down.

He'd just accepted the hug my mom forced onto him, the soft words she whispered into his ear for only him to hear, and because my mom didn't release until released, the hug had gone on for a while. Oliver's eyes were damp when they broke apart, but he didn't shy away. No walls came up, and then we'd all gone on to play a rousing game of Munchkin—complete with sabotaging and the special brand of Reid competitiveness to break the bit of lingering sadness.

Then we'd played UNO, because that, apparently, was a game the Jameses got down and dirty about—and seriously, Oliver had Skipped or Draw Two'd me at least five times on the way to winning that game.

After that was dessert.

Apple pie. Cheesecake. Chocolate mousse.

For four people.

But I wasn't complaining. I loved it.

"I'll wrap it up now," my mom said, taking the slice into the kitchen, and sure enough, I heard the Tupperware cabinet open and my mom begin digging around in it.

"My abs are going to suffer for this," Oliver said lightly.

I giggled.

My dad groaned and stood up, started gathering plates. "I learned long ago to give up on any abs in lieu of getting to enjoy that woman's cooking," he said, patting his belly—more beer than flat.

"I think that was the smartest call," Oliver told him, already on *his* feet, gathering up the remaining plates and leaving me with nothing to gather.

Rude.

"Damn right it was," my dad said, leading the way into the kitchen.

I grabbed a towel and the furniture polish and made my way back into the dining room, doing a post-dinner chore I'd done hundreds of times before.

Wipe the crumbs.

Polish the table.

Make sure the wood gleamed like it was brand new.

I was mid-wood gleaming when the doorbell rang. "Weird," I muttered, glancing at my watch. It was nearly ten at night, and Oliver and I would be heading out soon, since we had work tomorrow. So, it was late. Too late for kids selling candy bars or solicitors peddling vacuums. But it was also late enough that concern rippled through me.

What if it was an emergency?

Quickly, I set down the bottle of furniture polish and the towel, hurried to the door.

A flick to open the lock.

A twist of the handle.

Pulling open the wooden panel, and...gasping.

My mouth fell open, and if I'd been a cartoon, my jaw would have been on the ground. Because, seriously, what the *fuck?*

"Trevor?" I asked, and then continued gaping. My fingers clenched on the wood of the door, my knees went weak and then locked tight. He looked good.

He also looked like the most painful experience of my life.

A painful reminder of that time in my life.

I took a breath, regained my composure. "What the hell are you doing here?"

"Hi, Haze. I knew you'd be here tonight."

"I—"

And then he kissed me.

THIRTY-TWO

Oliver

I HEARD the doorbell ring and frowned.

Too late for visitors.

But then again, it wasn't my house. Maybe Toni had an open-door policy, or perhaps the neighbors were coming over for leftovers.

God knew there was enough wrapped-up food in Toni and Chad's fridge to feed an army.

I was setting the plates down when I heard Hazel's footsteps heading for the door, Chad right beside me, wearing a frown.

So maybe I'd been right about it being too late for visitors and something was off rather than the leftover train beginning. Toni seemed unaffected, humming to herself as she packed an obscene amount of food into a bag for me and Hazel.

Not that I was complaining.

Lunch and dinner this week were going to be *amazing*.

Voices filled the air, just a short burst of noise, but it was enough to send my nape prickling. Because it had been Hazel's voice.

And then a male voice.

But I was moving before I really processed the sensation. Not because of the male voice, but because of the tone of Hazel's.

It hadn't been happy.

In fact, it had been alarmed.

I strode for the hall, feeling Chad behind me.

"Babe—"

What. The. *Fuck?*

A man had his hands on her, his *mouth* on hers. Red hazed the edges of my vision, my stride—the one I'd worked so fucking hard to make steady after the injury—faltered, and I nearly ate it. But I recovered and did it in time to see Hazel shove the man roughly away from her.

"Haze, don't be like that—*ow!*"

And then she kneed him in the groin.

"Fuck you, Trevor!" She wiped her mouth with the back of her hand, spun away from the writhing, groaning piece of shit ex...and saw me.

Her expression fell.

Concern swept in.

Teeth found that bottom lip.

"Babe," I murmured. "You okay?"

Tears filled her eyes and she nodded. "I didn't—"

"I know." I gripped her shoulders. "Are you okay?"

"I'm—" A tear leaked out, and I wiped it away, struggling to be gentle when the sight of that glistening drop meant that my control was a hairsbreadth away from losing my shit. She was hurt—physically, emotionally, I didn't know which. Both were equally concerning, and both had me a heartbeat away from launching myself at the man on the ground.

"You stupid bitch!" Trevor moaned, cupping his crotch and rolling on the porch.

Hazel jumped and burrowed into me, her hands gripping my shirt tightly. I sucked in a breath, released it slowly through my nose. "I'd advise you to get your ass off this porch and to never come within a hundred feet of Hazel again," I said coldly.

The urge to punch the asshole was intense.

But Hazel didn't need me to lose my cool.

So, I sucked in another breath, released it just as slowly.

Even when Trevor pushed up to his hands and knees, still grabbing at his groin, and said, "Back the fuck off, asshole."

Hazel tensed.

I tucked her behind me, cupped her cheek, trying to get her attention, but her eyes were on Trevor, worry marring the beautiful lines of her face. "No offense, babe," I said, "but your ex is a dick."

That got her focus off the asshole and back on me. "I—"

"It's okay." I brushed a kiss over her forehead. "Everything is okay. Go into the kitchen, babe," I said, nudging her in that direction.

Chad nodded, tilted his head down the hall. "Go on, sweet pea."

I focused forward again, saw that Trevor was sneering... until Hazel started to move away. Then panic slid through his expression, and he jumped up to his feet, tried to push by me. "Hazel, *no*."

I stepped to the side, blocking him.

"Don't go," Trevor whined. "I made a mistake and—" He grunted as he tried to shove his way into the house again.

I slapped a hand to his chest. "Stop right there."

Trevor pushed me hard, rocking me back a step, forcing me to focus on balancing and keeping my feet at the unexpected contact. "Don't touch me, motherfucker," Trevor snapped, shoving me again.

"You need to leave," I said, keeping my feet, bracing myself, even as I felt Chad step up behind me.

But Hazel's dad didn't say anything. Just stood there in support and was letting me handle it. In his house. The trust blew me away, and despite the fury that was gripping my insides, I had more than a little respect for Hazel's father and was more than a little touched that he trusted me to take care of this situation.

That also bolstered my control.

"I...need...to—" Trevor's face clouded as he continued to struggle to force his way in. Finally seeming to realize I wasn't going to let that happen, he ceased, chest heaving, eyes wild. "Who the fuck are you, and why were you touching Hazel?"

I huffed out a laugh. "A little late for you to be worrying about who's touching her when *you* left her." I raised an eyebrow when Trevor rocked back on his feet as though he'd been gut-punched.

But Trevor recovered quickly, jabbing a finger into my chest. "Who. The. Fuck. Are. You?"

"He's *mine*."

The voice wasn't mine. Or Chad's.

It was Hazel's, coming sharp and fierce right as she slipped under my arm and moved in front of me.

"I love him," she announced.

Trevor's face paled. "I—"

"We're long done, Trev," she said, though her voice softened slightly. Probably because the fucker looked like he'd been hit with a two-by-four upside the head. But what did Trevor expect? Hazel was an amazing woman. Did he just think that she'd sit on the sidelines and wait for him to decide he wanted her back? "You left," she said. "You made it clear I wasn't a priority—"

"I made a mistake at the bachelor party."

Hazel leaned back against me, her curls brushing my chin. "And afterward?"

"I wasn't think—"

So on a roll, she didn't let him continue. "And before?" she asked, reaching back and lacing her fingers through mine, holding tight, her body to me, her voice calm and composed. "Because even before, you didn't treat me like I deserved." A glance up at me, her eyes warm, lips curved. "You didn't give me flowers or candles or music."

Trevor sniffed, drawing both of our focus. "That's bullshit society has made important because companies just want to make money, and you know it."

"Is it?" Hazel asked archly.

"I gave you flowers."

A sigh. A shake of her head. "Once. In our three years together, you brought me flowers *one* time. But it's not about the flowers, Trevor, not really."

"Then why bring them up?" he gritted.

"Because they're a symptom of why we would have never worked, not for me, anyway." Another sigh. "And not for you, either. Because you left."

Regret rippled through Trevor's face. "I—"

Hazel straightened her shoulders. "The problem was that *I* was the one giving. The *only* one. I was willing to bend over backwards to give you the world, just because you wanted it, because that's the way it works in a relationship." Her eyes came to mine again. "We give because we want to make our partner happy, to make them feel loved, feel whole." I brushed my knuckles over her cheek, and she squeezed my fingers again before she glanced forward at the man on the porch, the man she was eviscerating with her soft but firm words. "We wouldn't have worked in the long run because you couldn't give me that in return."

Trevor appeared devastated.

Probably because there was no soft in her tone, no avenue to negotiate.

Hazel was laying it out there matter-of-factly, baldly, not cruelly, but also in a way that the other man would know there was absolutely no chance of a future.

"Oliver gives it to me," she went on. "And I love him for it."

"Oliver"—Trevor's expression went sharp, locking onto me —"Oliver fucking *James*. I knew I recognized your face. I *knew* it." He glared at Hazel. "Are you fucking kidding me?" he snapped. "You'd rather date a fucking cripple than—"

He didn't even get to finish the insult before Hazel launched herself at him, fist raised and colliding with Trevor's nose.

There was a sickening *crack*.

Trevor wailed as blood began pouring down his chin.

But Hazel wasn't done.

She gripped his shoulders and lifted her knee, thrusting hard enough into Trevor's crotch that even I winced in solidarity. "Don't you *ever* say that about Oliver," she growled. "He is a million times the man you are." She stepped back when Trevor collapsed onto the porch, grabbing his balls for the second time that evening.

Oddly, I felt like laughing.

Poor guy had thought that his evening was slated to go a lot differently.

Hazel shook her hand and started toward me but was gently brushed aside by Toni. "Excuse me, Cotton Candy Boo." Her mom stepped forward and dumped a container of food on top of him—leftover pasta sauce, maybe? Though some salad was in there. Along with a pie crust. And half a piece of buttered bread.

Ah.

The scraps she'd been saving for composting.

I should have known Toni wouldn't waste food.

Not on a man like Trevor.

"Get off my porch," Toni hissed, "before I turn the hose on you."

Trevor's eyes went wide. He scrambled up to his feet, slipping on the sauce, leaving a wide streak of red on the wood. Toni was already making her way to the coiled up hose as Trevor shot down the stairs, ran across the lawn—

"Get off my grass, asshole!" Chad shouted.

Trevor veered, hit the driveway, and then was in his car, screeching down the driveway.

Toni turned on the hose, started cleaning off the deck. "Fucker messed with my composting." Chad moved to his wife, took the hose from her, and nudged her toward the house. Toni fought him, mouth opening, her expression one of protest, but that was all I saw.

Because Hazel turned to stare up at me with wide eyes. "Did I just punch someone?"

I cupped her hand gently in my, saw that her knuckles were already bruising. But other than that, nothing looked seriously injured or swollen. "Come on, babe. Let's get some ice for that."

"I punched him," she whispered.

"And kneed him in the junk twice."

More wide eyes.

"You did good, babe," I said. "Though you didn't have to punch him for me."

Those wide eyes narrowed. "He called you a cripple. That's—" A shake of her head. "Rage room aside, I'm not a violent person. I've never—" Another shake. "I never even played contact sports. I just...something inside me snapped when he said that."

"He's an asshole and deserved to get punched, Banana Muffin Munchkin," Toni said, having apparently lost the battle over who was going to hose off the porch. She stomped into the kitchen and put together a bag of ice, wrapping it in a towel and bringing it over to Hazel. Gentle hands placed it over the bruised digits. "Proud of you, Baby Cakes."

"For hitting someone?" Hazel asked, shock in every syllable.

"No," Toni said. "For standing up for what's important."

My throat grew tight.

But then Toni glanced at me. "Proud of you, too."

I blinked. *Why? Hazel had said and done it all.*

A kiss to my cheek before I could voice the question, followed by a hug that was tight and long enough to remind me of Teresa and the way she'd once held me. "Because you didn't lose your cool when Trevor kissed her. Because you calmly stepped in and protected her, made sure she was okay. And because, most importantly of all, you didn't take over. You let her say her piece. You supported her. You loved her." A sniff as she pulled back. "And then your first thought after that asshole insulted you was for her and to get her ice."

"Technically, *you* got her the ice."

Toni smiled, shook her head. "I hate to say it..." She trailed off.

I frowned. "What?"

"You're stuck with us now."

Hazel giggled.

Toni waggled her brows.

Chad came in and slung an arm around my shoulder. "At least you'll be fed well, son."

Son.

Stuck with us.

Family.

What I hadn't understood I'd been missing. Until Hazel.

What I was so fucking grateful for now.

"I love you," I said, smiling at the woman who'd stolen my heart and who I never wanted to give it back.

She smiled in response. A huge, gorgeous smile that made me feel whole, feel worthy, feel...like a man who loved a woman.

Not a man with one leg.

Nor one who'd lost everything several times over.

Not even one who'd never had anything to start with.

I just felt like Oliver James. And Oliver James was in love with Hazel Reid.

Which was why I crossed to her, brushed my knuckles down her cheek (because she liked when I did that), and kissed her.

And tucked all that love home.

Then pulled back and said, "But we've got to teach you how to throw a punch."

EPILOGUE

Hazel

GAME SEVEN.

The score was tied.

The Breakers were on home ice, exhausted, and looking like we might not be able to squeak out the win. We'd spent much of the overtime period in our own end, barely fending off an assault from the Gold's awesome offense.

Scrambling.

Desperate to stay in it.

I was in the owner's box, next to Oliver. Trying not to bite every single nail on my fingers down to the quick.

I'd already ruined my manicure, just by picking away at the polish.

But this shit was *nerve-wracking*. How did the wives and girlfriends do it? How did they stand the pressure of watching their guy on the ice fight for something they wanted so, *so* badly?

At least they only had one player to worry about.

I had twenty.

Was Marcel doing okay? What about Connor? His girlfriend had recently broken up with him, and he'd seemed down, like he'd really liked her, even though they hadn't been dating long. What about Luca? He'd made a bad play that led to the Gold tying the game in the final minutes of regulation. Was he kicking himself and in a bad mental space? And Theo. He was battling injuries and—

Oliver took my hand.

He'd been so still this entire game, a virtual statue.

As though if he breathed wrong, he'd sabotage the team.

But even while dealing with some pretty heavy demons—hello karma to swing its dick right in his face—Oliver was still aware of me.

"Breathe, babe," he said, not taking his eyes from the ice. "They have this."

"I—"

But I didn't get the rest of the sentence out because all of a sudden Marcel, Conner, and Theo were tearing up the ice, the Gold scrambling to catch up.

Too late. In a complete defensive breakdown, our team now had a three-on-none advantage in the Gold's zone.

Marcel fed the puck to Conner.

Who tapped it to Theo.

Who faked passing it to Marcel and instead fired it back to Conner.

Who shot it on net.

Brit, the Gold's goalie, was scrambling, challenging them, cutting off angles and sliding from side to side in the net. She stacked her pads, dove, and...

Saved the puck. It bounced off her into the corner.

The crowd released a disappointed breath, me right along with them.

And the Gold defense flew into the zone, tangled up with my guys, getting between them and the goal. But not between Marcel in the goal.

Somehow in the scramble, they'd missed Marcel.

Who suddenly had the puck on his stick and was firing it toward the goal.

Brit slid.

But she was too far out of position.

The puck flew into the back of the net.

Goal!

Holy shit. *Goal!*

The arena was quiet for a heartbeat and then absolutely exploded with noise. The bench cleared, guys flying onto the ice, everyone celebrating in a flurry of hugs and excited punches. Equipment was flung aside—gloves and sticks and helmets littered around the ice like a yard sale. The goal music came on. The crowd was roaring.

And the Breakers were gathered in a mass on the ice, hugging and smiling.

My eyes stung.

Hell, tears were sliding down my face. There was no point in hiding it. I was *so* freaking proud of them.

But when they turned, almost as one, their eyes on the box, and pointed at Oliver.

He pointed back at the guys.

And...I lost it.

Sobs wrenched through me, tears came in rapid succession, the scene on the ice going blurry.

"Babe," he murmured, cuddling me close, kissing my cheek, wiping the moisture away.

Then Conner gestured, and at first, my watery eyes didn't process it. I dashed the tears off my lashes, blinked a few times...then nearly lost it all over again.

Because once Conner had started, the rest of the team followed.

Pointing at Oliver.

And then down at the ice.

All of them.

Making it clear where they wanted Oliver.

I stood, tugging a now silent and still Oliver to his feet. Then to the door. Then to the elevator that led down to ice level. Then to the hall that led to the rink.

Conner stood at the end.

I smiled at him, having long given up on holding back my tears.

They dripped down my cheeks, and I tugged Oliver toward his friend, toward the bright lights and the roar of the crowd.

"Thanks, Haze," Conner said, quieter and more serious than I'd ever heard him. He wiped his thumb over my cheeks, pressed a kiss to the top of my head. "You going to be good?"

"Take care of him," I whispered, glancing at my lovely, good man, who was stunned silent.

A nod.

Then Conner slung an arm over Oliver's shoulders and drew him forward.

The crowd hit another level of loud when they realized who was stepping onto the ice, thankfully cut up so much that it was rough enough to walk on with normal shoes, and a carpet currently being rolled out on the edges if it wasn't.

I trailed quietly behind them, having to dash more tears away when I saw Marcel approach with a jersey—with *Oliver's* jersey.

That was when my man unfroze.

He took the jersey, tugged it over his head, and then hugged Conner and Marcel, their lips moving in rapid succession. The rest of the guys mobbed them, and I held my breath when it looked like Oliver might take a stumble.

But they righted themselves and him, and then there was nothing but smiles and pounding each other on the back...

And the Cup being brought onto the ice.

Oliver got it first.

I watched him lift it over his head, the crowd roaring. He held it up as he moved around the ice, taking the traditional circle in a way that was slower because he didn't have skates, but one that perhaps meant more to him than anyone else in the history of winning it.

Then he passed it onto Conner, who gave it to Marcel, who gave it to Luca, Theo, Raph. Everyone got their turn, and I knew that it was like they were getting their first-time celebration, too.

Because a year ago, it had been marred by Oliver's injury.

Because this year, there was only joy.

I leaned on the bench, saw that I wasn't the only one with wet eyes. All of the Gold players had stayed on their bench, were cheering just as loud. Including Brit, who had her helmet propped on top of her head, cheeks rosy, blond strands of hair gathering around her face.

And she was crying, too.

Because she got it. The players on the Gold got it.

Hell, *everyone* in the arena got it.

This was a painful loss and coming full circle, becoming whole when it seemed impossible.

It was endings and new beginnings.

And it was love...for a fellow player who'd been through a

lot, for a teammate who'd lost what seemed to be everything, for a man who was so damned good despite having been through more than anyone should have.

Oliver came back over to me, cupped my cheeks, and kissed my tears away.

Then I did the same for him.

Then I stared into his eyes and said, "I am *so* going to marry you."

I didn't find out until later that the moment was caught on the Jumbotron, that a mic was nearby, and my words had been captured on camera, replayed on the game coverage, on the local news.

I wasn't aware of any of that.

Not until my mom sent me samples for wedding invitations.

With a date set less than six months away.

With a Post-It stuck to the front of them that read simply, *Grandbabies.*

Marcel

She was...insane.

That was the only logical explanation.

I'd followed Prudence Hansley, retiree from the NWHL and current Scout and Development Coach for the Breakers, from the rink to this bridge.

And now she was strapping a parachute to her back.

It was late afternoon.

I'd attended the camp she'd been running because I was in town and liked to stay in shape, and I tended to get a little tetchy if I wasn't on the ice.

She'd run a tough clinic, put us guys through our paces, made some good suggestions and corrections, even to me, and then she'd released us. I'd showered. The young guys who'd attended camp all week had gone to do young guy things, but then as I was leaving, I'd heard Pru take a call that had concern rising in me.

The call had been an argument.

Ending with, "The conditions aren't too dangerous. I'm doing it, and I don't give a fuck what you say."

Obviously, that had prickled every cautious bone in my body.

Because I was a man who was cautious. Who planned and proceeded with care and didn't just dive in.

From the time I'd spent with her—she was my friend's fiancé's *friend*—our circles often crossing, and I'd heard enough about Pru's adventures to be seriously worried when she said she was doing something when clearly the person on the other end of the call was advising against it.

Now she was standing next to a bridge and strapping a parachute to her back.

What the actual fuck?

I popped open my door, stormed across the metal and concrete.

She glanced up, and though her eyes went wide at my approach, she didn't stop strapping it on. Was she going to jump? Off *this*?

Seriously.

What the fuck was wrong with her?

Did the woman have a death wish?

I grabbed her arm when she would have stepped over the barrier. "What the fuck are you doing, Pru?"

"None of your fucking business," she snapped.

I reached for the buckle of her chute, undid it before she could do something stupider.

"Stop," she growled, but was too slow. It was already undone, and I was yanking it down her arms, off her hands.

I'd barely gotten it off when she tried to yank it back.

So, I did the only thing I could.

Or maybe, more accurately, the only thing I could think of in that moment.

I launched it over the barrier.

Pru gasped and grabbed on to the metal, leaning over the edge. I moved with her, still not convinced she wouldn't do something stupid, like try to jump after it and strap it on mid-air, Black Widow style.

But all she did was watch it head to the river below us.

Splash into the water.

Then spun back and shoved me. Hard. "What the fuck are you doing?"

"Me?" I snapped. "*Me?* I'm not the one who was base jumping without anyone around after having an argument with a sensible person who said what is *obvious* and that being that the conditions are too fucking dangerous."

"I failed to get the memo telling me you have a say over my life."

"Do you have a fucking death wish?"

Her nostrils flared, and she took off for her car.

But she didn't get in, didn't take off and go home.

She went to the trunk and got out another pack. Another *parachute*.

My temper snapped, and I ripped it out of her hands, tossed *that* over the side of the bridge, and then braced myself because she was going to shove me again. "Any more in there?" I growled. "Because I'll throw those over, too."

"Those are *expensive*," she gritted.

"I don't give a fuck," I snapped. "You want to go base jumping, you do it as safely as possible with spotters or a partner, and you don't do it after someone advises you to not do it today because the conditions are shit."

The wind picked up right then, silently supporting my assertion.

She plunked her hands on her hips. "I do what I want."

"Yeah." I sniffed. "And you don't apparently care that you'll hurt people if you die doing something stupid."

Something almost like vulnerability crossed her face. "My parents are gone. I don't have siblings. It's just me, relying on me, living *my* life." By the time she finished, any trace of vulnerability was gone. Then it was just fire and temper and spunk.

All of which called to me.

"So, who's going to be hurt, huh?"

"Hazel. Oliver. The guys. Me."

She blinked.

Then lifted her chin. "You realize that I'm going to do this, and you won't be able to stop me."

I glanced in her trunk, her back seat, saw there were no more packs. "Today, I did."

"So what, you're going to stalk me?"

"If I have to."

She sniffed. "You made it pretty clear that you're not interested in me, so why care now?"

"Not interested?" I'd been lusting after her for months.

"You turned me down."

I scowled. "You were drunk."

"You *turned me down*."

I stepped closer. "I repeat. *You were drunk.* I don't fuck women who can't consent."

That stopped her for a second, and her face lost the rage. "You turned me down because I was drunk?"

"Do you need me to say it for a third time?"

Her eyes went wide, and then half her mouth turned up, her body drifting closer. "This is the most words I've heard you say at once."

I shrugged.

The other half of her mouth tipped up, and her body came flush with my. Long brown hair, lean and strong and with the most kissable set of lips I'd ever seen. Her breasts brushed my chest, her clean, fruity scent surrounded me. I settled my hands on her hips.

"Would you turn me down now?" she asked, dragging a finger down my chest.

No. I fucking wouldn't.

But she knew precisely what she was doing, could probably feel precisely what *she* was doing to me...and my cock.

"Would you take me home and—"

My fingers tightened. "I'll take you home, and I'll fuck you, princess, but only if you promise to not jump off this bridge."

She frowned. "I—"

"Until whoever was the voice of reason on the other end of that call, telling you today wasn't right"—the wind whipped around us—"says the conditions are good. And then if you still want to do it, you do it."

And I'd be here.

Making sure she was doing it as safely as possible.

Because despite what my ex said, I wasn't the kind of man who clipped someone's wings.

I just wanted the spreading of those wings and the leaping out of nests to happen safely and smartly.

Her hazel eyes swirled with emotions—heat, frustration, interest, attraction, annoyance, desire, and more that I couldn't discern. I watched and waited to see what she would do.

Her face went blank.

I braced myself again.

"Okay," she said, throwing her arms around me. "Take me home and fuck me, pretty boy."

Thank you for reading! I hope you loved meeting Oliver and Hazel! The next book in the Breakers Hockey series is BREATHLESS. Professional hockey players aren't supposed to get our hearts broken...but that was exactly what had happened to me.

CLICK HERE TO READ BREATHLESS NOW>

And if you enjoyed BOLDLY, you'll love the sexy, sweet, and close-knit Gold Hockey crew. The first book in the series, Blocked, is FREE!

IF YOU ENJOY MY SERIES, considering supporting me on PATREON! Get access to early releases, bonus content, character art, audiobooks, special edition covers, swag, and much more!

CLICK HERE TO SUPPORT ME>

.   .   .

I so appreciate your help in spreading the word about my books, including sharing with friends! Please leave a review on your favorite book site!

You can also join my Facebook group, the Fabinators, for exclusive giveaways and sneak peeks of future books.

SIGN UP FOR ELISE FABER'S NEWSLETTER HERE: https://www.elisefaber.com/newsletter

Hate missing Elise's new releases? Love contests, exclusive excerpts and giveaways?
Then signup for Elise's newsletter here!

www.elisefaber.com/newsletter

And join Elise's fan group, the Fabinators (https://www.facebook.com/groups/fabinators) for insider information, sneak peaks at new releases, and fun freebies! Hope to see you there!

If you enjoy my series, considering supporting me on PATREON! Get access to early releases, bonus content, character art, audiobooks, special edition covers, swag, and much more!

CLICK HERE TO SUPPORT ME>

I so appreciate your help in spreading the word about my books, including sharing with friends! Please leave a review on your favorite book site!

ALSO BY ELISE FABER

***Gold Hockey* (all stand alone)**

Blocked

Backhand

Boarding

Benched

Breakaway

Breakout

Checked

Coasting

Centered

Charging

Caged

Crashed

A Gold Christmas

Cycled

Caught

Cap

Covered

Crushed

Changed

Scored

***Breakers Hockey* (all stand alone)**

Broken

Boldly

Breathless

Ballsy

Bewitched

Blowout

Breathe

Blazed

Sierra Hockey Series

Over the Line

Caught from Behind

The Big Skate

On the Fly

Eagles Hockey Series (all stand alone)

Broken Laces

Lace 'em Up

Knotted Laces

Loaded Laces

Lucky Laces

Oak Ridge Vineyards

Bottles & Blades

Beauty & the Boardroom

Rush Hockey Trilogy #1

Big Puck Energy

Filthy Puckboy

So Pucking Over It

Rush Hockey Trilogy #2

Love, Pucks, and Other Stories

All's Fair in Pucks and War

No Pucks Lost Between Us

Rush Hockey Novellas

Puck and Make Up

Billionaire's Club (all stand alone)

Bad Night Stand

Bad Breakup

Bad Husband

Bad Hookup

Bad Divorce

Bad Fiancé

Bad Boyfriend

Bad Blind Date

Bad Wedding

Bad Engagement

Bad Bridesmaid

Bad Swipe

Bad Girlfriend

Bad Best Friend

Bad Rebound

Bad Romance

Bad Business

Bad Billionaire's Quickies

Love, Action, Camera (all stand alone)

Dotted Line

Action Shot

Close-Up

End Scene

Meet Cute

Love After Midnight (all stand alone)

Rum And Notes

Virgin Daiquiri

On The Rocks

Sex On The Seats

Life Sucks Series

Train Wreck

Hot Mess

Dumpster Fire

Clusterf*@k

FUBAR

Perfect Storm

Free Fall

Lost Cause

Roosevelt Ranch Series (all stand alone, series complete)

Disaster at Roosevelt Ranch

Heartbreak at Roosevelt Ranch

Collision at Roosevelt Ranch

Regret at Roosevelt Ranch

Desire at Roosevelt Ranch

***Phoenix Series* (read in order)**

Phoenix Rising

Dark Phoenix

Phoenix Freed

***Phoenix: LexTal Chronicles* (rereleasing soon, stand alone, Phoenix world)**

From Ashes

In Flames

To Smoke

***KTS Series* (all stand alone, series complete)**

Riding The Edge

Crossing The Line

Leveling The Field

Scorching The Earth

Cocky Heroes World

Tattooed Troublemaker

ABOUT THE AUTHOR

USA Today bestselling author, Elise Faber, loves chocolate, Star Wars, Harry Potter, and hockey (the order depending on the day and how well her team -- the Sharks! -- are playing). She and her husband also play as much hockey as they can squeeze into their schedules, so much so that their typical date night is spent on the ice. Elise is the mom to two exuberant boys and lives in Northern California. Connect with her in her Facebook group, the Fabinators or find more information about her books at www.elisefaber.com.

facebook.com/elisefaberauthor

amazon.com/author/elisefaber

bookbub.com/profile/elise-faber

instagram.com/elisefaber

tiktok.com/@elisefaberauthor

goodreads.com/elisefaber